About the Author

Gordon d'Venables was born on the land of the Wilman First Nation People and has been, inter alia, a farmhand, soldier, teacher, lawyer with predominantly international clients, and a university lecturer. He lives on Wardandi land in the southwest of Australia. The combination of his employment history, life experiences – including dealings and interaction with law enforcement agencies, the military, and global businesses – and extensive travel, has enriched his work. Gordon has published two books with Vanguard Press: *The Medusa Image and Hunted*. He also writes a regular newspaper column.

Star of the South
Kongal Djinda

Gordon d'Venables

Star of the South
Kongal Djinda

Vanguard Press

VANGUARD PAPERBACK

© Copyright 2023
Gordon d'Venables

The right of Gordon d'Venables to be identified as author of
this work has been asserted by him in accordance with the
Copyright, Designs and Patents Act 1988.

All Rights Reserved

No reproduction, copy or transmission of this publication
may be made without written permission.
No paragraph of this publication may be reproduced,
copied or transmitted save with the written permission of the publisher, or in accordance
with the provisions
of the Copyright Act 1956 (as amended).

Any person who commits any unauthorised act in relation to
this publication may be liable to criminal
prosecution and civil claims for damages.

A CIP catalogue record for this title is
available from the British Library.

ISBN 978 1 83794 074 5

This is a work of fiction. Names, characters, businesses, places, events and incidents are either the
product of the author's imagination or used in a fictitious manner. Any resemblance to actual persons,
living or dead, or actual events is purely coincidental.

*Vanguard Press is an imprint of
Pegasus Elliot Mackenzie Publishers Ltd.*
www.pegasuspublishers.com

First Published in 2023

**Vanguard Press
Sheraton House Castle Park
Cambridge England**

Printed & Bound in Great Britain

Dedicated to my late father, who instilled in me the values expressed in this book. To my great grandson, Koah, who will hopefully respect and treasure his cultural heritage as a descendant of the Badjiri First Nation people.

Acknowledgements

This book was written on Wardandi Noongar land in the southwest of Australia. I respectfully acknowledge the Traditional Custodians of this entire country. I recognise the strength and resilience of First Nations peoples; I respect their rich culture, the oldest continuous culture on the planet; I acknowledge their continuing connection to the land and waters; and the uniqueness many generations have brought to our nation's cultural and environmental distinctiveness. I pay my respects to Elders past, present and emerging.

In particular, my respects and gratitude go to three Elders from whom I have learned a great deal. Uncle Bill Turner, Uncle Dennis Jetta and Uncle Joe Northover. Uncle Bill Turner and I kept the coffee industry strong over many discussions before and during the time of researching and writing Star of the South. His input and advice was a constant and for that I am enormously grateful. His quiet words of wisdom together with the many books he gave me to read, written by and about First Nations people, influenced my writing. The most senior and highly respected Wardandi country Elder, Uncle Dennis Jetta, arranged for me to attend an Elder's meeting to discuss my writing objectives. He also read parts of the book that have cultural and spiritual significance and it is with his permission, on behalf of the Elders, that I have published Star of the South. Uncle Joe Northover is from the boodja, where much of the book was focused. He is widely known as the custodian of the river referred to as Cottam River in the book. He willingly provided valuable cultural advice on Wilman country.

A huge thanks to Max Retzlaff and Nick Martin, both of whom provided a great deal of information about the prison system from entirely different perspectives. Max gave me an understanding of inmate code, values, beliefs, social interaction, and behaviour from many decades ago. Nick's input was more current and in particular helped me understand an inmate's life, as well as the duties of Prison Officers in country and regional prisons. Both are friends who read several chapters and contributed to making the prison life of Boodjark realistic. Karim Khan has a deep understanding of country and bush tucker and was willing to share that knowledge. I am always determined to be as accurate as possible in my writing and I'm grateful that Karim read and approved of the relevant chapters.

At different times I had valuable discussions with Karen Jetta and Graham Ellis-Smith about a range of matters relating to First Nations people in the southwest of Australia. The range of subjects included, but was not limited to, bush tucker, the stolen generation, Noongar language and Indigenous culture. I am grateful for their time and friendship.

As always my wife, Diane, carefully proofreads and provides valuable editorial comments and recommendations. She is such a rock in my life. Thanks to the South West Aboriginal Land and Sea Council. Noongar words in Star of the South were taken from the widely acclaimed Rose Whitehurst dictionary. Copyright to the dictionary is vested in the Council, which kindly gave me permission to use those words.

Again, I called upon my old friend, Ian Cox. Ian has the incredible visual precision and ability to discern even the subtlest grammatical, spelling, and contextual errors that I didn't see. To Ian who proofread the final version before it went to Pegasus for final editing, thank you for casting your sharp eye over the manuscript. Any errors in grammar can only be attributed to me in the end.

Thanks also to the team at Pegasus Publishers (imprint Vanguard Press) for your thoroughness, for your positive comments, for your confidence and for distributing the book internationally.

Part One

Boodjark

Chapter 1

Heavy rain clouds blackened the horizon and moved slowly in the direction of the buildings that sat in the middle of a large area with an insignificant number of native trees. Most had been chopped to establish a farm of approximately two thousand six hundred hectares; geographical coordinates 34°38'12"S, 117°22'55"E. Nightfall was close.

For some reason, it rained more often at night in this part of the country. At least, that's what it seemed like to Prentice. Soon he would again hear heavy drumming on the tin roof, as the sky opened and shed its contents on his home of the last two years. Another sleepless night loomed.

Above the distant trees he could see a flock of black cockatoos moving towards him. His childhood friend told him the flight of *ngoorlak* was a telltale sign that heavy rain was imminent. The harbinger to mother sky shedding a deluge of *kep* to replenish the bush garden. They would noisily pass low overhead, above the structures, above the clearing, and seek shelter further inland where the rain would be less challenging; where the storm would weaken and lightning was less likely.

Prentice had been imprisoned, since his youth, for a total of sixteen years. On one occasion, the District Court Judge described him as a "recidivist" and said he would "likely become a career criminal". Initially his incarceration was for months at a time and later continuously for fourteen years. In that time, he had grown from a slightly built boy to a 188 cm, loose-jointed, rawboned, lean man of thirty-five years.

As usual, Prentice's mood was dark. As dark as the clouds. As dark as the approaching evening. He had removed himself from some of the social activities that other prisoners engaged in on a daily basis. He had no choice. Instead, he sat on the wide verandah at the front of his room waiting for the muster and evening dinner.

There were some activities in which he was required to participate but not all, and he chose not to mix with other inmates if he could avoid it. It was too dangerous, not only for him but for one inmate in particular. The inmate who called him 'Scarface', a name he detested despite the accuracy of its description. It was dangerous for him only in the sense that he might lose control and that would inevitably mean he would serve more time. Time back inside a strict security facility. Time would be his enemy.

Many hours in the workshop of the maximum-security prison had sharpened the skills he had acquired as an apprentice carpenter, before committing the crime that took away his freedom. It started at the Palmyra maximum-security prison with the introduction of the Long-Term-Prisoner Programme. The programme was designed to assist prisoners with potential reintegration into society. During his last twelve months at Palmyra, Prentice was an enthusiastic participant.

Later, at the medium security prison, most of his time was spent in the mechanical workshop, learning new skills that could mean a broader range of employment opportunities out in the real world. If that ever happened.

His early time at the minimum-security prison farm had been fruitful in learning new trades and further developing skills he had acquired over the years of his imprisonment. Although the farm provided plenty of options for skills development, he chose to minimise his involvement when possible. For Prentice, there was little else to do other than contemplate a chance at revenge. But he was mindful of the consequences of bad behaviour. Additional prison time would delay retribution.

Prentice had worked hard to earn a reputation as a model prisoner, resulting in his transfer to the farm. He had managed to keep his temper restrained but he wasn't certain he could exercise such control for the final years of his incarceration. Anger still brewed inside him. Absenting himself from social engagements meant he was less likely to reoffend. It also gave him more time to plan, not that he needed to plan much. One thing was certain: his proposed course of action would be inevitable, barring any unforeseen circumstances.

Several prisoners meandered past in the direction of the mess hall.

"Are you coming, Boodjark?" asked one of them, glancing over his left shoulder. The inmate with ginger hair. Prentice, who everyone knew by the sobriquet 'Boodjark', jolted upright. He had been deep in contemplation and missed the call for what was commonly known as 'the dish-up'.

"Yeah, sure," he replied, rising from the bench and rubbing his bony fingers across his buzz cut. With a surprising smile, he added, "I was miles away, Bluey. Planning to be, anyway."

"Planning to be," Bluey repeated. "Planning an escape?"

Bluey had a look of surprise engraved across his ruddy complexion.

"Only joking, of course, but ya never know what ya might be forced to do, don't ya think?" Boodjark said, still rubbing his head. An old habit when he was thinking.

His fellow inmates were surprised to hear Boodjark crack a joke. He never joked and rarely smiled. Behind his back, others sometimes joked about his inability to smile because his smiling muscles were underutilised. They were taut. Too stiff to activate in a meaningful way. To them, he appeared to carry a huge chip on his shoulder, the size of one of the great gum trees at the edge of the prison farm and beyond in the nearby bush.

Probably a broken man, Bluey thought. Prison without hope can do that.

Concerned, Bluey responded, "Nah, Boodjark. Too much at stake. You can't have long to go. Why would you walk out of here?"

Boodjark didn't immediately respond. His fellow inmates would soon understand.

He gazed skywards again as the flock of black cockatoos now flew directly overhead, squawking noisily. His colleagues followed his gaze. Looking to the sky signalled the end of the conversation.

There were over fifteen separate buildings at the minimum-security facility that usually housed about eighty prisoners. Near the cluster of buildings there were several market gardens with crops of vegetables that ensured the prisoners were well fed with seasonal produce. Garlic, tomatoes, and capsicum were abundant now. There was also a large glasshouse for plant propagation. Rows of fruit trees produced enough to also supply the medium-security prison that had previously been Boodjark's home. The kitchen and mess hall was in the centre of the complex.

Boodjark joined the three men as they walked the verandah of a brick building with cracked and crumbling mortar; an accommodation block. They turned onto another path and walked casually along the grey, uneven and well-trodden, concrete-covered walkway, past an ablutions block, past a laundry contiguous to a drying room, to the mess hall. This hall was strictly a chow facility. Most other indoor activities were conducted in a recently constructed purpose-built recreation hall.

As he pushed open the fly-wire door and held it in position for another inmate to hold for others behind him, Boodjark pointed at a prisoner taking his seat at the end of the first table.

"Him," he said sternly.

Bluey had thought the short conversation they had a few minutes earlier had ended and wasn't expecting anything further from the usually sullen Boodjark.

"What?" he asked, puzzled.

Boodjark nodded in the direction of the rangy, thin prisoner who was already spooning broth into his mouth as if it was his last meal. "Him," he said pointedly. "Hate his guts! If I smacked him, he'd probably break in half and I would get another ten years, but I might have to take the risk. Yeah, hate his guts."

Bluey and the other two in the group laughed at the imagery of the tall bloke, known as 'Shorty', breaking in two. A grim-faced Boodjark didn't laugh.

Chapter 2

Bruce Prentice was born in the small Wittekop hospital on a hot summer's day. Wittekop, population of five hundred, give or take, geographical coordinates approximately 32°78'S, 117°49'E, was situated in the middle of fields of wheat as far as the eye could see, about half way between the southern-most coastal town of Abannerup and the Big Smoke.

His arrival interrupted the wheat harvest for the town's only doctor, who had five thousand hectares of land thirty kilometres from the town. Normally the nurse wouldn't bother the doctor but it was a difficult birth and he was summonsed from his farm. It was an emergency.

As the doctor rushed into the corridors of the hospital, he peeled off clothes partially covered by husks and airborne grain dust from an early harvest. Thirty minutes later, Bruce arrived by Caesarean section with the umbilical cord twisted around his neck. Years later, Bruce's father joked that his son's problems in life stemmed from grain-dust inhalation. "Or perhaps his mother tried to strangle him with that cord," he would say.

Bruce's parents were regarded as good, solid citizens in the small country town, although that was more to do with the regard the local community had for his mother. He had two younger sisters and was the only son of a shearer. Shearing contracts took his father away from the family home for extended periods of time. For much of Bruce's life, his mother, Cheryl, was the sole parent.

Bruce was named after his father, the latter insisting that his first-born should carry his name and that of his father before him. A family tradition. Cheryl was happy for one of the baby boy's given names to be 'Bruce' but not the first name. Bruce Prentice senior demanded the boy would be named 'Bruce' and since he attended the Office of Births, Deaths and Marriages to register the child he ignored his wife's wishes. He registered the boy as he wished. Years later, Cheryl may have bemoaned the fact she didn't ask her brother to register the birth.

Bruce's childhood was best described as 'patchy'. His mother had patches of genuine concern for her son's future. His father had patches of benign neglect but more often, to Bruce, they seemed like patches of total disinterest. Probably more rejection than disinterest. The boy had no future. His mother's patches couldn't compensate for the bruised ego delivered during his father's patches.

If only his father weren't as cutting as a shearer's blade at those times. If only he cloaked his barbed, jagged criticism in one of the merino fleeces he forcefully separated from the powerless animals each day.

When young Bruce was in Year Five, at the Wittekop Primary School, his parents considered it was time to seriously contemplate a move to a larger town that provided more educational opportunities for the children. Bruce Prentice senior decided the boy, in particular, needed a greater range of educational opportunities. The girls didn't need higher education, the misogynist decided.

He didn't care where they lived. His work usually took him away from home for weeks and sometimes even months at a time.

Fortuitously, a prospect arose for Cheryl to be engaged as a senior nurse at a much larger hospital than the Wittekop District Hospital. Within months, the family had relocated to Cottam Mills, further west, geographical coordinates approximately 33°36'S, 116°15'E. Cheryl eagerly accepted the new position in a very busy Emergency Department at the local hospital. Busy because of the nature of work in and around Cottam Mills. Busy because the local men worked hard and played even harder.

Almost all of Cottam Mills' eight thousand people were, directly or indirectly, beneficiaries of the mining and timber industries. Those industries were substantially the solid foundation of all other businesses and employment opportunities in the area.

The town was renowned for its tough characters, including a disproportionate number of roughnecks. Miners and timber workers, whilst not all fitting into that category, worked long shifts and played passionately. Twelve hotels flourished as testament to that.

It didn't take long for Bruce's father to settle into his old drinking habits. When he returned from a shearing contract, he would spend most of his days either at his favourite watering hole – the Miner's Arms Hotel – at the home of a drinking buddy, or lounging next to a bar fridge in his shed he named his 'man cave', at the rear of his property. Wherever he spent the day, it mainly involved the heavy consumption of alcohol.

Unlike many of his heavy beer-drinking friends, Bruce senior didn't accumulate a beer belly. Shearing burnt the calories. He stood at 167 cm wearing his shearing boots and was 65 kgs wringing wet. On occasions he would be underestimated, considered a pushover because of his size, but he was a wiry and tough character.

Significant muscle mass doesn't necessarily mean significantly greater strength. Whilst some of his larger friends looked powerful, relative strength is an entirely different matter. "The bigger they are, the harder they fall," he often said.

The scrawny guy, Bruce Prentice senior, a bloke with slow twitch muscles, which provided continual strength over a long period of time, just like a long-distance runner, could bring down the largest bloke in the pub. It happened on numerous occasions but usually not without injury to both or all parties involved in a brawl.

Unfortunately for young Bruce and his sisters, Bruce senior had very little time for his family. Different priorities monopolised his time, notably the amber beverage known by those in his exclusive social circle as "Wife Beater". After drinking beer for the best part of the day, he would almost always finish with one or two snifters of whisky.

"How about a snifter!" he would shout to his companions after a long drinking session, the abundant intake of alcohol causing him to raise his voice. "A snifter followed by anothery. One for the road." He earned the nickname, 'Snifter'.

Snifter Prentice wasn't a wife beater. Inexplicably, that was just the colloquial term for his favourite beer. By late afternoon, when Cheryl returned from her duty roster at the local hospital, he was usually too inebriated to raise another can or stubby of beer, let alone a hand in anger.

Snifter claimed he loved his wife because she never objected to him being away from home for months at a time. Never objected to his penchant for heavy drinking, and always used her nursing skills, without the slightest complaint, to patch him up after he was in a fight.

Fighting between the miners and timber workers regularly occurred in the Cottam Mills hotels, most often precipitated by arguments over Australian Rules football. The town had two teams: the Cottam Mines

Rovers and the Cottam Millers. Fights between supporters of opposing teams would often start inside the hotel and, with the intervention of hotel management, spill into the streets. For Snifter they were a regular occurrence, even though he had never been a miner or a miller. He didn't need an excuse: he just loved a physical 'blue'.

In truth, Cheryl was very happy to have the space when Snifter had a shearing contract. When he was home, she always felt like she was walking on eggshells, such were his temperament and mood swings. She was most happy when he was away on a shearing contract and she could focus her attention on the children. They were in their formative years and needed parental attention and guidance. Within their household, only Cheryl would deliver that.

Cheryl had a Nursing degree and a Bachelor of Psychological Science. She understood from her studies that young Bruce's exposure to his father's violent tendencies could cause the circuitry of the boy's brain to change. Make him less likely to be inhibited in his actions as he grew older.

Snifter Prentice never stood a chance to be the Cottam Mills Bulletin Father of the Year. Not even a chance to be nominated. He wasn't a particularly good role model for his children. He didn't care. As far as he was concerned, he was the main family breadwinner and he could therefore do as he liked.

As a mentor for his son, he fell far short of acceptable parental standards. On numerous occasions, when young Bruce was told to wait in the car while his father went into the Miner's Arms for just 'one off the wood', he witnessed his father brawling on the footpath. An argument had spilled outside the pub. A physical altercation was something Snifter's children didn't need to witness but young Bruce did so on many occasions.

In Cottam Mills, Bruce didn't like his school. He wasn't motivated to study. He had no ambition, no sporting prowess and no interest in after-school activities with most other boys of his age. There was one exception. One boy he spent time with, his only friend, Mokiny, was from the Noongar Wilman nation.

Mokiny was welcomed into the Prentice household when Snifter was away from town with his shearing team. He loved to visit at those times and was made welcome by Bruce's mother and siblings. Mokiny considered Cheryl to be the best of all the mothers he knew outside the *karla* (camp).

When he visited on weekends, the house always smelt of freshly baked Anzac biscuits and cakes. In years to come, Bruce would appreciate that in particular.

Mokiny certainly didn't feel comfortable visiting when Snifter was about. On the occasion of his first visit to the Prentice home, Snifter hadn't said anything about his presence, but he had fixed an open-mouthed, frowning glare at Mokiny. A glare that told the boy he wasn't welcome. Mokiny sensed that Bruce's father was *wara* (bad). He didn't have to be told anything by Bruce. He sensed a *djinack*, an evil spirit.

Bruce was embarrassed. Lest he receive a back-hander after his father had a skinful of the Wife Beater, he didn't dare say anything. But Bruce knew the sole reason for his father's lack of grace, for his failure to offer warm hospitality, was to do with the colour of Mokiny's skin.

After school and on weekends, Bruce would spend hours in the bush with his friend. He learnt about bush tucker, *marany* or non-meat food, and survival in a harsh environment. Every day, Mokiny's tutelage provided new information. Lessons about the bush. Unlike his formal education at the local school, Bruce had an almost insatiable appetite for learning about bush tucker, the history of the Noongar peoples and their culture. He could not get enough of it and Mokiny obliged.

"One never knows when these survival skills might be required, Brewster," Mokiny Jnr told his friend on many occasions. He often laughed at the variation he gave to the name 'Bruce', thinking, *I bet his dad would like him to be a real brewster. A brewer of beer.*

At the same time, Bruce, in near synchronisation, would be contemplating, *Funny you should call me that, Mokiny. My dad would dearly love that. Would probably kill for an endless supply.* The boys were tight. Thinking alike.

As they grew older, Mokiny came to regard Bruce as a brother. Indeed, he often called Bruce *ngoony*, which meant 'brother' in his dialect. There was mutual respect.

Over time, having won the trust of Mokiny's people, Bruce was taught about Noongar culture and spirituality. As an Elder, Mokiny's father – also Mokiny, but known as Uncle Mokiny or Mokiny Senior – shared his wisdom and his vast knowledge of *boodja* (country). About the relationship between *boodja* and the people and stories of the Dreamtime. Uncle

Mokiny was highly respected by the Wilman people. The children would listen intently and absorb everything he talked about. "Uncle Mokiny, the old man, he the best," they would say and Mokiny Junior would beam with pride.

Bruce noticed how the people were inclusive and happy to share. The 'old man', in particular, shared knowledge and values. The children would grow to appreciate the Noongar law.

At young Mokiny's urging, his father, a *djenakabi* (a lawman), told stories of the *Walgu* and of his ancestors, their hunting and other business. But although he shared the stories, Mokiny Senior had an uneasy feeling about young Bruce. A sixth sense. Years later, his sense of unease was vindicated.

Importantly for Bruce, they shared the fruits of the land. Mokiny Junior taught him where to find the tastiest nuts and seeds and how to treat various parts of other native bush plants to make them edible. In his youth, Bruce had no idea how useful that information would become in later years.

In Australian rural country, most fathers would spend time in the bush with their children. Camping excursions, hunting rabbits, fishing, canoeing the river rapids, or simply enjoying the wilderness were normal activities for most families on weekends and especially during school holidays. Not so for Snifter Prentice. Indeed, he took exception to Bruce spending time on weekends with the Noongar people, who mainly lived in Nissen huts on the outskirts of town.

"Why do you bother with those blacks?" Snifter asked Bruce, one rare evening, when he hadn't been drinking. "Now that you're getting some hair growing on your top lip and probably growing on your balls for all I know, are you thirsting for one of those black girls? Hankering for a bit of black fluff?"

Disgusting, saying that to your son, thought Cheryl. She glared at Snifter but wouldn't dare comment.

Bruce was also puzzled and annoyed by his father's obscenity. He opened his mouth and words flowed faster than his brain could restrain. "I'm not like you! Don't judge me by your foul thoughts."

Before his mother could intervene to restore peace, the back of Snifter's right hand lashed against the side of Bruce's face, drawing blood from the side of his mouth where a tooth cut into his bottom lip.

"Don't talk to me like that! Show some respect."

"Respect… er… I'm sorry. Mokiny's family are my only friends," Bruce replied in a muffled voice, wiping his mouth with his forearm. "My friends…"

"Don't answer back, you little shit. Why do you think the blacks live in the bush on the edge of town? 'Cos they're no bloody good, that's why. They don't wanna mix with white people. One of them got a shearing contract for his team. The Fraser farm. My team has always had that contract. Cost me a bloody job, they did."

Bruce's thought process responded to the last comment but this time, in anticipation of another beating, he didn't articulate it. *Perhaps Mokiny's uncle is a better shearer. Perhaps he works harder. I know he doesn't drink alcohol and they're all at the end of the queue to get a house: that's why they live outside the town. They've gotta live somewhere.*

"But Dad, I'm white and they mix with me. Maybe it is something to do with respect. Mokiny and his father have taught me so much. They are fun to be with."

Snifter's voice again rose in anger. "So I'm not fun to be with, you good-for-nothin' turd? What about some of the white kids in town? Why don't you spend time with them and be normal? Normal! Do you hear me?"

Normal? What's normal? thought Bruce. *Is it normal to be disrespectful to others who are just trying to make a life for themselves?*

There was no further discussion on the matter. Although tempted, Cheryl didn't contradict her husband. She didn't dare to do so.

But that exchange may have precipitated a change in how young Bruce Prentice started to view others. That may have been the precise moment when doubt emerged.

No-one is born a racist. They are taught.

Chapter 3

Snifter Prentice was determined to see that his only son should have what he described as a "decent education". An education that would provide opportunities in life that he never had. Snifter had left school when he was thirteen years of age but the law had changed since then.

"He's in year nine, right." Snifter told his wife firmly. It wasn't a question. "He can't legally leave school and get a job until he finishes Year ten."

Cheryl nodded in agreement, before adding, "And even then, he needs to have the permission of the Education Department. Training to be a shearer like you might not cut it." Euphemistically thinking, *Bruce can do much better.*

"There's nothing wrong with being a shearer and earning good money, but that boy isn't cut out for hard yakka," Snifter insisted. "He needs a proper education. He's not gettin' one 'ere. With the right education, I can see him being a desk jockey in a secure Government job, or perhaps even learning how to run his own small business. Maybe even become a policeman, although I'm not sure he has what it would take to be a cop. Nah, coppers need to be smart and tough to advance up the ranks. The kid hasn't got it."

Snifter was determined to ensure his son was removed from an environment where, in his mind, he was learning stuff that was meaningless. "He'll never be any good if he just spends time with that black kid. He's learning nuthin," he told his wife.

Bruce is learning good human values about sharing, caring and respecting others. He's not getting that from a male role model in this household, Cheryl thought. But she also knew there was no point in arguing with her husband. His mindless bigotry was ferocious.

The discussion about Bruce's schooling continued and was extended over several weeks, before it was finally decided he would be sent to a private school in another town. A larger town seventy kilometres from Cottam Mills.

Bruce wasn't happy with the plan and entered his new school in a bad frame of mind. The school, exclusively for boys and accommodating a much larger number of students than his old school, was located in Ditchingham, geographical coordinates 33°32'70"S, 115°64'09"E.

About two hundred boys were boarders. Some came from mining towns, particularly the goldfields; some from rich, agricultural areas and others were from the capital city. Bruce was the only boy from Cottam Mills.

He resented the forced relocation. He resented his father for the enforced move. Disgruntled, in the first few months, he felt isolated.

Surprisingly, some of the senior boys ignored his dark moods and encouraged him to become involved in sporting activities. They sensed a rough edge to the school's newest boarder and decided he would be a handy addition to the football team, when they played other private schools. Most importantly, those rough edges could be honed to a sharpness their opponents would feel.

"If you follow instructions from some of the seniors and rough up opponents on the footy field, you'll be rewarded. Win friends," one of the other school boarders told Bruce. "Nut if you don't – well, you'll soon find out."

"What do you mean by that?"

"What?"

"Your comment that I'll 'soon find out'?"

"You need to understand who the leaders are at this school and what problems they can create for boys who don't fit in. I thought you'd know that by now. Nuthin' else."

There was a lengthy silence as Bruce contemplated what he had just been told, before responding, "Sounds like a threat. I need to sleep on it."

"Not a threat, Brewster. Just a fact. The senior boys can make your time at this school much more interesting and exciting. Watch them and learn, not just on the footy field but after school."

Bruce smiled at the use of the name 'Brewster'. *Perhaps I might be able to fit in. 'Brewster'*, he thought. *That's what Mokiny called me. I like it.*

The biggest single factor shaping an adolescent's values and behaviour is parental influence. When influence normally provided in the family setting is weak or non-existent, other social influences come into play. Peer influence is more important than peer pressure. Bruce hadn't previously experienced peer pressure. Only the influence of his mother and his friend Mokiny, but neither were present in his life right now and were unlikely to be for a considerable time.

It was apparent that Bruce's social network could be widened if he followed the advice and influence of his fellow boarder. He was torn between the expectations he knew his mother would have of him and the processes he could follow at school to ingratiate himself with others.

There was a social motivation. There was choice. Safe decisions and behaviour his mother would expect, or more risky choices that his new friend had alluded to. At his age, the social motivation was powerful.

It's not as if anything I do would have any life-long consequences, he thought. *I'm stuck in this environment for the next few years, so I may as well make the most of it. Fit in, otherwise it could be a lonely existence here.*

Bruce started training with the school football team. He wasn't a particularly gifted athlete, but just as the senior boys had observed, he possessed a country boy's hardness. A willingness to play rough gained the praise of his teammates. He was hard in the contest and even his coach made approving comments after his first game.

"You mustn't overstep the mark though, Bruce," his coach warned him. "Playing good, hard footy is fine but try not to be too aggressive. I like the way you meet the contest head-on but be careful to stick within the rules of the game."

The school captain, who was also the popular captain of the football team, whispered, "Take no notice of the old fart, Bruce. The boys loved what you did. Loved the fact you smacked hard into that Aboriginal kid. Really crunched him. He was almost single-handedly winning the game for Centrals until you got him. His silky skills weren't so silky afterwards."

Bruce's ego was almost at boiling point. He'd been noticed. The most popular boy in the school had praised him.

Working hard at his game sometimes meant he overstepped the bounds of fair play. The senior boys, the influencers, continued to praise him for it. Risk-taking became increasingly more appealing. In this social context, with the senior boys taking an interest in young Bruce, at last he had a sense of belonging. That sense was amplified by taking even greater risks. Especially when the risk-taking was extended beyond the sporting field.

At the time Bruce attended the private school, it had a policy of providing a handful of scholarships to boys the Registrar regarded as being 'from a disadvantaged background'. A formal application was not required as long as other essential criteria were met.

The Registrar visited outlying country towns and in discussions with teachers from those areas, students were identified to fill vacancies that occurred at Ditchingham from time to time. In that way, the school was able to promote itself as an 'equal-opportunity' establishment, demonstrating a strong social policy, thereby attracting government funding to supplement fees paid by the more financial parents.

Aboriginal students were chosen on the basis of what the Registrar described as their 'ability to assimilate'. Of particular interest were boys who met three criteria. First, they must not be impudent and must cast their eyes to the ground when being addressed, unless told otherwise. They must never talk unless being asked to speak by a teacher. Just as important, the third requirement was they must be good at sport. After all, there had to be a purpose in having them attend a private school, apart from the school's image and the funding it attracted.

Now almost regarded as a legend on the football team, Bruce displayed an air of arrogance in the school grounds. He joined with a group of boys who considered themselves superior to the school's Indigenous boarders. Bruce belonged to a gang regarded by others as just a bunch of bullies. With a new sense of belonging, Bruce experienced an adrenalin rush when he joined in the taunts. This reward grew out of proportion, when he knew his friends were watching him. Eventually the taunting became violent.

When he physically assaulted a much smaller Indigenous boy, who was unable to defend himself, he was praised by his friends for his 'courage'. There was no apparent reason for the assault. Bruce's friends had convinced him a reason wasn't necessary. The fact the smaller boy was different, even if only in one respect, was reason enough.

"Father Thomas wants to see you during the lunch break," one of the teachers told Bruce the following morning. "He will see you in the chapel at twelve thirty."

"You're in for it Brewster. Someone has pimped on ya," the school captain told him. "Probably that black kid with the blacker eye," he laughed and Bruce joined in, standing taller in his own mind.

In the chapel, the priest told Bruce to enter the cubicle, where he would hear his confession. The confessional was partitioned into two cubicles. There was a small opening in the solid, timber dividing wall, level with the priest's head when he sat. This allowed the confessor's voice to be readily heard. The priest slid the small wooden door that covered the opening to the side. He could see the top of Bruce's head, partly obscured by latticed timber strips. There was silence. Bruce nervously picked his fingernails.

Father Thomas coughed. Bruce shuffled his feet on the wooden floor and continued to pick his fingernails. The only sound.

"What have you to tell me, Mr Prentice?" the priest asked, eventually.

Silence. Bruce wasn't sure of the reason for the chat. He hadn't previously been to confession and didn't know what to expect. *You only go to confession if you've done somethin' wrong. Not me.* Bruce laughed at his thought, almost but not quite silently.

"What is funny, Mr Prentice?" Father Thomas said slowly.

"I got into a fight, Father. Some black kid started it. I don't normally do that sort of thing," he lied. "But I had to defend myself, didn't I?"

"No, Mr Prentice, you didn't. Today we will ignore what actually happened but remember this: having those boys in this school is important for our funding. If we didn't have them your parents would have to pay more. Understand? Now keep your nose clean, young Bruce Prentice, or I might have to take action against you. We don't want that now, do we?"

Bruce left the confessional feeling vindicated. *"Today we will ignore what actually happened."* Father Thomas's words resonated as he left the chapel. Bruce could celebrate with his friends. A throng of boys from his age group gathered as he proudly walked outside into the sunshine. All were eager to learn of his punishment, if any.

"What happened, Brewster?" the school captain asked, as he pushed to the front of the group. "Did old man Thomas give you the cane? Did he make you drop your pants and whip your arse or did he give you six of the best on your hands? Give us the drum."

"Nah, nuthin' like that. He said I should have done a better job at beating the shit out of that kid," Bruce lied, laughed and added, "I reckon

Father Thomas was getting all excited and was probably even doing something unthinkably insane when I told him how that pretty boy Abo looked before and after I finished with him. I heard a groan from his cubicle when I told him how tough I was and how that kid's thick lips were now even thicker."

The boys joined in with Bruce's laughter and fell in behind him as he walked towards the playground, where the Indigenous boys usually gathered under an old eucalyptus tree. For a short time, pumped by the attention he was receiving from his friends, Bruce considered testing the extent of Father Thomas's instructions. Testing the boundaries. As he neared the group, he changed his mind and instead shouted a warning, informing them to be very careful in the dark of the night.

He thought himself a hero.

Chapter 4

After a time, Bruce's taunting and physical aggression became even more appealing to his friends, when it manifested itself in the form of risk-taking of a criminal nature. Initially, it was relatively minor – petty theft and similar. But over time it progressed to breaking and entering, and stealing from a local Ditchingham delicatessen.

Inevitably, Bruce was caught and charged by the local police. He was released after his mother was contacted and quickly arranged payment of a surety to bail him out. Cheryl Prentice was devastated. A sullen Bruce showed no remorse and even seemed, to his mother, to be resentful of her intervention.

I would be further elevated in the eyes of the other boys if I had spent a night or two in the can.

By the time Bruce was returned to the school, it was common knowledge he had been arrested and taken into custody. As he entered the compound after the final siren when school was finished for the day, he was spotted by a group of local boys standing by the bicycle racks. Upon seeing him the boys responded unexpectedly.

"Three cheers for Brewster!" one of the boys yelled and others joined in the chorus. Bruce's chest bulged with pride. Final confirmation he belonged.

Father Thomas informed Cheryl Prentice that the school would not take any action at that time, pending the Magistrate's decision.

"Everyone is entitled to the presumption of innocence," he insisted. "The burden of proof is on the police or prosecution to make their case. Until then, Bruce can stay here on the understanding he behaves himself."

Bruce's mother engaged a lawyer for his first appearance in the Ditchingham Regional Children's Court. Determined to ensure her son had the best legal representation, she had increased her house mortgage with the

Cottam Mills Rural Bank to pay the legal fees. A good lawyer would surely see justice was done – a 'not guilty' decision.

Ignoring his mother's urgings, Bruce entered a plea of guilty. His lawyer then successfully argued that he was remorseful and as he had no prior convictions his actions should not attract a punishment. She stressed that any other form of punishment would be excessive as it was highly likely he would be expelled from his private school. His parents would undoubtedly lose the school fees already paid. That was a condition of a students' entry to the school.

The Magistrate determined that Court costs were required to be paid. Restitution and a small amount in compensation to the shop owner were also applied.

Following the Court appearance and guilty plea, the school Principal summoned Cheryl Prentice to a meeting at which she was informed of the School Board's decision to expel her son. "I'm sorry it has come to this, Mrs Prentice," Father Thomas said in a forlorn tone. "But I hope you understand we need to protect the school's reputation."

Bruce sat in silence as his mother pleaded with the priest to show leniency. On Bruce's behalf she pleaded for a second chance. When Father Thomas shifted his gaze to her son, who reciprocated with a wide-eyed stare, he merely shook his head. Cheryl begged sympathy for her financial plight.

"Father, I must tell you something very personal. In the six months since Bruce has been gone from Cottam Mills, his father and I have separated. I confess to be struggling but I want Bruce to have the best chance in life, the best possible education, even though it is at great personal cost. Unfortunately, his father won't pay but I guarantee I always will." Cheryl paused to let that sink in and then reinforced the message. "In fact, I have increased my mortgage to ensure I have the money. I can give you a letter from the bank, if you wish, Father."

Father Thomas appeared unmoved. Cheryl sensed the argument was falling on deaf ears and finally pleaded, "I am a sole parent now, with two daughters to support. If you insist on Bruce's expulsion, I really need a reimbursement of fees paid for the balance of the school year."

"Mrs Prentice. I'm afraid the Board has made its decision, not just on the basis of his recent criminal offence." Father Thomas had raised his voice and glared at Bruce as he uttered the last two words. "But also on the basis of his repeated poor behaviour. His attitude cannot be tolerated any longer. We have tried to guide Bruce along a moral path, a path he seems unwilling to walk. A Christian path of understanding, a path of sympathy and decent moral standards."

"The school fees," Cheryl asked in an attempt to deal with the heart of the matter of most concern to her. A forlorn hope. "I struggle…" Her voice faded as she realised the irony in the Principal's comments. *A path of understanding, a path of sympathy and decent moral standards.*

Father Thomas continued to shake his head and then reinforced the school policy with, "A contract is a contract."

Chapter 5

At his Ditchingham school, Bruce had experienced a growth spurt that now placed him at the size of some of the senior and larger boys at his old school. He now stood at 180 cm but possibly looked shorter because he slumped his shoulders.

Forced to return home, he soon discovered there were two aspects of his recent new reputation that preceded him. Already other boys at the school knew of his misdemeanours: the Children's Court appearance and the guilty plea.

Street gangs were a thing in Cottam Mills. The putative leader of the reprobates at the fringe of the adolescent population was eager to recruit Bruce to his gang.

"He's one of us now," he informed his fellow misfits. "He left town as a wimp and in a short time grew up and found his place in society. I hear he even threatened to punch one of his teacher's lights out," he exclaimed. That brought raucous laughter from his friends.

Usually there would be a vote on whether or not a potential new recruit should be included as part of their group. A vote would be taken but only after an applicant or nominee had shown his mettle by performing a significant, meritorious accomplishment. Something that might attract the attention of the constabulary. Not so on this occasion. There was no need. Bruce's actions and exaggerated rumours that circulated about his toughness and newly developed aggression were enough, and Bruce made no attempt to dispel the rumours.

Although happy to return to Cottam Mills, Bruce still disliked the idea of attending the local Senior High School, but he very quickly began socialising in a way he never did before his departure. He had been a loner. Now, in his mind, he was a hero. Spending time with boys regarded as the town bullies, just like his old friends at the private school, became an important part of his lifestyle.

The second aspect of his new reputation was soon apparent to everyone, although it, too, had arrived in town before him. Bruce was unsure how. To his knowledge, none of the Indigenous boys at his last school were related or in any other way connected to the Noongar people at Cottam Mills, the Wilman nation. Somehow, perhaps carried by *maar wirnkoorl* (the westerly wind), Mokiny knew that Bruce had taunted and was violent towards those boys.

Mokiny Jnr was extremely disappointed and sought the advice of the Elders to determine if there was anything he could or should do to refocus Bruce. To encourage him to revert to his former self. Adopt the values that he had been taught by the Noongar Elders, his father in particular, whilst he was in primary school.

Mokiny was the son of a *djenakabi* (law man). His father, known to his mob as Uncle Mokiny, was now solid in his belief that Bruce was *wara* and instructed young Mokiny and his friends to keep well away from him. Uncle Mokiny Snr told his son and his friends that he sensed Bruce was *wara* inside and carried an internal *djinack* (evil spirit) that had previously not revealed itself or had been well disguised. *Maar* had confirmed his feelings of unease. Had revealed the truth and told the Wilman people that Bruce was *kaat wara* (sick in the head).

Uncle Mokiny Snr, the 'old man', as the Noongar Wilman children called the senior *djenakabi*, had attempted to guide young Mokiny and his friend Bruce on a path of strong human values. To teach them both right from wrong. Teach them the law. But the boys took different directions.

Mokiny Jnr now realised Bruce never was a *ngoony*. The Noongar peoples of Cottam Mills instead called him 'Boodjark'. That name very quickly circulated around the school and the town. Even Bruce was happy to adopt the name. To him it sounded 'really cool'. Only Mokiny Jnr and his friends knew its meaning. Maggot.

Boodjark was unhappy at school. He approached his mother with the suggestion that he could help support the family if he left school and was able to obtain employment. "I hate school and I'm no good at it. I don't like the teachers, I don't like the subjects. What's the point of learning French? Let me leave," he implored, "I want to get a job."

Cheryl thought about the idea. *We could certainly do with extra money to more adequately feed the kids and pay the bills.*

The catalyst for Cheryl deciding to discuss the matter with Boodjark's school form teacher and the Deputy Principal was the arrival of the Shire Council rates. They had increased well beyond what she had budgeted for.

The teachers were unanimous in agreement that her son was not academically inclined. That his failures in Year Ten would undoubtedly be repeated at upper secondary school. It would be surprising if he were to advance to tertiary education. There would have to be a dramatic change of attitude and the evidence suggested that would be highly unlikely. Cheryl was convinced. Her son would leave school and get a job.

Since the breakup in marriage between Cheryl and Snifter, Boodjark's uncle had provided constant emotional support to his sister. Although not sure if Boodjark would respond to his moral guidance, Cheryl's brother believed he needed to try. The best way was to have the boy under his nose on a daily basis.

A respected businessman, employing six men and four women engaged in domestic and commercial bar and kitchen design and manufacturing, Boodjark's uncle also employed several apprentices. In recent times, the construction industry had slowed and there was little demand for new kitchen installations. The renovation side of the company's activities continued to do well, to some extent filling the void. He had sufficient work to offer his nephew an apprenticeship at Prestige Designs and Installation.

For almost twelve months Boodjark's apprenticeship proceeded without incident. He wasn't a particularly hard worker although he contributed, mostly performing menial tasks. But he was bored. He still associated with the miscreants of his age in Cottam Mills. It was only a matter of time before he joined the hoodlums in an unlawful endeavour. Peer pressure, peer influence, the adrenalin rush, could be offered as reasons but not excuses.

Boodjark's apprenticeship at Prestige meant he would often accompany a skilled tradesman to private domestic and commercial properties for fit-outs. It occurred to him that his knowledge of the premises, including the awareness of security systems and where they existed, would enable him to gain easy access whenever he chose. Possessing that knowledge, he believed he wouldn't be caught. *Wara*, evil thoughts.

Encouraged by his friends, Boodjark borrowed some carpentry tools from his uncle, ostensibly for the purpose of doing woodwork in the shed at the rear of his mother's property. His uncle was mistakenly pleased that his nephew would be using the tools to improve his woodwork skills. He knew the shed was well equipped with benches but he also knew Snifter Prentice never bothered to acquire tools. He had no time for their use and even less use for the time.

The night-time breaking and entering started with premises that were unoccupied due to refurbishments. Some of those occurred in Ditchingham, where Prestige had won significant renovation and modernisation contracts. One of Boodjark's older friends, Simon Patterson, had a driver's licence and car. The car wasn't fast. Not a serious get-away vehicle from any criminal act. But Patterson liked to think it was.

Ditchingham was on the flats below the escarpment, conveniently only forty-five minutes drive from Cottam Mills. The old Holden sedan rattled its way along the potholed bitumen road that could be mistaken for a corrugated gravel road, so frequently were the potholes encountered. Contractors had re-sealed some patches for the local Council but it appeared budgetary restrictions had limited the repairs. Where the road narrowed, as it wound down the steepest hill, the road worsened. *No problem*, thought Patterson. *No need to speed on the return trip*. He was right.

Established businesses, bars and a hotel that were undergoing renovations suited Boodjark for the break-ins. The owners needed their business to continue operating while the work was being undertaken, which meant there was often cash or other valuables on the premises. He decided the Ditchingham Arms Hotel would be easy pickings.

Large rewards were not always readily available. That didn't bother Boodjark. His friends boosted his ego with praise and encouragement. That was enough. There was still a thrill in the risk-taking, especially when watched by his friends, who usually didn't enter the premises but waited nearby, car engine running.

"Come in with me tonight, Patto," Boodjark urged Patterson, as his older friend slowed the car in a lane at the rear of the Ditchingham Arms Hotel. "It's my birthday. Help me clean out the grog. We'll have a party back at Cottam. Whadya reckon?"

Patterson turned the key to shut down the engine. It coughed black smoke, an audible complaint. A complaint that caught the attention of the resident who lived directly behind the hotel. The hotel proprietor.

A light sleeper, Bob Rendell was surprised to hear noise in the laneway at the rear of his property late at night. It was usually a quiet area. He rose from his bed and pulled the blind aside in the family room to peer out. Before it was extinguished, he saw what appeared to be a car light reflected off an upstairs hotel window.

Rendell listened intently for any unfamiliar noise. There was a faint sound of footsteps on gravel. The footsteps stopped. A thud and then another. The sound of two pairs of feet hitting the concrete beyond the wall, inside the hotel yard.

His wife joined him at the rear of the house as Rendell was pulling on a pair of running shoes.

"Don't do anything silly, Bob," she whispered. "Call the police."

Her plea fell on deaf ears. Bob stubbornly left the house. Catherine Rendell made the call instead.

Celebrating his sixteenth birthday at a Ditchingham hotel, late at night when the bar had long closed and in total disregard for the security system, several bourbons may have affected Boodjark's judgment. When he drank, like his father, he thought he was invincible.

Boodjark came of age back in the days when men were like his father. If there was a fight to be had, count him in. The weak wouldn't survive in that man's world. Timid, shy people, like the blacks, who would look away if challenged, even verbally challenged, were regarded as weak by real men. Real men knew how to drink and knew how to fight.

A few swigs of Jack Daniels would be enough for him to stand toe-to-toe with anyone within sight. Rules didn't apply in a punch-up. Hands, fists, feet and the use of any potential weapon within reach would be used. Although scrawny, Boodjark could go a few rounds when the grog took effect.

Snifter Prentice was in better physical shape. For him it took at least a quarter of a slab of beer. Not so for his son. Boodjark and Patto believed themselves immune from detection. They were becoming inebriated. The alcohol made them indestructible.

"Kind of the manager to leave so much Jack Daniels for us," Boodjark slurred, before taking another mouthful. "Fill the bag with the bottles of Scotch, too, Patto. There's no money in the till but there has to be a safe around here somewhere. I'll find it and we'll take that with us."

"The hell you will!" shouted Rendell, having quietly entered his hotel from a side door and now interrupting the party. He rounded one end of the bar and confronted the intruders. Fists clenched, feet planted firmly apart on the timber floor next to an open tool bag. The apprentice's tool bag.

Patterson was in front of the bar. The customer's side. He lifted a heavy, oversized, canvas duffle bag, bottles clinking. He didn't wait to see what his partner in crime was planning. He struggled his way towards the rear hotel door where the pair had entered.

Boodjark defiantly took another mouthful of bourbon before lifting the near-empty bottle above his head. The remainder of the amber liquid ran down his arm and spilt onto the floor. He hesitated only a second and then charged, catching Rendell by surprise. The proprietor was shocked at the effrontery, took a step backwards and tripped over the bag of carpenter's tools, hitting his head on a barstool as he fell. Rendell lunged sideways endeavouring to find a weapon in the open bag, any weapon. An empty bourbon bottle crashed across his right arm, disabling it.

Patterson heard the commotion and stopped at the door in time to witness Boodjark hasten towards his tool bag, procure a screwdriver as a makeshift weapon and thrust it into Rendell's leg. Boodjark scrambled to his feet and shuffled towards the door.

Rendell screamed painfully. Patterson watched. Frozen in place. He stood near the doorway, mouth wide open as Boodjark rushed up to him.

"Let's get out of here," Boodjark urged, grabbing Patterson by the arm.

"You shouldn't have done that," Patterson cried out, head spinning in confusion.

"I had to. We needed to get away from that madman."

Who is the madman, thought Patterson, now regretting the decision to accompany Boodjark. That regret would shortly be deepened and carried by him for many years.

As the pair stepped outside, they were greeted with, "No, you shouldn't have done that. Now, place the bags on the ground, boys. Lay flat on the ground, face down!" The burly policeman had one hand on the Taser in a holster attached to his belt. Another equally large police officer moved towards the pair of malfeasants. Without hesitation, instructions were followed.

Boodjark and Patterson appeared before the same magistrate who heard the matter Boodjark was last charged with. It was Patterson's first offence and he was afforded some leniency, but not his accomplice, who faced more serious charges. Caught trespassing on the premises with stolen goods and the hotel proprietor found with a screwdriver in his leg, his lawyer was never able to mount a solid defence. He had little room to move.

In an attempt to reduce the inevitable penalty, he admitted to trespass but argued against the other charges. He further argued his client had a reasonable belief the property owner intended to cause him grievous bodily harm and accordingly, he acted in self-defence. A long shot rejected.

The charges stood. Aggravated burglary, because the overwhelming evidence was that he used a weapon (the screwdriver) with intent, plus assault occasioning bodily harm. The magistrate believed Boodjark must now be taught a lesson and told him so. His history was noted and he was sent to a juvenile detention centre for two years.

Believing two years to be excessive, the lawyer tried to persuade his client to appeal the term of the sentence but Boodjark declined.

"Nah, don't worry, mate," he said, and then as an afterthought, he added, "Can we appeal on the grounds the bloke I stabbed was attacking me? I had to act in self-defence. I had to subdue him. If not, I'll be out soon enough. Good behaviour 'n all."

He had no sense of responsibility for his actions. Lessons from the 'old man' had fallen on deaf ears.

Chapter 6

The strength of one's character can be measured by how well we meet and handle challenges that are inevitably thrown at us throughout life. The demonstration of character can be seen in how we bear the discomfort of negative challenges; how effectively we take them on board, accept the difficulties, the pain, and live with the thought that we've been lucky to have had that experience. A strong character can see a vision worth pursuing. A positive outcome. A glass half-full type of person.

Boodjark didn't find the juvenile prison a challenge. Nor did he believe the experience to be character building. For him it was a temporary interruption to his exciting and preferred lifestyle. Inside the can, whenever he could, he would spend time in the gym, working on building a physique that would be intimidating. There's no challenge in that and nor is it character building but it occupied time.

Two years in the juvenile penitentiary should have introduced him to new, positive ideas but that is not what a prison necessarily provides. Although one might argue it should be, the effectiveness of a prison is not measured by its capacity to rehabilitate. In reality, the Ditchingham institution had the opposite effect.

Boodjark wasn't interested in changing his life. To his fellow inmates, he appeared aloof. Disinterested in them. The only time he would converse was when they shared their experiences of antisocial life on the outside. In turn he would exaggerate his delinquent activities, possibly to seek peer approval or alternatively to claim he was better than the others. His ego meant one-upmanship was always on the agenda.

He exuded an impression of superiority. An air of arrogance that didn't cut it with most of the other young crims. What did cut it was a bread and butter knife repeatedly bent until it snapped, exposing enough blade just above the handle to be used as a weapon when required. It was comfortably concealed in the large hand of one of the bigger and more aggressive inmates.

"You're an asshole, Boodjark," raged the offender carrying the hidden makeshift weapon.

Boodjark was regarded as a newcomer, even though he had served two months of his sentence. They walked laps of the yard whilst the agitator maintained his verbal abuse. The bigger boy had been confined for eighteen months and was described by most as 'stir crazy'. An expression that was insensitive to some in the institution who suffered actual mental illness. An unnecessary expression, but one that was frequently used by prisoners as well as prison officers, most frequently called the 'screws' by offenders.

Attempting to cause trouble the haranguing continued. "That attitude may have worked with your scaly mates at school but it doesn't wash in here, you arrogant, good-for-nuthin' son-of-a-bitch!"

Eventually, Boodjark succumbed to the provocation. The resultant brawl left him with serious gashes the length of his face, requiring stitches from the prison nurse. Both inmates spent two weeks in solitary confinement. Following this further confinement, Boodjark sank deeper within himself. Unless essential, he avoided mixing with the other offenders at all times. Prison officers believed his disconnection from the malcontents as an acknowledgement of his rehabilitation. A mistaken belief. Nevertheless, eventually his good behaviour resulted in an early release.

When he returned to Cottam Mills, Boodjark was sullen and moody. Unforgiving towards his former friends, who had abandoned him. Total disregard for his former work colleagues, including his uncle who would not reinstate him in his apprenticeship. No third chance. Even his sisters avoided him.

During the time of Boodjark's departure from Cottam Mills, the local economy had been hit with the closure of several mines and a downturn in the timber industry. The national economy was on the verge of a recession. New-home construction numbers and demand for timber had slumped. The building industry was in decline, suffering its worst downturn for many years. Millers and miners lost their jobs.

With no work, unskilled and little chance of employment, Boodjark wandered the streets, occasionally mixing with others whose deviant behaviour readily fitted the profile of his preferred companions. That behaviour was most often of a violent nature. Most often violence against vulnerable teenagers from the Indigenous community.

The Noongar youth had been taught by the Elders to turn the other cheek. Walk away from confrontation. They were naturally shy and, if possible, would stay well clear of whites of their age group. They were vulnerable because they avoided hostile situations and were wrongly perceived to be weak. They had been taught to show respect for everyone, no matter what their colour or creed.

The bullies in town didn't recognise that the reticence to mix was shyness. They had a lack of awareness or understanding of the character of Indigenous people. They only saw what they believed to be weakness. It wasn't. It was strength. It took strength to walk away. Ignoring the taunts showed strength of character. The old man, respectfully known to the young Noongar boys and girls as 'Uncle Joe', had instilled that belief.

For Boodjark, a confrontation would prove beyond doubt that he was superior. He always had something to prove. He had to prove he was strong. Prove that he had power. Prove that he could do as he pleased; after all, he had a good teacher in his father.

He was joined by two other young thugs lurking nearby the Noongar *karla* on the edge of town, looking for trouble. Verbal abuse wasn't enough.

"You're nothin' but a bunch of cowards. Don't walk away and hide!" Boodjark yelled at a group of Indigenous youths returning from town in the late afternoon. "You're nothin' but a bunch of weaklings. Gutless," he taunted, chest pumped out.

One of Boodjark's companions joined in with, "Yeah, gutless – the lot a ya! You blackies didn't put up a fight when white man came and took this country. Let's see if you've learnt anything. Got any courage now?"

The three *koorlamidi wadjala* (young white men) laughed as the Indigenous group, head down, walked across the street and disappeared along a dirt track that led to their *karla*. The *wadjala* decided they would return later that night.

Yabini was one of Mokiny Junior's younger sisters. At fourteen years of age, she was a pubescent beauty. Her fifteenth birthday was only a few days away but she could be mistaken for being in her early twenties. She was elegant, mature and carried herself with dignified poise. Dark hair shone down her slender back. Equally dark but sparkling eyes shone. An ever-present smile that flashed lightness, brightness and happiness crossed her face. Her personality raised the spirits of everyone with whom she came into contact.

She was born in the bush under a beautiful *dirdong* (spring) night sky. An unblemished night sky. Almost every star of the Milky Way could be seen brightly stretching across the sky and the Southern Cross was readily visible to guide lost souls throughout *boodja* that night. The artificial lights of the town had been turned off, making the stars brighter than ever. Her parents named her Yabini, meaning 'Star'. She brought light into their life. As she grew older, she brought light into the life of everyone with whom she came into contact.

Yabini was employed after school, stacking grocery shelves in a Cottam Mills privately owned supermarket. The owner paid her cash, not having to worry about holiday pay, superannuation payments, or a loading for weekend work. Not surprisingly, she was not given the appropriate rate of payment for her work. It was an exploitative, menial task but she was satisfied in the knowledge that every little extra income benefited the family and her Wilman community.

Punctual in her attendance, methodically following instructions and diligent in performing each task, Yabini was a good worker. She never complained, always happy to help. She hummed a beautiful tune whilst working. Her employer believed that to mean she was happy with the meagre income she received.

It was a dark, moonless night. Spring rains had returned and darkened the night even more. There was an occasional clap of thunder, preceded by flashes of lightning. For Yabini, those flashes were enough to illuminate the bush track. They were also enough for the three young men who watched as Yabini strolled casually and carefree towards them on her way home from work.

Boodjark stepped onto the track from behind a large tree, in front of Yabini. She stopped and turned to look behind but found the path of retreat blocked by his two companions.

"Please, I just want to go home," Yabini said. There was silence. "I have money. I'll give that to you if you just allow me to pass. My dad will be along soon," she said in a panicked voice. "We don't want trouble.

Please let me pass, please. I just want to go home to my family." Those pleas were her last words.

Without any further warning, a hand from behind covered her mouth, muffling a cry for help. Flailing arms were tackled and she kicked at Boodjark as she was dragged through shrubbery into a small clearing near the large gum tree. Yabini was repeatedly punched in the stomach and then, continuing to struggle, she was punched to the side of her face. Losing consciousness, she fell.

"My idea and I silenced her, so I'm going first," Boodjark insisted.

Beautiful, helpless Yabini was raped. Pack-raped.

"She saw you, Boodjark. I swear she saw you. I saw your face when there was a lightning flash and I was standing behind her. She would have seen you, too. You shouldn't have shown your face," Boodjark's friend muttered with panicked anxiety.

"Don't worry. She's worthless now. Won't tell. Too ashamed to tell her mob." As an afterthought, he added, "Maybe I'd better make sure of it."

He reached for a large rock near where Yabini had fallen and lifted it in his left hand. It felt unnatural and less likely to be effective for what he had planned. Being right handed, he passed the rock to that hand. That's when he felt it. Sticky moisture covered the surface. Blood.

Boodjark felt for but was unable to find a pulse. They had assumed Yabini was unconscious. She had hit her head on the rock with an unchecked fall from a coward's punch. Her seemingly lifeless body gave a slight shudder. Boodjark again felt for a pulse. Nothing.

"Let's get out of here," he said cold-heartedly but with urgency. He stood and brushed past his companions. They followed Boodjark's instructions but also knew there would be dire consequences should they not do so.

Beautiful, innocent Yabini lay motionless. Dead.

At that precise moment, there was another bright flash of lightning and a much louder and immediate clap of thunder. The noise caused Boodjark and his two friends to simultaneously look skywards. Surprisingly and suddenly, they saw the rain clouds part. An exceptionally bright star appeared in the sky directly above them. Astronomers would likely say it was Sirius, because it's the brightest star in the sky. Sirius normally rises after midnight but strange things happened that October night.

Mokiny Junior's older cousin, Bessie, was one of the few Indigenous people who were fortunate to have State housing in Cottam Mills. She normally would not venture out of her home at night, especially when there was *kep boolarang* (much rain). But something caused her to visit her uncle that night. Her Uncle Mokiny Senior, the *djenakabi*. There was no particular reason to see him and the family but she had strongly felt the urge.

There were seven Nissen huts at the *karla*: one for each large family, including aunties, uncles, cousins. The Nissen huts were ex-military and very old. Rust had formed at the edges of the half-cylindrical huts where the corrugated steel sheets were wedged into the ground. In addition to the Nissen huts, four corrugated steel shacks completed the circle of accommodation. Some families patiently waited for a State house but most were happy to live in the *karla*, close to family. Family bonds were, and always would, remain strong.

Numerous members of Bessie's family occupied a Nissen hut. Water seeped into the hut through holes originally made by tek screws and was collected in several buckets. Most rain ran off the rounded steel roof and crept into the edge of the hut where it was rusted at its base. Water dripped audibly into a bucket near the centre of the hut, dropping from three metres. It didn't interrupt the enthusiastic but serious discussion.

Bessie sat with the extended family, while they talked about their daily activities. They happily shared experiences. Parents beamed with pride as they conveyed the news of their disabled boy participating in the school sports carnival. Everyone applauded with delight. They all laughed at the small things that made them happy. Smiling faces of the newborn in the mob, a toddler losing a front tooth, a girl achieving good grades in a school exam. They even laughed at their misfortunes.

When the Elders spoke, they gave their unmitigated attention. They listened eagerly at the storytelling from a respected Elder who told of their ancestors, some of whom camped in this same area where they now lived. They heard how *mar* (the wind) told them when it was time to move to the coast for the best fishing season and how *djindang* (the stars) gave them directions. They knew the *djindang* well, especially the Southern Cross group.

Bessie had heard many of the stories before. Storytelling was truth telling. They were truths passed down through the family for generations. Always *boonda* (true) and captivating. She watched Mokiny Jnr's face light up when the Elders spoke. She could see how much respect he had for one Elder in particular, his father Mokiny Senior. Bessie had always been fond of her cousin and was very proud of the young man he had become.

The story Mokiny Jnr always loved the most was the story of the *Ngarngungudditj Walgu*. The bearded serpent had created the river that meandered through Cottam Mills and another two rivers near Ditchingham. In its travels, *Walgu* nestled into a valley near where the coastal town would be built, creating an inlet to the sea. It had returned to rest in the river near Cottam Mills. Near where the *Beelagu* (river people) lived. Sometimes, at night, the *Walgu's* silver beard could be seen resting on top of the river.

The *Walgu* was important. It gave life to the Noongar people by creating a valley for the collection of fresh water. Water that attracted animals. It also greeted and cared for the spirits of ancestors in the Dreaming.

After only a short time with the family, Bessie stood, ready to leave. The rain had stopped. Time to head home. Everyone, especially Mokiny Jnr, was surprised when Bessie wrapped her arms around the young man and gave him a firm and prolonged hug. A surprising display of affection. Without a word, Bessie turned and walked out of the *karla*.

Strolling back towards her house on the *karla djooroot* (track), the *malkar* (thunder) spoke again for the last time on that night. Bessie was surrounded by the brightest flash of *kilang* (lightning) she had ever seen. It may have flashed downwards and touched the earth nearby but to Bessie it felt like the *kilang* was projected upwards. She heard the *malkar* and felt *mar,* the wind. She shivered.

Bessie paused, deep in contemplation about an expression she had once heard. *Someone just walked over my grave*. A feeling of coldness, skin crawling, and she sensed goose bumps on her arms without explanation. She was engulfed by a strange sensation. It felt like her heart stopped, or at least paused for a moment. Perhaps it did. Unexpected, unearthly. Was it a *kaanya* passing by? A soul? Someone travelling to the Dreaming? That thought lingered.

She gazed skywards at the trees moving in the wind. Shadows cast by the clouds moved almost solemnly across the trees and shrubs below. Mother time always hastened the family to come together but not usually on such a night.

Why this night? What caused me to join the family tonight, of all nights? On such a wet and windy night. Why did I have such a strong urge? Was it one of our ancestors Uncle Djarraly spoke about? Calling out to me. Was I called to the karla for any particular reason? Perhaps something will be revealed.

Time stood still for Bessie. An unearthly experience, as if in a spell. Glimpses of an exceptionally bright star materialised. Bessie had never seen that star before, at least not this early in the night. Only glimpses emerged from the blackness of the night clouds directly overhead. Despite strong gusts of wind, trees lining the track now seemed to move in slow motion. *Mar* took control and gave Bessie time to think. *Kaanya, yes – a soul travelling.*

The coldness, the crawling skin, the goose bumps, and the sensation. A soul passing, travelling to the Dreaming. A profound display of Noongar spirituality. That is what Bessie told the family several days later.

"Yabini has met her ancestors in the Dreaming," she later said. "Our beautiful girl is at peace now. Resting with our ancestors who were also killed by the *wadjala* when they took our *boodja* and those that died in the sixty thousand years before."

Ahead, there was a slight rustle of bushes. Bessie didn't move. Not a *ka-rda* (racehorse goanna) prevalent in these parts. Too much noise and too big. Was it a *yongka* (kangaroo)? She listened intently. The sound of movement continued and then she heard humans whispering. *Wadjala.*

Three young men hustled out of the bush, thirty metres in front of her. They didn't look sideways. They didn't see her.

Chapter 7

Yabini was found the next day. Three days before her fifteenth birthday.

The people of Cottam Mills, not just the local Noongar Wilman people, were shattered. Yabini was well liked in the community at large. Always greeting townsfolk with a beaming smile, anxious to chat. A willing worker at the supermarket and always happy to volunteer her time at community events.

At school, Yabini had many friends. She was renowned for her sporting prowess, was an outstanding athlete, and was an important member of the girl's basketball and cricket teams. To her classmates, it was beyond belief that she would be murdered. She would always be remembered.

All Noongar people in and around Cottam Mills were heartbroken. For many it was the most difficult time they had ever experienced. Some chose not to speak her name. Some of the older people from the Wilman nation believed her name mustn't be spoken. They believed to do so could mean her spirit might return to cause harm. For them, she would be forever remembered and talked about, but not by name.

Others, especially the younger people, spoke her name freely, recalling all of the beautiful times they had spent with her. For them, it was an important part of the mourning process to call her name. They decided Yabini must be remembered and talked about, to remain connected to the family. She would want that connection and her memory to live on.

Her immediate family remained indoors, refusing to talk to anyone. They couldn't. It was simply too difficult. For some Aboriginal and Torres Strait Island people, the law required them to remain silent and in mourning for three months. For some, it would be much longer. The period of bereavement for the Wilman nation was usually four weeks but Yabini's loss would be felt for much longer. Her family and close friends would mourn for years.

Only the Elders could address Yabini's parents and siblings. The Elders arranged for their care during this difficult time. The parents and siblings could not leave the hut. It was wrong to step outside their tribal community and to talk about the evil that had occurred. Family members would daily deliver food to their hut. As is customary when a death occurs, the hut's furniture was removed because it may contain an evil spirit. It would be replaced some months later.

Uncle Djarraly and the other Elders believed the police should stay away. They didn't need to talk to the family. They should just get on with the job and solve the crime. Bring justice to the people.

Over the years, Cottam Mills had more than its share of violence but nothing of this nature. Nobody had ever been murdered. Nevertheless, with one exception, the police acted professionally and were quick to cordon off the area with scene-of-crime tape. Police officers worked in shifts to stand guard near the crime scene, awaiting the arrival of the forensic pathologist from the city. The crime-scene investigator arrived in Cottam Mills, late morning, on the day Yabini's body was found.

The main track to the Noongar Wilman people's *karla* was impassable, cordoned off by the police. Nobody was permitted to use that route. It meant only a few people familiar with alternative routes to the camp would enter.

The police wanted a statement from family members but the Elders insisted they should not enter their hut. A junior officer with no understanding of Noongar culture threatened to charge Uncle Djarraly with obstructing the police. He was an exception to the professionalism of the police officers who were generally respectful.

A Police Aboriginal Liaison Officer from Ditchingham stepped in and instructed his colleague to leave them be. To show respect to the family during their sorry business, their time of mourning. He was supported by homicide detectives who were summonsed to the town immediately the body had been found.

An area within fifty metres of the crime scene was the immediate focus of an intense search for clues. It started mid-afternoon, several hours after the body had been found and continued into the evening, under torchlight. After ten hours, the search was halted for the night, to resume at daylight the following day. It was then extended further through the bush to the *karla* and nearby streets. Unrelenting rain on the night of the murder had washed footprints from the *djooroot,* but the main focus of the police was to find the murder weapon.

The coroner could not conclusively determine the cause of death at the crime scene, though an initial examination of the body indicated the likelihood of blunt force trauma to the head and torso. The head impact was almost certainly enough to cause death. The search for a weapon continued.

On the afternoon of day two, an observant young female police constable found a rock that looked out of place in the bush. It was approximately thirty feet from where the body was found. There were no other similar rocks nearby and it appeared, to the constable, that it had been thrown there, breaking a branch from a small shrub before landing and being partially covered by mud. After photographs were taken, the forensic pathologist carefully removed the rock with gloved hands before taking it to the police station for further analysis.

Noting blood on the rock, the forensic pathologist first undertook a uhlenhuth test, a test to quickly determine if the blood was human or from another animal. A species test. They had to be thorough and record every step of the procedures undertaken.

Expeditiously completing that test, they proceeded to check the deoxyribonucleic acid. As expected, DNA of the deceased was found but further close examination found that was the only detectable DNA recovered from the rock.

Next, an examination for fingerprints, however incomplete they may be. Fingerprints can sometimes be found on the hard surface of a rock but the process is difficult. The forensic pathologist used ninhydrin solution in the hope that the rock was porous enough to highlight some ridge detail. Even though the granite rock had some porosity, it was insufficient to absorb the solution. The fingerprint test was negative.

Other than discovering the rock as a probable cause of death, a thorough search of the bush revealed nothing that could be linked to the murder. Time was of the essence. The trail would become cold if Homicide was unable to quickly find clues.

Police officers had gone from door to door, within the neighbourhood of the crime, urging residents to share any information they may have. A plea for help was broadcast on the radio and published on the front page of the Cottam Mills Bulletin. Homicide detectives were becoming frustrated. They had made no progress.

Late on the afternoon of day two, Mokiny Jnr visited Bessie. He needed to talk to his older cousin. It had been impossible to talk to his parents or siblings in the last two days. The grief they felt was so powerful, they couldn't talk at all.

Mokiny Jnr had recalled how his cousin had unexpectedly and uncharacteristically given him a prolonged hug on the night of the murder. Perhaps at the exact time of the murder. He had always been close to Bessie but her show of affection that night was different. Unusual. He had to get to the bottom of it and there was something else he needed to tell her.

As he walked up the front verandah steps, crossed the creaking boards and knocked on the door of Bessie's timber house, he thought, *My ngany moort* (cousin) *knows something. It may be hidden deep in her soul but it is there. Perhaps our ancestors are using ngany moort to help bring justice to our moort* (family).

He was again greeted affectionately and ushered inside. There was a table in the kitchen with a pale green linoleum top edged by a hard plastic strip. Four chairs with a dark-green cushioned base and backrest edged by chrome metal surrounded it. Mokiny sat on a chair by the unlit wood stove and watched his oldest cousin fussily wipe the table with a damp cloth.

As is customary, Bessie boiled the kettle and made a pot of tea. Extra strong tea on this occasion. Noticing Mokiny's eyes were red – he had been crying – Bessie took her time to gather two mugs and milk from the refrigerator. The *nyorn* (sorry) time was difficult for both of them. They both needed time to compose themselves. Tea was poured and the pair sat in silence at the kitchen table, waiting for the other to speak.

Bessie knew Mokiny wanted to talk of the nauseating, horrendous event from two nights before. Wanted to express his sadness. Her head was lowered, peering over the steam rising from her mug of piping-hot tea. Mokiny gazed directly at his beverage. At first, all that could be heard was the sound of the green grocer cicadas at the rear patio.

Minutes passed in silence. After a time Mokiny rubbed his eyes and asked, "Why did you visit the family on that night?"

"I don't rightly know," Bessie whispered with eyes still downcast. "Something told me I needed to see you all." As she spoke Bessie slowly nodded, elbows on the table, wringing her hands together.

Suddenly Mokiny sat upright, his head swivelled, and eyes searched the room. "There it is. I heard it yesterday. It's what brought me here. Can you hear it, Bessie? And her perfume, Bessie," he whispered hurriedly.

He raised his eyes to see tears flowing down his cousin's cheeks. She had heard it, too. The sound of a sweet, mellifluous voice hummed quietly nearby. The beautiful tune that Yabini hummed whilst she worked.

Bessie knew exactly what Mokiny was thinking. The spirit of his sister had returned to help the family find justice and give purpose to their grieving.

"I know, Mokiny, I know," Bessie said forlornly, tears still flowing. "Yes, I hear it. She is wearing her favourite perfume, too. She has visited me constantly in the last two days. I saw her briefly at the front door yesterday and her perfume has followed me around the house."

Bessie raised her head and gazed at Mokiny Jnr, who looked directly into her eyes, mouth agape. His eyes were moist. They sat in silence again.

After a few moments Mokiny broke the silence.

"What to do?" he asked. "You need to help her, cousin. She's returned for a reason and you're the only person who can help her. She needs your help to free her to the Dreaming."

Bessie raised her right hand, palm facing her cousin and with a look of determination in her eyes, said, "I know what I must do, Mokiny."

Day three. Overcoming her immeasurable and overwhelming grief and fear, Bessie attended the police station. She was grieving for her loss and for her extended family's loss. She was fearful of not being believed. Afraid that, like so many times in the past, the colour of her skin would taint the police attitude towards her. Fearful of what might happen if the murderers knew she had spoken out. But speak out she must.

It was a hot day and Bessie carried an umbrella to shield the sun. The air was still. As the door to the Cottam Mills Police Station slid sideways with a shudder, triggered by a sensor above the door as Bessie approached, the stillness was suspended by a sudden but slight movement of air. The breeze carried the scent of Yabini's perfume.

Bessie paused, smiled and found the courage to enter. *I know you're with me, beautiful girl.*

"My name is Bessie Brenting. People just call me Bessie," she introduced herself quietly.

Initially, the constable at the front desk was disinterested in the hesitant approach of an Indigenous woman standing, head bowed, at the front counter. When Bessie was eventually able to muster a confident and convincing voice, she insisted she had solid information on the murder. Since no arrest had been made, shy Bessie told the junior Officer, the information she was able to provide might assist their investigation.

"I need to talk to the Homicide Squad," Bessie insisted. "So far you mob haven't been much good, have ya. Hear me out."

Bessie was not deterred by having to wait for the two homicide detectives who had been summoned to return to the Police Station. During the several hours before they arrived, Bessie sat nervously waiting. The events of that terrible night played over and over in her mind. She had hoped her evidence would not be necessary, that the police would have made an arrest by now, but for whatever reason they had failed to do so. She feared the murderers might not be caught. But she had Yabini by her side. That made her determination stronger.

Eventually, Bessie was escorted to the operations room at the rear of the police station. Photographs of the crime scene were pinned to a board. There were numerous photos of her young cousin. Unable to look at the macabre pictures, she turned away and cried. It was a natural reaction.

Sensitive to Bessie's grief, the detectives waited a few moments before making introductions.

"I'm Detective Sergeant Langford and this is Detective Hopkins. Take your time and when you're ready, we would like to hear what you have to say. Please, take your time," Langford said politely.

After composing herself, Bessie quietly, almost inaudibly, told them what she saw on the night of the murder.

"Can you please speak a little louder, Mrs Brenting."

"Bessie. Call me Bessie."

"Okay, Bessie. Can you provide an accurate description of everything you saw and heard? Anything, no matter how insignificant you think it might be. Tell us about whatever you saw and heard." Langford was now convinced the nervous woman sitting across from him was genuine.

With tears streaming down her face, through hazed vision, Bessie described in detail the three young men she saw walking out of the bush. This was the investigation's first breakthrough. Although it was a dark night, Bessie was able to provide an accurate description of what the young men wore, their approximate height, colour of their hair and skin and their general demeanour. Throughout the interview, Langford noticed Bessie's right arm was extended slightly away from her body, as if she was holding an invisible hand. She was.

"One of them fellas had a scar on his face. The right side of his face. A long scar like he had been struck by the foot of a *yongka*." As she gave that description, Bessie raised her left hand, fingers curled inwards and dragged it suddenly near her face. Noticing Hopkins raising his eyebrows, Bessie quickly added, "A kangaroo. Them fellas was in a hurry to get away. *Ket-ket,* in a hurry."

"It was a dark night," Langford asserted. "How can you be so sure? Do you think you saw the murderers?"

Langford was observant. He saw a slight twitch of Bessie's right hand that was still extended about thirty centimetres away from her side.

"I don't think: I know. I seen them fellas. And I seen that scar face before, too. He no good fella in our town."

"But it was a dark night," Langford repeated. Bessie thought he was beginning to doubt the accuracy of the detail she had conveyed to him, but for Langford it was about ensuring the evidence could survive the closest scrutiny from a defence lawyer.

Bessie didn't want to tell the detectives she had a dream that night. She didn't want to tell them that in her dreams she saw three young men, one with blood dripping from his hands, emerge from the bush. She couldn't tell them she saw the image whilst her body hung in the air above the bush track a few feet from the *wadjala*. That the image was sent to her by a *kwobali kaanya,* a very good soul. That Yabini or her ancestors in the Dreaming had told her conclusively. She couldn't tell them that Yabini was standing next to her, holding her hand, encouraging her to truth telling.

"That night was very strange," Bessie told the detectives. "It was dark for most of the night but for a brief moment, as if the spirits had meant this to be, there was a break in the clouds and a bright star gave enough light for me to see those evil fellas. I saw 'em," Bessie said emphatically, attempting to leave no doubt she would be a strong witness.

For a long minute, neither detective said a word. They simply looked at Bessie as if trying to decide if this woman was truthful. Langford could see it in her eyes. Eventually, he turned to his colleague and murmured, "Write this up straightaway. Don't let her leave until she has signed a statement."

Langford left the room. He had decided there was a possibility the man with the scarred face could have a criminal record and he needed to check local photographs on the computer network. It didn't take long. He directed another police officer to print copies of ten photographs, one of which included Boodjark. A local man who had a criminal record and carried a scar the length of his face. Down the right side.

By the time Detective Sergeant Langford returned to the operations room, photographs in hand, Bessie was reading the statement prepared by Hopkins. It wasn't a long statement but it was enough and, most importantly, reflected clarity of recollection. Langford waited until she signed each page of the statement.

He then laid the photographs on the table in front of Bessie before asking, "Can you tell me if one of these men is the same man you saw at the murder scene? The one with blood on his hands." Gently, he added, "Bessie, take your time to look at each photograph. Can you say if one of these is one of the three you saw that night?"

From left to right, Bessie slowly cast her eyes over the photographs. She stopped at the sixth. Without hesitation, Bessie pointed at the image of Boodjark and said, "That's 'im!"

"Are you certain?" Langford asked. "Could it be one of the others?"

"No. That's 'im, I said. That's definitely 'im. Yep, I'm certain."

The police had a witness. A confident witness that placed Boodjark at the scene of the crime. The likely killer.

An arrest was made the same day.

Chapter 8

From inside a heavily barred control room, a prison officer pressed a button at the maximum security prison, geographical coordinates 32° 3' 25.0056" S, 115° 44' 38.0004" E. Two massive, barred gates at the entrance to the prison slowly opened inwards, without sound. Electronically controlled and well-oiled. The prison van slowly passed through the vehicular entrance gates, drove ten metres into an enclosure and again stopped. There were barred gates in front of the vehicle and at the rear.

The van driver alighted and passed a document to another prison officer who had stepped out of the gatehouse. He gave the document a cursory glance, already familiar with its contents. Only the name near the top of the page interested him. He walked casually to the door at the side of the van and waited. Like the prison officer, the driver wasn't in a hurry. He rattled a bundle of keys, found the one he wanted and strolled to the door to unlock it.

With a metallic squeal the door swung outwards, revealing only one handcuffed passenger with a chain joining his wrist and his ankle. He was seated on a bench opposite the door, head bowed. The driver unlocked the manacle held by a large ring attached to the floor of the van.

"Out, Prentice!" yelled the prison officer, with the nametag 'Martin'.

Boodjark blinked several times, his eyes adjusting to the light. He moved slowly. As he stepped onto the grey and cracked concrete, the same Prison Officer, without giving any further verbal instructions, used a wooden baton to nudge him towards a side gate. Boodjark turned his head to look at Martin, who then pointed his baton in the direction he should walk. A signal to move.

He shuffled forward still chained and handcuffed. Another prison officer scowled at Boodjark as he neared the barred gate. It was immediately unlocked and the prisoner was nudged through. More old, grey and cracked concrete met him in a central courtyard.

Boodjark raised his head, casting his eyes towards a pale blue sky perfected by a mid-afternoon ball of fire.

The senior prison officer gazed at Boodjark and saw a familiar manifestation of alcohol and substance abuse, in his case evidenced by facial lines and darker-than-normal circles around his eyes where chook claws hung.

"Welcome to our resort," said Martin in a sarcastic tone. "We hope to make your stay as miserable as possible." He laughed at his own joke. "Move along now. You have a busy schedule and haven't got time to gaze at the sun or try for a sun tan." Martin laughed again.

Other nearby officers joined in the laughter, even though they had heard Martin's expressions many times before. It was politic to laugh and it told the incoming crim they were a unit.

Although Boodjark didn't appear interested, Martin had an audience and took advantage of their attention by adding, "See those birds?" using his baton to point to a flock of seagulls landing on top of a nearby brick wall. "See those birds, I said," he repeated, jabbing the prisoner with his baton. Boodjark raised his head. "They're the only birds you're gonna see in a long time. Only the feathered kind." Labouring the point, in case Boodjark didn't get the message, he added, "None wearing a skirt." That brought more laughter. Boodjark lowered his head.

When the laughter subsided, another officer pointed in the direction of a building at the side of the courtyard. The building, like all others in this complex, was constructed of heavy limestone bricks, 450 mm wide and 350 mm high. Mould ran along the edges and in the joints between most bricks. Where there wasn't any mould, the bricks were stained by a combination of dirt and salt from the nearby ocean, transplanted there by the regular afternoon light breeze, quaintly and colloquially known as the 'Palmyra puff'.

The wall facing the courtyard was absent windows but a wooden door with peeling green paint was positioned in the centre. Boodjark was given a gentle encouragement towards that door as it was opened. The welcoming room.

Inside, Boodjark became prisoner 20797. A prison officer, wearing a nametag 'Lewis', rounded a desk and roughly removed Boodjark's handcuffs and chain. The manacle had chafed his ankle and as Lewis twisted it, the side of the fetter dug into flesh, causing the prisoner to involuntarily flinch. Lewis was squatting whilst removing the manacle and Boodjark thought how easy it would be to crunch his head. He didn't, of course, but such aggressive thoughts were constantly at the forefront of his mind.

"Toughen up," Lewis grunted. "If you don't, others will see to it in here. Now, remove your crappy, smelly civvies."

Boodjark was puzzled by the instruction and showed it in his facial expression. A look of bewilderment.

"Get undressed and put your stuff in the cardboard box," ordered Lewis, pointing at the table upon which sat a weather-stained, well-used 400 mm square box. Boodjark slowly removed his outer clothing, folded his jeans and denim shirt, and placed them carefully on the table next to the box.

"Everything I said!"

No you didn't, dickhead!

"Take everything off and be quick about it," Lewis barked his instructions.

Boodjark hesitated but decided to follow orders. There really wasn't any choice. A man held in remand with him, before his trial, had told him if convicted he should "Follow orders from the screws, otherwise, when alone, they can make your life hell." He didn't know if that was true but decided to accept the advice.

He repositioned the neat pile of clothing from the table into the box. The perspiration-stained clothes he had arrived in would be placed in a storage room nearby.

He stood naked in front of three prison officers, unsure of what would happen next.

"Open your mouth," Lewis sneered. "Lift your tongue."

Lewis carefully inspected the inside of Boodjark's mouth and said, "You need some dental work but it won't happen in here. Turn around and bend over, spread your legs and pull the cheeks of your butt apart."

Again Boodjark hesitated but followed the instructions, after noticing the glaring look of determination on the three faces. Any remaining dignity the prisoner had was gone.

"Now, lift your scrotum." Boodjark didn't move. Lewis raised his voice and snarled, "Lift your ball sack!"

Satisfied there was nothing hidden on Boodjark's person, he pointed at a door that led to a room known to the prisoners as 'the wet room'. Inside, there was a row of showers. Painted brick walls that rose only to waist height partitioned narrow cubicles.

Another prison officer handed Boodjark a green towel and his first issue of prison garments. One pair of green underpants, a green sweatshirt, dark green shorts and green loose-fitting trousers.

Moving more freely now, he crossed the room and opened the door. He stepped down from wooden floorboards onto a cold, concrete surface and glanced around the room. To his left, bolted to the wall and floor, was a narrow wooden bench that ran the length of the room. On the right, there was a shorter bench fixed to the wall adjacent to the door. Also to the right, there was a wide drainage channel in front of a row of showers.

"Take a shower. Be quick and don't use much soap on your dick." Lewis chuckled quietly whilst looking at his colleagues, again demonstrating a combination of his sense of humour and desire for control over the new inmate. The other prison officers nodded in unison.

Satisfied he had again impressed his colleagues, Lewis continued. "Shower and get dressed in your new uniform. Then you'll be shown to your luxury apartment. Hurry along, 20797. Get your arse into gear and don't use much water."

Boodjark walked to the furthest shower in the row of ten.

"Not that one!" yelled Lewis. As prisoner 20797 took two steps back towards the bench, where he left his clean prison garments, where Lewis stood with his colleagues, the message was repeated as he stepped into each cubicle. When he reached the first cubicle he glanced at Lewis. The prison officer said nothing, so he stepped over the drain and opened the faucet. Cold water dribbled from the shower rose. Boodjark turned and looked pleadingly at Lewis, who smiled knowingly.

"Get yourself wet, 20797; turn the shower off and soap up. Then wash the soap off. Haven't you ever showered before, 20797? You smell like you haven't seen water in a long time. For the next twenty years you will shower three times a week, but not in this luxurious spa. The shower shed has even colder water." Lewis chuckled quietly but loud enough to gain the nodding approval of his colleagues.

Boodjark didn't move, watching the water trickle onto the concrete floor near his feet.

"If you have any complaints, complete a blue slip and put it in a box near your slot. Your Divisional Unit Manager collects the blue slips and gives them to me. I file them." Lewis smirked as he looked at the other prison officers.

"Yeah, in the bin," one of them said and they all laughed extravagantly.

Like their other colleagues in Palmyra Prison, these prison officers aimed to dehumanise the inmates. Call them by a number. Belittle them. For that reason, the prison was colloquially named 'gestapoville', 'castle con', or 'crowbar cooler' by the prisoners, depending upon their state of mind and the particular situation they found themselves in at the time.

Some well-read inmates called Palmyra Prison 'the valley of tombs', a reference to the ancient city of Palmyra in Syria. The name 'valley of tombs' acknowledged that many offenders died whilst incarcerated. It also made a comparison with the ancient, desert city's extremes of temperatures with those inside the slot. Extraordinarily hot summer days and cold nights.

After his cold shower, Boodjark dried himself and quickly dressed.

"Follow this prison officer, your Unit Officer" barked Lewis, nodding at his colleague. "He will show you to your new home, cell 15. Listen carefully to his instructions and all will be sweet. Step out of line and your life won't be worth living. Behave yourself, 20797 and we'll all get along just fine. You'll love the resort." Lewis laughed sarcastically as he turned and left the wet room.

The officer with a nametag 'Somerville' led Boodjark outside into the baking sun. Somerville was a large, overweight man. Boodjark sized him up. Looked at his arse and thought of two sumo wrestlers struggling to gain ascendancy inside a tent.

He followed Somerville into a courtyard where ten-metre squares of lawn were disconnected by three-metre wide concrete paths. Several prisoners who were working in the area, kneeling and extracting nuisance weeds from the well-manicured lawn, rose to their feet and stared at the new arrival.

There were four hundred and seventy-eight prisoners in the overcrowded, high-security facility designed for less but the arrival of a newbie always aroused attention.

What are they staring at? I'm just another victim of the so-called justice system. Probably like many of them.

"Get back to work," yelled Somerville. "You can make your acquaintance later." He turned to Boodjark and said, "A little piece of history for you, 20797: this area was the Convict Parade Ground when Palmyra was first built. Behave yourself and you can have some privileges just like those scumbags over there. Get yourself some fresh air. But create trouble and you'll get the same treatment as the original cons."

One of the prisoners looked at Boodjark and winked before returning his attention to the lawn.

Why the wink? Don't get fresh with me. You might be a big boy but I'll smash your fucking head in if you give me the chance. I remember my dad saying, 'The bigger they are, the harder they fall'.

Boodjark turned directly ahead looking at a building with a portentous aspect, four storeys high with rows of small barred windows. The main cell block. Home for the foreseeable future. Shoulders slumped, he moved more slowly now.

Entering Main Division, Boodjark was directed into a small office. He was given his rations. Two cakes of soap, a toothbrush, a tube of toothpaste, shaving soap, a single disposable razor and a pack of coffee.

Cell number 15 was at the top landing. When he stopped at the door, Somerville placed his hand on Boodjark's back and nudged him inside the three-metre by two-metre cell. His new home. There was a bunk bed, a small wooden stool, a tabletop bolted to the side wall under which a slop bucket partly protruded. On the top bunk mattress was a pillow, a neatly folded dark green towel, two single bed sheets, a pillowcase and a blanket.

Somerville glanced at his watch and said, "Three forty-five. Work parties finish now and your new family will all return to their slots. Get changed into your night uniform. Roll call and muster is in half an hour. Tea is at five thirty."

As Somerville spoke, Boodjark couldn't take his eyes from the floppy skin under his chin. *Triple chins,* he thought. *I could grab that and squeeze the life out of you.*

Somerville paused, curious to know what 20797 was thinking but he decided not to ask. That would be treating the prisoner like he actually meant something. *Like a person and not the animal he is*, thought Somerville.

He handed Boodjark a pale blue booklet and added, "This is your Information Booklet. Don't lose it. Read it carefully, follow the daily timetable and instructions. Now put your mark on here," Somerville said, handing Boodjark a biro. He was expected to sign a slip of paper to acknowledge he had read and understood the contents of the booklet.

"But I haven't read it," Boodjark spoke for the first time since his arrival at Palmyra.

"Yes, you have. Don't mess with me 20797!" And then more loudly, "Sign the fucking piece of paper! You're not gonna be trouble, are you, 20797?" reinforcing that Boodjark was now nothing more than a number. Boodjark signed.

Satisfied the first stanza of 20797's initiation was complete, paper in hand, Somerville turned and immediately left the cell. He walked as briskly as possible to the stairs at the end of the landing. He knew what would happen next. *The proper introduction to Palmyra. No handbook can prepare you for this, 20797.*

Boodjark sat on his bunk bed, legs dangling over the edge, just as his cellmate arrived. It was the same prisoner who winked at him in the courtyard. A big, muscular man. He stood at 195 centimetres and carried 120 kilograms. He wore a blend of scars and crude, bodged tattoos, most of which were chiselled into his flesh during one of his numerous stays in Palmyra prison. He paused in the doorway, allowing time for his eyes to adjust to the poor light angled between the bars.

Small, hooded eyes fixed on Boodjark. "They told me I had a newbie joining me. How nice. What's your name?" A voice that sounded like a rasp file dragged across solid timber. "I'm called 'Horse'. Why horse? You'll find out soon enough."

"My name is Bruce but my friends call me 'Boodjark'."

Horse stood directly in front of Boodjark and placed his left hand on Boodjark's right leg. He grinned, to expose tobacco-stained teeth, and said, "I can be your friend. I'm the boss in this division. Do as I say and I'll look after you. Give you protection. You'll need it, a sweet boy like you."

"Take your hand off my leg."

Horse ignored him and instead placed his other hand on Boodjark's left thigh. In an instant, Boodjark's clenched right fist found the side of Horse's head. Left ear ringing, Horse stumbled to the side and kicked the slop bucket as his knees buckled but he didn't fall. He was caught by surprise, gathered his balance, emitted a sound like the growl of a wolf, and charged at Boodjark.

The noise advertised a fight. Some inmates on the landing quickly became spectators, jostling for space in the doorway, rubber-necking as the newcomer was taught a lesson in prison ethics.

"Return to your cells or I'll lock the landing down!" yelled Somerville after a few minutes, returning with three prison officers who, batons raised, pushed spectators away and burst inside. One of the inmates in cell 15 quickly succumbed to the fury and swiftness of prison summary justice. A severe cudgelling.

Through a stupefied haze, Boodjark heard Somerville instruct his colleagues to "Take 20797 around the back. Single storey housing." He was soon to learn the phrase 'around the back' to be a euphemism for solitary confinement.

Horse, unscathed save for the red left ear, walked swiftly to the second landing, to the cell he had occupied prior to Boodjark's arrival. His personal belongings were still there. Photographs and paintings adorned the walls. A television sat atop a chest of drawers, next to a CD player. Horse was clearly privileged.

After two weeks in solitary confinement, the offender in his adjoining cell informed Boodjark that Horse was his welcoming party. An initiation. Horse was favoured by some officers to keep the peace in his division. In return, they turned a blind eye to some of his activities: the treatment he dished out to the vulnerable.

Chapter 9

Over the next twelve months Boodjark was sent 'around the back' on numerous occasions. Horse never bothered him again but for a time, Boodjark created trouble without the help of others. For a while he refused to work. As a consequence, he was placed in the Detain Party, forced to remain in the yard at the rear of Division 3 without privileges. Being detained in the exercise yard for several months made him even more mentally troubled and aggressive.

Consumption of alcohol made matters worse. Whilst alcohol was not permitted in the prison, he accumulated a substantial supply of Old Spice Aftershave and Cologne, both of which had heavy alcohol content. The liquid was filtered through stale bread. The taste wasn't pleasant but for Boodjark its consumption sometimes helped him through the night.

Often the targets of his depravity and aggression were the quieter Indigenous men. Even though at least one prison guard would be stationed in an enclosure with an unimpeded view of the yard, hits on the Indigenous prisoners by whites were rarely sighted: not so, if a fight broke out between Indigenous prisoners. Usually anyone within the vicinity would spend time 'around the back', unless they had white skin.

On some occasions Boodjark used his toilet bucket, complete with contents from the previous night, as a weapon. He had spent many hours at bodybuilding and would use his fists but that usually meant time in solitary. Evidence of fighting engraved on his knuckles could not be ignored. In any case, the bucket was certain to inflict more damage.

Time in solitary exacerbated his depraved state of mind. Boodjark would obsessively recall the events of the court room that led to his incarceration. He ruminated on the evidence that had been presented by a woman he considered a low-life. He contemplated acts of vengeance. Contemplated how his hatred would eventually be manifested in an act of vengeance that would free him from depression. That time would come, he was certain.

To achieve his objective, he needed to be a model prisoner. To demonstrate to the authorities that he was remorseful, that he had been rehabilitated; ultimately, to convince the Parole Board to reduce his time inside.

To have his freedom, he changed his behaviour. He avoided confrontation. With monotonous regularity, he had previously lodged a blue request form in a box on his landing for the attention of the Unit Divisional Manager, his old 'friend' Somerville. The requests were regarded as complaints.

He had compared his mother's freshly baked biscuits and cakes with the bread the screws left in the sun to dry, before giving it to the inmates. He had incessantly complained about the lack of good-quality, fresh fruit and insisted on greater variety in the main meals.

Suddenly, he stopped complaining.

Chapter 10

The first twelve months of Boodjark's time in Palmyra Prison had been horrendous, not just for him but also for other inmates with whom he frequently argued and fought. After his first Christmas locked away, the change in his behavior was so dramatic that, after a time, senior prison officials became convinced he was well on the path to rehabilitation.

Could his good behavior be sustained? He worked hard at convincing the screws he was a new man. Although he hated the woman who was the only witness for the prosecution in his case, seven years before, he held that hatred internally. It didn't manifest in poor behaviour as it had in the past. But it didn't diminish, either.

Hatred is a dark emotional force that can cause irreparable damage to one's personality. It can cause deep depression. It can make a person crazy. Is it the most powerful driving force? More powerful than love or hope? To a large extent, it depends on role models during one's formative years; if one has a role model.

For Boodjark, hope and hatred were intermingled. His driving force. Hope for vengeance. Hope that could only be fulfilled if he was a free man. He thought about escaping but in the knowledge that past prisoners who had made such attempts had failed, costing them more time in the slot, he decided to bide his time. He had to be free. To be free, he had to behave himself.

Security at Palmyra was at the highest level of all prisons within the jurisdiction. There was no chance of escape. Some prisoners tried but none were successful.

The closest any offender got to achieve ultimate success was when he leapt three metres from the roof of New Division to the outside wall. But like the other attempts, that failed miserably. The would-be escapee landed against and grasped the wall but couldn't pull himself to the top, to freedom. After hanging for a few minutes, prisoner 19572 fell to the concrete, thirty feet below, breaking both legs. After being cast in plaster, 19572 was taken by wheelchair around the back. Two months in solitary, plus an increase in his time in the can. A lesson for all inmates.

Boodjark's hopes were raised when his early-morning work schedule in the carpenter's shop was interrupted by a call to attend the Superintendent's office. His first and only visit to the Super's office. It had to be positive.

"Prentice," the Superintendent greeted him bluntly. "You had best get used to being called by your surname. You are to be transferred to a medium-security prison, where the esteemed prison officers will no longer call you by number." The last comment was made with undertones of sarcasm. The Superintendent believed the 'esteemed' prison officers at medium security were too soft.

"You will serve the balance of your sentence at Ditchingham Regional Prison. Now go and pack your things. The prison van leaves in thirty minutes. But I know your sort. A recidivist. You'll be back."

That was it. No explanation. No praise for his good behaviour. Nothing further.

Thirty minutes to pack. No opportunity to say goodbye to other inmates. Not that Boodjark was concerned about that. He didn't regard any of the others as 'friends'. By necessity, he occasionally mixed with inmates participating in the Long-Term Prisoner Programme. That programme had been introduced during his last twelve months. It was designed to assist prisoners develop skills for post-prison life. He had to interact with those inmates but largely ignored everyone else.

Lewis, who had been promoted to Captain during Boodjark's incarceration and was present in the Super's office when he was delivered the good news, handed him an empty 500 x 400 x 300-millimetre cardboard box. "Pack your stuff in here, 20797." Lewis emphasized the number. "The smellies you wore when you arrived will be in a plastic bag in the van. Now go!" With that, Lewis walked away. No goodbyes.

Up yours, too, Lewis. I'll be glad to see the back of you. Your victimisation, discrimination against long-termers.

Several prisoners working in the garden saw Boodjark walking in the direction of the main gate and carrying all of his worldly goods in a cardboard box. They knew what that meant. One stopped weeding and yelled out, "See you when you get back!"

That was a common saying directed at prisoners leaving Palmyra. There was always an expectation the exit door was revolving and it was only a matter of time before the outgoing would re-enter.

Chapter 11

Whilst incarcerated at Palmyra, Boodjark's mother travelled by bus once a month to visit him. His sisters refused to visit. They never forgave him. Neither did Cheryl, but she felt the need to try and add some normality to his life and retain the familial connection. She hoped and prayed he would be rehabilitated. Soon after Boodjark turned twenty-four, Cheryl stopped visiting but he didn't know why and his only letter went unanswered.

Cheryl had breast cancer. Her health deteriorated very quickly, despite several bouts of chemotherapy and a mastectomy. Boodjark was unaware of his mother's situation. Snifter was also unaware but even if he had been, he was uncommunicative and so estranged from his son he would never have bothered to inform him. Within months, Cheryl passed away.

Knowing Boodjark originally lived in Cottam Mills and expecting him to have family who would likely find it easier to visit, several months before Cheryl had passed, the authorities made the decision to transfer him to Ditchingham, the nearest multi-security prison to his old town. They believed rehabilitation was more likely, should he be closer to his family.

After Boodjark was handed the cardboard box, he left the Superintendent's office and rushed to his slot. He had gathered his possessions and without much order or care, threw everything into the box that Lewis had given him. At the cell door, he stopped and looked back inside one last time. He spat on the floor, turned and walked briskly away.

Three hours later, Boodjark went through a similar routine to that which met him when he first arrived at Palmyra, seven years before. There was an exchange of documents between prison officers, before his handcuffs were removed and he was escorted into an office. He was immediately issued with a parcel of clothes, toiletry requirements, and a new Prisoner Information Booklet.

Unlike his introduction to the Palmyra strict security prison, he felt the major difference this time was that he was being treated with dignity.

Certainly more dignity than he had encountered in his early years of incarceration. He wasn't poked with a baton, he wasn't required to widen and stretch his gluteus-maximus muscles for inspection and he didn't need to shower in front of the prison officers who met him upon arrival.

Palmyra would soon become a distant memory. His new home had a mixture of medium and maximum-security prisoners. The latter group was smaller in number and had separate accommodation. The prisoners mingled most of the time, especially for their work schedule, but at the end of the day the two categories of prisoner went their separate ways.

Boodjark willingly participated in work activities where he would be most noticed by the prison officers. He was determined to convince the screws that he was a reformed man. It worked. Within a relatively short period of time, he was transferred internally from the dormitory-style accommodation to a minimum-security, self-care unit. Here, he enjoyed more freedom. He was required to clean his own room, cook for himself, do his own washing and other 'household' chores.

To the prison officers, it was noticeable Boodjark didn't have any visitors at all in the six years he was at the Ditchingham Regional Prison. That made their decision to transfer him to the Abannerup Regional Prison an easy one. He had been exemplary in his behavior, seemingly rehabilitated and remorseful. Seemingly.

Chapter 12

A flood of memories greeted Boodjark as he was transported 380 kilometres from Ditchingham to Abannerup, geographical coordinates 35°1'23"S, 117°52'53"E. The trip presented views of the countryside he had missed over the last thirteen years. Tall stands of trees, shrubs of creeping wattle, kangaroo thorn, golden wattle and other wildflowers lined the highway. Flashes of childhood memories passed quickly by. Fleeting images of Mokiny and the bush.

The van passed a turn-off to Cottam Mills and he gazed at the road that snaked its way across rolling hills in the direction of the town and its memories. An unwanted vision was inadvertently retrieved from his amygdala, a memory part of his brain. A storage place for a mental photograph of Ditchingham Courtroom 1. A repository which, in a millisecond, processed an emotional connection between that flash of vision and an Indigenous woman. Boodjark shuddered. He could feel anger rising in his body. He quickly looked to the front of the van, in a different direction, to temporarily erase the picture.

A large green sign at the side of the highway indicated the turnoff to Wittekop was a further thirty kilometres ahead. Positive memories drifted to the forefront of his mind. Memories of his early years at Wittekop Primary School. In his mind's eye he could see his mother hanging the week's washing on the iconic Australian invention, the Hills hoist. There emerged some vague recollections of his father. Only vague because most had long been erased.

Boodjark vigorously shook his head, as if that sudden burst of energy would forcibly remove the visions permanently. Cast them free.

Soon after, the van stopped at a roadhouse near the turnoff to Wittekop. Boodjark remained with a prison officer in the van, chain bolted to the floor. The driver added 65 litres of diesel to the van's fuel tank, while the most senior of the three prison officers, with the nametag 'Simpson', entered the roadhouse. A few minutes passed and he returned, wrestling with several rounds of bacon and egg sandwiches, three beef and cheese sausages, a 600 ml bottle of still water, Nestle Choc Milk and a strong, extra shot, flat white coffee for the driver.

The three prison officers sat at the front of the van facing the offender and ate as if this would be their last meal. Simpson made loud chewing noises and licked his lips between bites of his sandwich.

"I don't want the sausage, Simmo, after you dropped it on the floor," the driver said. "Shall I give it to 20797?"

"Nah. Nobody said anything about feedin' 'im. Before leaving Palmyra, he coulda gone to the kitchen and made 'imself a sandwich but chose not to. Nah, stuff 'im," Simmo spoke as he slurped the last of his Choc Milk. "Kick it under the chair. Not our job to clean the van," he concluded with a conceited smile.

Yeah, sure. I had time to make a sandwich, didn't I? Boodjark didn't articulate his thoughts, not wanting to give the screws the satisfaction of knowing he might be hungry.

As the van continued further south, the landscape changed. Undulating countryside revealed bright yellow fields of canola awaiting harvest. Dietary fibre shaped as grain crops, including wheat and oats, moved like capillary waves rippling steadily across paddocks in the breeze. Slight but majestic movements. An occasional harvester could be seen sending plumes of grain dust and seed husks billowing into the air.

After just over six hours, the prison van skirted the town of Abannerup and entered the grounds of the Regional Prison. From the van window, Boodjark immediately noticed a wire fence surrounded the perimeter of the prison with rolled razor-wire atop. Two fences, about ten metres apart, ran parallel around the entire complex: each carried rolls of razor wire about a metre in width and height. Freshly cut grass was between the fences and although not visible but nevertheless known to the prisoners, laser sensors were fixed in place. Hidden from view and emitting an infrared frozen rope to trip any would-be escapee.

A large, steel, barred gate opened inwards as the van approached. It rolled to a halt on the tarmac between the two fences. The gates closed with a loud, metallic clunk. Another vehicular gate in front of the van remained closed. To the left of the large gate, a personnel gate opened. A prison officer passed through the smaller gate and approached the van with a sniffer dog. The van driver electronically opened the side door, allowing the dog to enter to perform its assigned task. It was very business-like.

Boodjark reached as far as his chains allowed in an attempt to pat the dog. He hadn't seen a four-legged animal in seven years, only the two-legged type.

"Don't pat the dog," the controlling officer barked.

Whilst the dog conscientiously and briskly walked, almost trotted, along the van's aisle, darting in between the rows of seats, head down, another officer circled the outside of the van holding a large mirror attached to a pole to peer underneath. Neither the dog nor the mirror man found any contraband. Satisfied with his work and that of the sniffer hound, mirror man signalled for the second gate to be opened and for the van to proceed to the main administration block.

At the final stop, a man whom Boodjark recognized to be a senior officer, because his uniform's epaulettes carried several stars, emerged from the office building. The driver passed a two-page document to him through a side window. The officer took his time to read both pages, then raised his head and peered into the side window where Boodjark was seated. He signalled to have the van's door opened.

Stepping into the van, the officer with a nametag 'Prentice' said, "Welcome to Abannerup Regional Prison, Bruce Prentice. We have the same surname but I can assure you we are not related."

No number, Boodjark thought. *A good sign.*

"It was a long drive. Have you eaten?"

Have I eaten? Another good sign.

Almost in a state of shock for being spoken to in a civil manner for the first time in many years, Boodjark didn't answer. *Is this a trick?* he asked himself. *Is this real?*

"We offered him food but he declined," Simpson lied. Simpson's colleagues nodded in unison like a pair of mascot nodding dogs attached to a car's dashboard, moving to the rhythm of the car. Head moving, body fixed and stationary.

Senior Officer Prentice grunted. He didn't believe Simpson. "Unshackle him." The instruction was barked and directed at Simpson. Turning to Boodjark he added, "I'll arrange for an officer to take you to the mess, get you some tucker and then escort you to your cell. I think you'll notice a difference in the way we operate here. Vastly different from where you have served time."

For the first time in many years, looking at Simpson, Boodjark smiled. A smile that didn't linger, possibly because of the strain on infrequently used facial muscles. He desperately wanted to give Simpson 'the bird' – extend his middle finger vertically in an 'up yours' gesture – but resisted the temptation. The constrained smirk was enough.

Senior Officer Prentice changed his mind. "Actually, I'll take you to the mess and my assistant will take your belongings to the cell. We'll have a chat about what is expected of you here."

As he walked Boodjark away from his last connection with Palmyra and Ditchingham Prisons – the van and three disgruntled prison officers – he continued his introduction to Abannerup. "You have twelve years to serve, Boodjark. I see from these papers that is the name you go by. Noongar, meaning 'maggot'. Still, if that's your preference, that's what you'll be called even though you're not Aboriginal. Our focus at Abannerup is on rehabilitation and respect. You'll be given the opportunity in a variety of workshops. All being well, in time your status might be changed to low risk. Let's hope so."

Six years later, after many interviews and various other forms of assessment, having earned the reputation of a model prisoner, Boodjark was assessed as low risk. He was transferred for the last time. This time, to a minimum-security prison seventy kilometres from Abannerup. Kolbang Prison Farm.

Chapter 13

A second flock of *ngoorlak* flew directly overhead. A cacophony, squawking, seemingly yelling to each other to fly harder before the thunder and lightning arrived. At the edge of the prison farm, a mob of *yongka* moved in the direction of the tall gum trees to the east. Some stretched their great hind legs with a huge *barding-iny* (hop), not waiting for the slower animals that didn't appear to be in a hurry. Some moved slowly to give time to their *djoodiny* (joey kangaroos) to keep pace with them.

"It's gonna be a big storm," Bluey said, as the men left the mess after dinner. "The roos are on the move. Black as hell. Unusual for October. Must be this climate-change thing people keep talking about."

"Dunno about that," said Shorty, at the rear of the group, as they started along the path leading to their quarters. "I reckon it's a load of bullshit. What do you reckon, Scarface?"

Shorty stood at 194 centimetres and possibly weighed 80 kilograms fully clothed and wringing wet. The tall, skinny but wiry man with a ruddy complexion and closely cropped hair wasn't liked by many of the inmates because he frequently made insulting remarks to others, believing he was immune to physical retaliation in the low-security prison. He was always polite and well-mannered with the screws. They would have his back. He particularly disliked Boodjark because he always seemed disinterested in mixing with other prisoners.

He thinks he's better than me and the boys, Shorty thought.

"I said 'Whadya reckon', Scarface," he repeated.

No response. Boodjark reached into his inner reserves of strength to exercise control. He hated being called 'Scarface'. Only this man they call 'Shorty' taunted him with that nickname.

Keep your cool Boodjark, he told himself without articulating the thought. *Not worth the risk.*

"Scarface. I'm talking to you, you cocksucker!" Shorty yelled. He turned to one of his friends, who was holding the mess door open to allow other friends to exit. "I guess Scarface is too dumb to have an opinion about anything."

That was it. Enough to send Boodjark into apoplexy. In a frenzy of rage, a red-faced Boodjark lost control. *Enough is enough*, he thought. He swivelled on his heels and pushed past several inmates, who were shocked to see the angry reaction from a hitherto laconic and compliant man. Bluey and another inmate attempted to block his path. Unsuccessful, they grabbed his arms to stop his progress and pulled him back from the confrontation.

Bluey pleaded with his friend. "Don't do anything silly, mate. He's not worth it. You don't want to go back to Palmyra, do you?"

At that, Boodjark stopped. He pointed his trigger finger at Shorty and growled, "You're a dead man walking. Sleep with one eye open tonight, 'cos I'm coming for ya, you motherfucker. You're dead meat. Do ya hear me? Dead!"

When the storm subsided and the sun rose over the tall gum trees the following morning, Shorty lay motionless on his back at body count. A pool of dark blood sat ominously under his bed. He wore a new gash the length of his face that, if he lived, would form a terrible scar from his hairline to his jawbone. He had a deep incision the width of his neck, exposing a lacerated windpipe. An incision across a throat that would forever remain silent. Dead.

Boodjark didn't make muster, either. He was gone.

Part Two

Bessie

Chapter 14

Storm clouds seemed to gain momentum as they drifted northwards towards the Cottam Mills valley. Whilst it wasn't unusual to have some wet weather in late *dirdong* (spring), rarely did it approach from that direction and rarely was it as vicious as the looming storm. There was a sudden, loud, explosive clap of thunder. It sounded like an asylum of drummers had simultaneously hammered their bass drums. A flash of lightning preceded the synchronised drum roll.

Heavy rain clouds blackened the horizon. It was impossible to see the line between the top of the hills and the clouds. It was still well south of the town but Bessie knew the storm would soon be bearing down on Cottam Mills.

There was the flight of the *ngoorlak* noisily passing low overhead, squawking a warning to anyone who bothered to listen. Announcing to anyone who understood their message that a storm was approaching. The Noongar people understood. This would be a fierce night.

Her border collie dog was restless; bright eyes flashed from side to side, alert, black ears erect, mouth open, he panted incessantly. After her husband had gone to the Dreaming, Bessie had the need of a companion and a watchdog. Buster was perfect. He was an intelligent and loyal friend. To a limited extent, he added some meaning to her life. A life lost with Jimmy's passing.

Buster sensed the imminent change in weather and every few minutes left his dog mat and walked to the side of the verandah, appearing to gaze into the distance. The drum roll had him on edge.

Reaching down from her sofa, Bessie reassuringly petted Buster and thought, *From the south. Unusual. The same direction as the storm on that terrible night so many years ago. A night of kep boolarang and malkar. Yabini, how I miss your beautiful smile. How I miss the core of your personality.*

Bessie had an uneasy feeling. She was somewhat alarmed. Uncertain, not knowing what brought forth the same feeling of unease. It aroused the same sensation that she felt on a night of *kep boolarang, malkar* and *kilang* in that October night sixteen years before. The feeling that someone had just walked over her grave. Now, as then, her skin crawled. A clammy feeling engulfed her, and then unexpectedly, goose bumps crept along both arms.

Buster could sense his owner's unease and gave a slight whimper.

Bessie glanced at her little friend and spoke quietly in a reassuring tone. "Nothing to be concerned about, Buster."

Ngadi ngadi mar, she thought. *The wind is picking up.*

Every night, after dinner, Bessie would make a pot of tea, take two mugs from her kitchenette, pour a little milk into a small chinaware jug and place everything onto a silver tray. It had become a tradition and Bessie was big on tradition. She would carry the tray to the rear verandah of the same State Housing Commission house she had rented for the last twenty years. A quiet moment she and her late husband had always enjoyed. But for the last four years, she sat alone and sipped her tea. The second mug was for her absent, but in her mind, her ever-present husband Jimmy.

'Time for you and time for me…' Bessie would often recite the words of TS Eliot. '… Time for a hundred visions and revisions before the taking of tea.'

The rear of the house had commanding views of the hills beyond the river, created by *Ngarngungudditj Walgu*, the bearded serpent. The Cottam River. Tonight, heavy clouds swallowed the top of the hills beyond.

Bessie always enjoyed this time of the day, despite the prevalence of uninvited flying insects. She swiped and clasped her right hand near the side of her face in a vain attempt to catch one. The thrust of air caused the mosquito to teasingly buzz out of reach, not to return having associated the potential victim's scent with danger. As if working in tandem, another drove its proboscis into the soft skin near her ankle at that precise moment. It was preoccupied with filling its abdomen with good blood and was slow to move. Bessie successfully swatted it, prematurely ending its meal.

She reached for a personal, organic, mosquito-repellent spray sitting on a tray table against the wall and applied it liberally. Apart from the annoyance of the nightly invasion, most evenings offered peace and quiet.

Bessie enjoyed the tranquillity and the time to cogitate about the happenings in her extended family. To her, family was more important than anything else and she knew that view was reciprocated. That was the Noongar way. Family first.

Notwithstanding family support, without Jimmy in her life, Bessie was lost. Her sadness was compounded by Yabini's passing. Having Mardoo visit regularly helped, but not enough to overcome her heavy heart.

On this night, Bessie's thoughts of family were interrupted by *malkar* and *kilang*. But there was also a strong, unearthly feeling. An ephemeral feeling of unease. After only a few moments of unease, bordering on trepidation, for what the night might unexpectedly bring, Bessie rose from her cane sofa and walked to the edge of the verandah. She looked to the sky directly above, expecting to see a very bright star. But it wasn't there. For a moment she closed her eyes and visualised the night sky from sixteen years ago to that very day. The bright star. She shivered. So did Buster.

After a few moments, Bessie gathered the teapot and mugs, and returned them to the tray. She peered over her shoulder at the gathering rain clouds and then slowly walked along the verandah towards the kitchen door.

Although she was light of frame, some of the verandah boards, nevertheless, groaned. They had been weathered by the effluxion of time combined with the impact of winter rains from the south. She glanced down, cast her eyes along the verandah, and thought, *I need to ask Mardoo to bring an American screwdriver and knock down these protruding nails.* She smiled at the name her late husband had given to a hammer: 'an American screwdriver'.

Mardoo was Bessie's second cousin. Mokiny Junior's son. Mardoo Trunning would often ask Bessie if she needed any help around the house. He would help with the gardening. Pull weeds, plant annuals, plant perennials and undertake whatever chores Bessie required of him. Assist with whatever his oldest cousin needed, as there was no man in her life to help.

At the fly-wire door she stopped and moved the tray to her left arm so that she could more easily open the door. Before doing so, her right hand touching the brass doorknob, she turned one more time to look beyond the hills. Another flash of *kilang* again sent more shivers down her spine.

Was that a *birnt* (death cloud) beyond the hills, behind the *kilang*?

Tomorrow, if weather permits, I'll go to the river and throw a handful of sand into it, just like I did years ago to call her spirit home. That's the law. The Beelagu law. On the anniversary of her passing to the Dreaming, I must talk to her spirit.

Bessie didn't move. She stood with the door slightly ajar, as if there were an unearthly force keeping her from losing this moment. A *kwobali kaanya*. She again closed her eyes. Eyes held firmly shut, she could see three *wadjala* men hustling out of the bush below her. One had a scar the length of his face and blood dripping from his hands.

Shaken, Bessie opened her eyes. Inexplicably, she now stood in her lounge room, gazing at a photograph of her husband. Teleportation. She didn't remember walking into the house. She didn't remember placing the tray in the kitchen, walking along the passageway and into the lounge room. But there she was, holding the picture frame so hard, her knuckles almost burst through her skin.

Tears rolled down her cheeks. Exactly sixteen years ago, on this very day, *wadjala* had taken her young cousin, just like they took the lives of tens of thousands of men, women and children after European occupation of their *boodja*. Over three hundred massacres, not counting individual killings of First Nations people. Many in retaliation for the theft of livestock – a cow or a sheep. Murder was hardly a just form of punishment. *Wadjala* killed their *yongka* – their food – was taking a sheep any different?

Wadjala had taken her cousin and her husband.

Although she had every reason to be bitter, Bessie wasn't. Just deeply saddened.

Chapter 15

Bessie was born in a humpy – a small shack in the general area of the bush where many generations of her family had primarily lived. For thousands of years, her ancestors had nurtured the native plants, hunted the *yongka*, the *ka-rda*, the *yorndan*, fished, celebrated the birth of *koorlangka* with corroborees and taught them the law. The Noongar way.

She could never permanently leave these beautiful, ancestral grounds. This was her *boodja*. Her country. A connection to this land was in her blood. From generation to generation, over thousands of years, the Elders had told many stories about the river and its creation. Passed information about the law and the Dreamtime through generations. Stories about every aspect of *boodja*. Stories that she understood as an important part of her identity.

Bessie's immediate family had always worked and lived in the area. Her father had been employed in the mines and her mother toiled hard for minimal wages as a cleaner at a local shopping centre. A menial task that didn't pay well. The money was just sufficient to maintain a roof over the heads of a growing family, put food on the table and pay for the children's education. They didn't have many possessions but what they did have was derived from hard work and would be shared with family and other folk when needed.

Their main hope was for a good education for their children. The local State school would deliver that. A chance to provide the children with an opportunity for a better life.

Bessie's father told her how his father had helped construct a nearby earthen dam on a subsidiary of the Cottam River. He had been assured by the government *wadjala* that the dam wouldn't impact the water flow downstream or any of the Noongar *karla*, their littoral or riparian rights. The *wadjala* misinformed the Indigenous people. They knew – or, at least, should have known – the impact of the dam on the surrounding area and further down the river. They lied.

Her parents had a special connection with the *boodja* where their parents, Bessie's grandparents, had raised their family. Bessie's father was from the Wilman language group and her mother from the Pibulman mob, but they had settled on the traditional lands where many generations of Wilman had lived. Their old *karla* site was now permanently covered by water.

A large tract of land was flooded, destroying other traditional *karla* sites, engulfing sacred caves and paintings that would never again be accessible. To the First Nations people, that was a heinous act; a flagrant disregard for the oldest continuous culture on the planet, akin to mining companies setting dynamite and forever destroying marks and sacred messages left by the *nyidiyang* (ancestors). But there was money to be made by so doing.

Downstream, the riverbed was mostly dry. Small billabongs would be formed during the winter months and remained an important source of water for wildlife, but the valley would never be the same.

Bessie remembers her grandfather, tears rolling down his face, telling stories of how the river created by the *Ngarngungudditj Walgu* had been decimated. She remembers him telling the story, when she was little girl, of how the *Walgu* would sometimes rest in this area, a subsidiary of Cottam River, when the river was in full flood. The *Walgu* would have a long rest before travelling downriver to its masterpiece, the Cottam River.

But the dam meant *Walgu* could no longer rest there. It had been disturbed. Having helped the *wadjala* destroy the valley forever saddened him. He felt guilty. He passed away, broken-hearted at what had happened to his spiritual *boodja*. His passing, caused by a broken heart, had an indelible and long-lasting impact on Bessie. It was impossible for her to identify the major cause of her sadness compounded by many events in her life.

Once her grandfather had gone to the Dreaming, there was no possibility of Bessie's family leaving the area. There probably wasn't any chance of that, anyway, but the ties to *boodja* would always be strong. They continued with the traditional ways of the Wilman people, hunting freshwater crayfish or *maran*, the *yongka* and the *ka-rda*. But they were forced by necessity of work to relocate into Cottam Mills. A new *karla* would be formed on the outskirts of town, close to the Cottam River.

Chapter 16

It was a traditional wedding by the river, near where the *Walgu* rested after creating an estuary at Ditchingham. A deeply spiritual place for the *Beelagu* people – the river people. A place where they would come to pay their respects to the ancestors. It was known as *Karla koorliny* (coming home). Where the ancestors are forever *danjoo koorliny* (walking together) with the *Beelagu*. It was the place where Jimmy Brenting had pledged his commitment to Bessie and it was now fitting that the marriage contract should be formalised there.

In many years past, the Noongar law was strict when it came to relationships. A marriage between members of the same Skin Group was forbidden. Bessie and Jimmy still held those values. Jimmy was from a different language group to Bessie. Bessie was from the Wilman nation and Jimmy from the Pibulman nation.

They never knew that an autosomal recessive disease could result from marrying a relative. They never had the scientific knowledge. It was just instinctively wrong. Law did not permit the connection. There could only be a 'Right-Way Marriage'. That had been the Noongar way for thousands of years. Most of the disorders were finally acknowledged by medical science in the twentieth century.

Jimmy and Bessie lived in a small, pale green weatherboard and asbestos State Housing Commission house: 31 Banksia Street, Cottam Mills.

Indigenous families were not allocated a State house without considerable sacrifice. The *wadjala* government demanded they ignore their Noongar culture and language. They must agree not to remain connected to family. If these conditions were agreed, they were required to carry a certificate that stated, "This is your chance to live with freedom like a white person." Those whom were given such 'privileges' usually honoured the commitment only for a short time. Family, community and culture were more important. Rightly so, they ignored the *wadjala's* outrageous demands to forsake their heritage.

The Brenting house had a corrugated tin roof; a small porch and a gravel driveway leading to a carport at the side were other features. Two bedrooms, a bathroom and toilet on the rear verandah, which was the width of the house, a wood stove in a kitchen-cum-dining room, and a lounge room at the end of a passageway, near the front entrance to the house.

The lounge room had two recliner rocking chairs and a three-seat sofa acquired through the classified section of the local newspaper. There were two items of Ikea second-hand furniture – a white sideboard and a television stand. The walls were bare, save for a small, unframed Albert Namatjira print attached to one wall with Blu Tack. Bessie was proud of her belongings. They were hard-earned. The sofa was from Jimmy's salary, the kitchen table from her savings, and the kitchenette inherited from her parents.

All of the houses in the street were State-owned, where the tenants paid a relatively small sum for rent. Once a month, on behalf of the landlord, with leather bag slung across his shoulder, the rent man called and collected the money. He issued a paper receipt. No matter how late he was in the rent collection for the day at number 31 Banksia Street, he would sit by the wood stove in the kitchen and have a cup of tea. Bessie's fresh homemade ginger biscuits or fruitcake were irresistible.

"Time for a cuppa?" Bessie always asked.

"Is the Pope a Catholic? Does he wear a funny hat?" the rent collector always said in response.

To which Bessie would reply, "Does a *kwernt* (bandicoot) defecate in the woods?"

For years the exchange had been the same. Tradition. The rent collector, known only as 'Rent Man' because he never shared his given name with the tenants, had no idea what a *kwernt* was but he never asked. Like most *wadjala*, not even this friendly man was sufficiently interested to learn the Noongar language. Most *wadjala* had no interest in understanding the oldest culture on the planet.

Rent Man always complimented Bessie on the state of her garden. It was eye-catching. The neatest and best garden in the street. It compared more than favourably with the next door neighbour's yard. The *wadjala* had a rusted Zephyr sedan jacked up on concrete blocks. It had stood in their front yard for years. Wild oats surrounded the running board and couch grass infiltrated the cracks created by rust at the bottom of the doors. Rent Man wasn't concerned. He wasn't responsible for property inspections; just the collection of money.

Jimmy's family had been very happy with the marriage. They believed it would give him a chance to find himself. To remove the shackles of depression that enveloped his soul.

His family was large in number, spread throughout the Pibulman and Wardandi areas, but was disparate in character. Some had not experienced the trauma Jimmy had and didn't understand his morosity. They hadn't suffered the sense of worthlessness, the sense of not actually belonging anywhere. A generational state of mind.

When Jimmy's mother was only a toddler, two *wadjala* men wearing suits and driving a shiny black government car drove into the Pibulmen *karla* where she lived. The community was puzzled by the arrival of the government officials. They had heard stories about the *wadjala* taking Indigenous children from their parents for no reason, but they were unsure if the stories were true. For the first time, this community witnessed a child being stolen from her parents because of her skin colour.

From early in the last century, the *Aborigines Act* had a far-reaching affect and underpinned government policy to segregate what the Act described as "Aboriginal Natives", from white people. It's hard to believe but the Act specified that the Chief Protector of Aborigines was the legal guardian of all Indigenous children until they attained the age of sixteen.

The Chief Protector could appoint honorary Protectors, thus a system analogous to a police State was applied. For some citizens, at least. But then Indigenous people were not regarded as 'citizens' until 1944 and nationally until many years later, depending upon the law in each State.

Government control over the lives of Indigenous people was extreme. Controls extended to almost every area of life – employment, personal relationships, and most profoundly, the life of Indigenous children.

The practice of taking children from their parents and either having them adopted or placed in religious missions was *wadjala* government policy for about seventy years. Police officers, Justices of the Peace and Protectors had the right to send children under the age of eight to missions without parental consent. Shortly after birth, many babies were immediately taken from their mothers to be adopted by a white couple incapable of otherwise having children.

This policy was, arguably, an extension of the Aboriginal massacres nationwide, except in this case lives were taken without a weapon being fired.

Many families were divided. Government policy was to attempt an assimilation of children into the non-indigenous community, while their parents were being herded into segregated settlements to provide labour where there was a shortage of workers. It was exploitative, the cost of labour being the provision of some food and shelter. For some *wadjala*, the cost was a combination of food and alcohol. Cheap labour – food and grog for wages. Malnutrition was rife. Living conditions also meant a high rate of disease and infant mortality.

The most profound cost was not easily identifiable. The disconnection between family members. The loss of close contact, the estrangement from love and resultant inadequate emotional development resulted in generational loss of self-esteem. Mistrust of everyone. Especially distrust of government and authority.

The problem was compounded by many children being told their parents didn't care for them. Most were denied information about their background and grew up with a loss of identity.

As they matured, the mistrust and internal guilt made it difficult for them to form or manage relationships. Mental health was not a priority for the *wadjala* community: 'Toughen up', they would say. A depressed state of mind often led to alcoholism and substance abuse. For many young, traumatised people, suicide was an easy way to erase the loneliness, the internal guilt and low self-esteem.

When Jimmy's mother was taken from her parents, she didn't know the reason. As she grew older, through chance meetings with similar 'incarcerated' children in institutions, she became aware of her tribal background. She didn't know her parents had never stopped trying to find her. When she eventually, spasmodically, learnt of her family background, she found it impossible to bond with others from the Pibulmen mob.

Robbed of family and robbed of her childhood; distanced from her community until it was too late. No sense of belonging, this mindset was gifted by the *wadjala*. It played on the mind of her son. A domino effect.

Jimmy was bequeathed a loss of identity. There was very little Bessie could do to help him. His parents had difficulty in parenting. His mother was distant and seemed uncaring. He didn't have a role model. She was burdened by a feeling of anger that was impossible to explain. This was the legacy she unknowingly left young Jimmy.

Over time Jimmy's mental health deteriorated. It was inevitable. The State did nothing to help, despite Bessie's pleas to her local Member of Parliament and to the State Health Department. It seemed the Government Departments didn't rate mental health as an issue. It wasn't a serious budgetary consideration. Of even less concern was recognition of the long-term and inter-generational impact of the stolen generations.

Jimmy's family was unable to expunge the black dog from his disposition. Medication helped but, from time to time, when he felt physically strong and emotionally capable, he would not take his pills. The black dog would inevitably return.

Bessie attempted to comfort him but was brushed aside. She knew the problems of the stolen generation's people and their offspring but wasn't able to help the man she loved. She did her best to support her husband emotionally and for a time succeeded, but the traumas of his mother had attached themselves to Jimmy like a blood-sucking leech.

Eventually the 'leech' sucked the life out of Jimmy. His state of mind became too difficult for him to overcome. He felt suicide was his only option.

Chapter 17

Bessie never remarried. Despite being frequently approached by admirers, she believed any new relationship would be a betrayal to Jimmy's memory. Instead, she spent more time with her family at the Cottam Mills *karla* and Jimmy's family on the outskirts of Ditchingham. She bought a dog for a companion.

Because of her familiarity with the language, and her detailed knowledge and understanding of Noongar culture, she was offered a position at the local primary school. The progressive-minded school principal had a discretionary fund and chose to use it to employ Bessie.

Although not a qualified teacher, Bessie had a comforting and positive manner in dealing with children. Teaching children about the oldest culture and language on the planet came naturally to her.

Even though her job was only a part-time position, teaching at the local school kept Bessie occupied for much of the week. When she wasn't teaching she spent time planning the following week's lessons, visiting family and gardening. She took enormous pride in her garden.

One of her pupils was her cousin, Mardoo. When he wasn't playing with his close friend Ozzy, he would often help Bessie in odd jobs around the house. In particular, he would gladly assist after school in maintaining the best garden in the street. Bessie and Jimmy never had children of their own. To some extent, little Mardoo filled that void.

Mardoo willingly helped Bessie and the time spent with her further broadened his education. Like his father, Mokiny Junior, he had an insatiable appetite for the stories passed down by the Elders through the ages; especially stories and truth-telling passed down from his grandfather. Mardoo would lap up the stories like the dogs in the *karla* lapped up the morning's leftover porridge.

As they planted petunias, trimmed dead or dying bright, multi-coloured zinnia flowers, pulled weeds and trimmed hedges, Bessie would give her cousin language lessons. He was eager to learn the language and more importantly, to understand tribal heritage and family connections.

It was the day after the storm. Boodjark had escaped from Kolbang Prison Farm. Bessie and Mardoo were busy in the garden at 31 Banksia Street.

"The ground is still heavy from the *kep boolarang*. Last night's storm," Bessie opined.

Bright sunlight and the *dirdong* heat generated humidity but it was not yet enough to dry the soil. The pair tilled the ground in preparation for planting zinnias that had been sown in small containers in the warmth of her garage. Five days after the seeds were deposited in small individual plastic boxes, the seven-centimetre seedlings would always be planted neatly in two rows alongside the path leading to the front porch at number 31.

"The storm was horrendous, wasn't it?" Mardoo commented rhetorically. "It came from nowhere and caused some damage at our *karla*. Nothing that couldn't easily be repaired at daylight."

They busied themselves in silence for a short time, before Mardoo muttered, "You have never talked about Uncle Jimmy."

Surprised, Bessie didn't respond. *That remark came from nowhere*, she thought. *Just like the storm*.

Mardoo thought she hadn't heard him and repeated the comment. "Aunty, you never talk about Uncle Jimmy. You once told me he had a heart attack. Is that true? I think you were trying to protect me, and Uncle Jimmy's name. Whatever really happened to him?"

No response. Bessie tried to avoid eye contact with Mardoo and for a long minute succeeded. When her young cousin planted the last of the zinnias, he sidled over to a kneeling Bessie and placed his right hand on her left shoulder. She realised then that her cousin could not be fooled. He had an intelligent and intuitive ability.

The boy has a sixth sense. It's time to tell him the truth.

"Let's go to the river," Bessie said solemnly. "I need to tell you about the sorry time."

"Tell me here."

"No. The river. Wait by the car. I'll get my keys."

Bessie frequently visited the *Ngarngungudditj Walgu's* resting place, seeking solace in the tranquillity and nearness of the spirits of her loved ones. Without Jimmy in her life, she was lost. Jimmy's spirit rested there. Her parents and their parents rested there.

Some *wadjala* would seek peace and hope from their religious belief by attending their church with a cross atop a spire, a mosque with a minaret attached, a shul or a temple. All with symbolic ornamentation. There were no spires, minarets or ornamentation at the river. Just nature, knowledge and spiritual connection.

Bessie sought only peace and proximity to the spirit of her ancestors who had been permitted by *Ngarngungudditj Walgu* to rest there. She knew the day would come when she would join them. Soon. Life didn't offer her much. Each day was a grind to survive. Every day she would wake in the belief that another of her relatives would likely have passed to the Dreaming. It was too common. She would welcome that day for herself.

Within about ten minutes Bessie reappeared, having quickly changed from her gardening clothes. She wore jeans, a black blouse and her long dark hair that had been tightly tied into a bun was now loose and flowing over her shoulders. She now wore modest jewellery. Imitation pearl earrings given to her by her late husband on their wedding day.

Thirty metres from the riverbank, Bessie parked her late model two-door Ford Escort sedan on the gravel car park, contiguous to a narrow beach leading down to the water. She turned and looked into Mardoo's eyes and saw his concern for her. There was something else. As she stepped out of the car it came to her. He had Yabini's eyes. Dark, but sparkling and asking questions, just like his aunt Yabini. She had never noticed it before.

I've never seen Yabini in him before. His father – yes, but never his aunty. Definitely not. This is some type of transformation. A rebirth. Could it be...?

The pair walked slowly down the gradual embankment onto the beach. This area was known as *karla koorliny* (coming home).

Several hundred metres downriver, a group of children were swinging on a rope tied to the branch of a very large tree growing on the riverbank. They would run, rope in hand, and fling themselves into the air well above the water. Some squealed as they hit the water in a belly flop. Laughter could be heard in the distance and caught Bessie's attention.

"You should be playing with those kids," Bessie said.

"Nah, not those kids. They're not like Ozzy," he emphasised. "They never play with a black kid. At school they sometimes say racist things to me. Call me hurtful names for no reason. I don't understand why."

"What do you do?"

"Nothin'. What can I do?"

"Nothing. That's our life. Just stay strong."

Bessie bent and in her right hand gathered a handful of yellow beach sand. With her free hand, she grasped Mardoo's right hand and led him along the embankment to a special part of the river. In the traditional time-honoured way of the Noongar Beelagu people, she sat on a large granite rock near the water and gestured to Mardoo to sit next to her, facing the calm water. This sacred area was absent of any other people.

They sat in silence for a few minutes before Mardoo said, "You carry too much sadness, Aunt Bessie. I can see it in the lines at the side of your eyes. I can see it in your face but mostly your eyes."

Without responding, Bessie looked away. She threw the sand into the river. Bessie gazed into the still water at her feet and saw her reflection. She looked to the side and saw Mardoo's reflection and then a third image suddenly appeared. The image of a young woman smiled at her. Knowingly, she returned the smile.

She nudged Mardoo and pointed at the images in the river. He raised two fingers like a victory signal. Just as she thought, Mardoo only saw two reflections.

One day he'll see her. I know he will. He has an instinctive, sometimes even foreknowing sense.

Bessie took a deep breath, filled her *walyan* (lungs) and sucked in the cool air that drifted silently and unseen across the water. Sent by the Beelagu ancestors to comfort the visitors. She loved the river, especially this sacred spot where *Ngarngungudditj Walgu* rests. The Beelagu people regularly visit here for the tranquillity. For many, it's their church.

Bessie knew the law. The law said she must show respect and throw sand into the river before talking to the *wern*, the spirit of the dead. That was an important custom passed down over the generations. A law that cannot be ignored.

Having respectfully waited a reasonable time after throwing the sand, Bessie commenced to quietly sing. She sang in the language of her mob, the Wilman First Nations people. A song calling to the spirit of her long gone ancestors and her recently deceased family members. A song of respect to the Elders, past and present. A song that announced their presence, that stated who she was and the purpose of their visit.

Mardoo understood an occasional Noongar word, but didn't interrupt. He knew this was important to Bessie and he had been told how significant the river was to his people.

The song tailed away. The third reflection also drifted away. Neither Bessie nor Mardoo moved. Time for truth telling.

Bessie began. "I think you know Uncle Jimmy never had a heart attack. I'm sorry you were never told the truth but it was hard for me to accept."

Mardoo reached sideways and tenderly touched her forearm, understanding her difficulty in dealing with Jimmy's passing.

"Most of our family and friends had a mistaken opinion about him. It was their personal choice about how they saw him in life. Sadly, many people saw him as humourless and moping. The attitude of some people who did not try to get to know him or were unaware of his family story only made him worse. For all of his life, he was angry. A suppressed attitude of guilt mingled with anger carried by his mother also manifested in Uncle Jimmy. He inherited it."

For several minutes Bessie described how her mother-in-law had been taken from her family as a small child. Mardoo sat quietly. He politely and intently listened as he always did when older family members talked about family. He was respectful.

Bessie recounted how Jimmy's mother was initially taken to a Catholic mission to be educated in the white man's way. A religious education. But a year later, she was again taken. This time she would be raised by a childless couple. She had no connection to *boodja*, no understanding of her culture, no knowledge of her real family. All she knew was that she was different.

Bessie told of the perpetual emotional and mental damage caused by those policies. More than a generation of children stolen from their families. Their family connection stolen from them. She told of the burden Jimmy carried and then she lowered her eyes to the water.

"Uncle Jimmy could no longer carry that burden and decided to set himself free. He is with our ancestors, Colby. They understand."

Mardoo was surprised. *Colby,* he thought. *Nobody ever calls me that.* Bessie noticed the look of surprise. The name Colby was derived from a coal-mining location and was given to Mokiny Junior's newborn. Because of the baby's size, it wasn't long before everyone called him 'Mardoo', the Noongar word meaning 'mouse'. It stuck.

"Mardoo," Bessie corrected and continued. "Before you were born, there was an unthinkable tragedy in Cottam Mills. A tragedy that had a profound impact on our family. It is why your papa is sometimes difficult to talk to. I want you to understand why he is often so very sad. Moody. Your papa may not show his emotions. Like so many Noongars of his generation, especially men, he conceals them. He loves you more than you'll ever know, Mardoo. He has high hopes for you. Says you can be whatever you want to be. I'm sorry, I digress. But I wanted to assure you of your papa's good intentions. Despite that, he cannot bring himself to tell you the sorry story – but you should know."

For the next fifteen minutes, Bessie told Mardoo about the sorry time. She told him about his beautiful aunty Yabini. That she was a ray of sunshine in the Wilman community and was well liked in Cottam Mills. She told him that beautiful, sunny, bright Yabini had been murdered near the *djooroot* to his *karla*. The rape and murder had emotionally scarred those who were close to Yabini, especially her brother: Mardoo's father.

Bessie gave an account of the police investigation and how she assisted law enforcement to find the killer. Without her evidence, they had nothing. She told him about the criminal trial and the evidence she gave. She was the main prosecution witness.

"How did you know this man was the killer, Aunty? You said it was night-time… er… *kedaluk,* that's the right word, isn't it? It was dark, wasn't it?"

"Yes, that is the right word. Yes, it was dark but I was able to make a clear identification. There was absolutely no doubt."

There was a splash in the water a few metres from where they sat. They turned and watched a fish in the shallow water. In the clear water, they could see stripes and as the fish turned, a distinctive red ventral fin. It was a redfin perch opportunistically hunting for yabbies, scrubworms or minnows at the edge of the reeds. Another splash and a ripple of water as the hunter swam away having satiated its hunger.

"Mardoo," Bessie continued, "You might find this hard to believe, but on the night of the murder I had a *koondarm*, a dream. In my *koondarm* I saw three young men in the bush where Yabini was killed. Now, this is the bit that's hard to believe. Strangely, my body floated in the air above the bush track a few feet from the *wadjala*. I have always believed the image was sent to me by a *kwobali kaanya*, a very good soul. It was a clear message.

"Yes – it was dark for most of the night but as if arranged by the spirits, there was a break in the clouds. A bright star, the brightest star I have ever seen, and the *kilang* gave enough light for me to see those evil fellas. I saw 'em."

Bessie spared Mardoo a complete account of what she had witnessed. The description of blood dripping from the killer's hands. She decided that detail might be too much for young Mardoo. Indeed, it was even too much for her to relive. She felt nauseous just thinking about it.

She paused for a moment, deep in thought. Mardoo didn't speak. He gazed at his older cousin and read the emotion that crept across her face.

"As I said, there were three *wadjala* in my *koondarm*. My guess was they were in their late teens. Three, evil young men. The worst of them had a scar the length of his face. On the right side, from just below his eye right down to the side of his chin. A jagged scar. A wound that hadn't properly healed. Perhaps a wound from a *yongka* had become infected."

As she spoke, she ran her index finger down the side of her right cheek, just as she did sixteen years before when describing the killer to the police.

Bessie realised she was rambling to gloss over the really horrific part of the story, the blood on the *wadjala's* hands.

"When the police showed me a number of photographs, I was able to identify him. It was unmistakable. The killer showed no emotion when he was found guilty and sentenced to life in prison. There was no sign of remorse. Before two burly prison officers took him from the dock, he glanced around the Court House, made eye contact with me and glared. A hate-filled glare. It sent a shiver down my spine as it does now, just thinking about it. I'll never forget the look of evil on that boy's face."

She told Mardoo about the storm from the *boongari* (south) that had unexpectedly thrust itself upon Cottam Mills that night. As if an evil spirit had descended upon the Noongar community.

"Like the storm last night?" Mardoo asked.

"Yeah, exactly like that storm. The storm came from the south. A dreadful night. *Kep boolarang*, *malkar* and *kilang*. Much rain, thunder and lightning. Mardoo, I hope you never have to say those three words in the same sentence in *dirdong*, in spring."

"Why is that, Aunt Bessie?"

"Because it was exactly sixteen years ago that Yabini was taken from us. A night just like last night. It brought back very bad memories for me."

Nothing further was exchanged for several minutes. Bessie looked quizzically at Mardoo, who appeared to be deep in thought. Eventually she broke the silence. "Is there something you need to tell me, Mardoo?"

Mardoo hesitated and then responded in a constrained fashion, "No, Aunty."

Mardoo had listened to his aunty, open-mouthed. He wasn't sure if he should tell her of his epiphany. The vision he had in his dream during the storm, the previous night. He dreamt of a man dressed entirely in black walking boldly through the streets of Cottam Mills, going from house to house as if searching for something. Or someone. The man had a scar the length of his face. On his right cheek.

Chapter 18

For the next two days, Bessie tried to erase the memory of the murder, the crime scene photographs and the trial. Starting with the night of the murder, her visit to the *karla* to spend time with her family and the walk home on the bush track had all been revisited. So, too, had all of the worst aspects of those days.

She had slept uneasily on the night of the storm, but the following night felt a sense of comfort having visited the Cottam River and the resting place of *Walgu*. It was cathartic to have such an attentive listener in Mardoo as she retold the story of her experiences sixteen years before.

Talking about the passing of two of her loved ones to the Dreaming had helped her. Had provided a sense of relief. She had bottled some of the information within her and needed to empty the vessel. It was only right that Mardoo should drink the same knowledge of his family as everyone else. He also needed to know why his father, Mokiny Junior, was sometimes difficult to live with. The chat by the river about Yabini and Jimmy had been good for both of them.

Without doubt, it was good for Bessie. She had talked to her ancestors. Just like many times before when she had gone to the river and thrown sand, Yabini's image had appeared in the still of the water. Her soul was happy. Settled with her ancestors from thousands of years before. At peace. But Bessie always knew Yabini would be at peace because she was such a beautiful soul.

***

It is written that purebred dogs have an uncanny sense of imminent danger.

On the third evening after the storm, exactly sixteen years since Bessie gave her statement to the Homicide Squad, she made a pot of tea, poured a small amount of milk into her chinaware jug, selected two mugs from her kitchenette, placed the items on her favourite silver tray and stepped outside onto the verandah. A tradition that would never be broken. She walked carefully along the groaning verandah, again reminding herself to talk to Mardoo about hammering down the nails.

Tail wagging as usual, Buster stepped lightly along the verandah next to Bessie. He sniffed at his plate of dog biscuits as he sauntered past and stopped briefly to lap some water from a bowl.

"C'mon Buster," Bessie instructed. "Come and sit with me. There's a good boy."

Buster took a last mouthful of water and enthusiastically ran to sit on his mat next to his beloved, tail still energetically wagging, head tilted slightly and eyes beaming. It was as if Buster was waiting for a friendly chat with his owner. They often chatted at this time of the evening, when Bessie had her dog's complete attention.

It was a very pleasant evening with a slight easterly breeze, signalling to Bessie that warmer weather was on its way. Hot days always followed the easterly spring wind. She sat and breathed deeply, taking in the cool evening air from across the valley. *Could this be the last of the cool nights before the summer heat?*

No sooner had she sat on the cane sofa and poured herself a mug of tea, when she heard a slight sound coming from the direction of her carport. The side of the house where there was a personal gate. It sounded like the scratch of unoiled hinges. Buster had heard it too and uttered a deep growl in anticipation of an unwanted visitor. He stood.

"Who is it?" Bessie murmured.

"It's only me. Just wanna talk, Aunt Bessie."

Mardoo rounded the corner of the house and stood momentarily at the bottom of the stairs, waiting for an invitation. He realised that was unnecessary and slowly scaled the wooden steps leading to the verandah. He noticed the thick jarrah boards groan. *I must tighten the steps; hammer the nails down for Aunt Bessie.*

At the sound of the voice, Buster scampered along the verandah, tail wagging furiously. Mardoo stopped on the last step and bent to ruffle his favourite dog's ears. Buster licked Mardoo's arm at the inside of his wrists. Requited love. He then let out an excited yelp and ran back to his owner, tail still wagging.

There was no need to invite her cousin to talk. The tone of Mardoo's voice told Bessie there was an addendum to their afternoon's discussion by the river. That afternoon she had a sense that Mardoo wanted to tell her something. His presence confirmed that.

Bessie patted the seat next to her. Mardoo sat after giving his cousin a kiss on her cheek. Such affection was not common amongst the Wilman mob, but from a very early age Mardoo had been told by his father that he must always greet Bessie with a kiss. "Bessie is a special woman", Mokiny Junior had insisted, "And must always be respected and loved." After the chat that day, Mardoo knew exactly what his father had meant.

"I need to tell you something, Aunty. It might be nothing to be concerned about but as I have told you before, sometimes my dreams become reality. I worry about that."

Tension was written across his face. A look of genuine concern. Mardoo's eyebrows were tightly knitted, his forehead was deeply lined and his mouth was shaped as if he was clenching his teeth.

Bessie eyed him carefully without commenting on his demeanour. Embarrassed by his cousin's gaze, Mardoo looked away. In the direction of the river.

"I had a *koondarm*, a dream. I think that's the correct Wilman word, *koondarm*. Is that the right word, Aunty?"

He received a nod of approval in return.

"In my *koondarm*, Aunty, I was visited by a *warra wirrin*. A wicked man full of hatred, an ugly man. He was dressed in black."

"Did your *koondarm* tell you more? Where was this man? Who was he? Where did he come from?"

A rush of questions and then, realising she might cause unease, and wanting to allay any fear that Mardoo might have, Bessie calmly added, "By the way, I haven't mentioned this in class, but a wicked, ugly man is *wara maaman*. *Warra wirrin* means bad spirit." She laughed lightly.

Mardoo attempted a smile but it was unconvincing. The pinched eyebrows were revealing. Betrayed his intense nervousness. Not for him but for his Aunty, after he learnt of her role in having a murderer sentenced to imprisonment for life.

"I didn't mean to alarm you by the truth-telling, Mardoo. I thought you deserved an explanation for your father's moods and an understanding of what being a Beelagu person really means. The significance and sacredness of the river. Please don't be alarmed. That *wara maamam* is securely in prison. I suspect our talk might have triggered some strange thoughts in your sleep. You needn't be concerned."

Mardoo was pensive. "Perhaps, Aunty," he eventually said. He again gazed into the distance, past the river and into the hills beyond. Buster looked at Mardoo and followed his gaze to the south. He gave a deep-throated growl.

"What's wrong, Buster?" Bessie asked, attempting to comfort her dog.

"Aunty, in my dream this *wara maamam* had a scar on the right side of his face and he was here. In Cottam Mills."

Buster hadn't averted his eyes from the horizon. He laid his ears back tightly against the side of his head and again uncharacteristically growled.

Part Three

Mardoo

Chapter 19

Mokiny Junior and Jodi Trunning had two children, eleven-year-old Mardoo and his younger sister, Heather. The family lived in a corrugated iron shack situated at the *karla* which had been part of Mokiny Junior's family for several generations. A well-established and liked family, the Trunnings would always be treated with respect, despite the noticeable mood swings of the oldest family member.

The shack was basic but served the family's needs. A central kitchen and dining room was the largest and most frequented room for extended family gatherings. Much of the cooking was undertaken in a lean-to that housed a barbecue, a smoker and an outdoor sink. There were three wooden doors – one at the end and the other two at the long side of the dining room. The end one opened into a bathroom that had a shower, a separate bath, a medicine cabinet and a hand basin over a utility cupboard. Two doors led to separate bedrooms; one for the parents and one for Heather. Mardoo's bedroom was a sleep-out near the rear entrance and alfresco kitchen.

Mardoo liked his room. It enabled him to rise early in the morning without disturbing the family. He would sneak about a hundred metres along a winding grey sand path, flanked by marri and river sheoak trees, to the Cottam River. There, he would watch the sun rise above the trees on the opposite side of the river.

He loved the early morning when there was dampness on the leaves and a mistiness moving in a snail-like manner along the river. After a good night's sleep, he would sit on a log overhanging the riverbank and deeply inhale the fresh, early-morning river air. A perfect start to the day. Sometimes he had the good fortune to witness a *yongka* emerge from the brush to rehydrate, hear a *kaa-kaa* (kookaburra) stretch its vocal chords to welcome the daylight, or a *koolbardi* (magpie) warble to the rising sun.

Recently, his sleeping patterns had been disturbed. Over the last few nights he had been annoyingly tossing and turning for most of the night.

Something was bothering him but while he could identify the source of the problem for last night's disturbance, the truth-telling, he was unable to erase an image from his mind. It wasn't just a general sense of unease but a more specific *koondarm* had uncloaked a portrait of moral depravity.

The day after the truth-telling chat with Bessie, near the river resting place of *Ngarngungudditj Walgu*, Mardoo had woken with a start. Another very restless night. He couldn't shake off the image he had told Bessie about. The image of evil personified visiting Cottam Mills.

A few hours after Boodjark had commenced his unauthorised circuitous route out of the Kolbang Prison Farm, wearing civilian clothes, Mardoo rose from his bed and reached for the clothes he had placed on his bedside chair before sleeping. He slipped on a pair of black cotton shorts and his favourite t-shirt with an Aboriginal designed motif. A fishing theme. He ventured outside carrying his Adidas running shoes. He would be dressed for an early morning jog, beside the river, on a track that emerged from the bush at the nearby horse-race track.

Near the Prison Farm, Boodjark had hitched a ride in a box truck bound for a nearby winery. The countryside was quiet, save for the sound of a throbbing truck motor driving Boodjark to freedom.

It was dark. The moon had slipped below the horizon. Mardoo's *karla* was quiet too. He stretched and blinked several times to adjust to the sight of the campfire nearby. A man was silhouetted against the open fire in the communal area, thirty metres from the Trunning family shack. He was stoking the embers still burning from the previous night. Sparks escaped and fanned out over a short distance, reached skywards but didn't find anything to which they could become attached. It was like the powdered metal and potassium nitrate oxidizer of a sparkler on Guy Fawkes night. They soon dissipated.

Mardoo recognised the shape. *An early start for Pa.*

Mokiny Jnr faced the direction of the river, back towards his family home and didn't see Mardoo. Sharp hearing picked up the near-silent snap of a twig and instinctively he knew who was approaching. He slowly turned to greet his son.

"You're up early, Pa."

"Couldn't sleep. You're up early, too, Mardoo."

"Couldn't sleep either, Pa. Had a bad *koondarm*."

Mokiny grinned and pearl-white teeth glistened. Although Bessie was Mardoo's second cousin, it was polite and respectful to call her 'aunty'. "Your *maam yok* (aunty) has been teaching you new words. *Koondarm*. Tell me son, what was your dream about?"

"I'm not sure. It was hazy. Crazy scenes drifted past. Every now and then, Buster would appear with pleading eyes. There was a strange man growling like a dog. Do you understand dreams, Pa? Can you read them?"

Suddenly Mokiny's mood changed. He stood upright and snapped at his son. "No. I can't read them and I don't know what your stupid dream would be about. Have your breakfast and get ready for school."

"School holidays started yesterday, Pa. No school for two weeks."

"Have your breakfast," Mokiny repeated, louder still. "Go!"

In a prickly mood today, thought Mardoo. *I'll spend the day with Ozzy. I'm staying away from you today, grumpy.*

Mokiny couldn't tell Mardoo that his own dream was similar. Bessie's dog didn't feature, but evil in the form of his childhood friend, as he imagined he would appear as a young man, was present. It was inexplicable. He had a distinct feeling it was something to do with the anniversary of his sister's death. His nightmares had returned on the sixteenth anniversary of her passing to the Dreaming just as they did for weeks after every such anniversary.

The family tragedy had a ripple effect. Not surprisingly, given the horrendous nature of the murder, it had grim, even nightmarish consequences extending into the Indigenous community.

Several years after the murder, Mokiny's father, still consumed by grief, simply disappeared. It was initially believed Uncle Mokiny Snr may have gone for a *dombart yabera* (lonely walk) and, in fact, he may have, but the family became concerned when he hadn't returned after two days. Members of the *karla* searched the area. They visited all of Uncle Mokiny's favourite places in his *boodja* but to no avail. The police posted 'missing persons' photographs around Cottam Mills but the community, both black and white people, was convinced not enough had been done. Uncle Mokiny Snr was never found.

Mokiny Jnr decided he had to find a way to peel away the gross morosity that haunted him. Melancholy caused by the loss of his sister and his father. He recalled how heartsickness got the better of his cousin,

Jimmy. He wouldn't let it get the better of him. Jimmy's suffering was different; he permanently had the black dog because his mother unwittingly passed on her emotions from the stolen generation. Mokiny was different still. It wouldn't destroy him. He was a *kabap* (witch doctor) and the power within him would overcome his sickness.

After placing two logs on the fire, Mokiny left the *karla*. He walked slowly along the track that was the main entrance to the community from the direction of the centre of town. He usually took a different route to and from the *karla,* even if it took him longer to get to town. Terrible memories haunted him if he walked on this particular *djooroot*. But today he felt the need to. Somehow, after all these years, he had to find a way of dealing with Yabini's death.

A very large tree rose up in front of him at a bend in the track. He stopped, took a deep breath and stepped off the track amongst the thick undergrowth. He walked heavy-footed to scare any poisonous snakes that may be present and hidden out of sight. Hearing the noise and being sensitive to the vibrations on the ground, most snakes would make themselves scarce, slithering away quietly. If one couldn't see them in the shrubbery, a bite may be deadly. One couldn't be too careful.

There was a clearing fifteen metres ahead. Mokiny ceased stomping at the edge of the open area, breathed deeply and attempted to calm his anxiety. Head down, he took several deep breaths and then shuffled forward into the clearing, crossed to the other side and sat on the stump of a tree that had been deliberately felled about fifteen years before.

A few feet away near where she had been found, sixteen years before, was a small shrine consisting of ochre-painted rocks, a small wooden cross and some ceramic ornaments, personal to Yabini. He wasn't sure who had constructed the shrine in the memory of his sister, but he suspected it was his late parents. His father had disappeared, presumed dead, and his mother had died with a broken heart two years later.

Mokiny buried his face in his hands. Tears flowed.

How can I tell Mardoo about the rape and murder of his Aunty Yabini? How can I tell him that my old friend was responsible? Could it have been avoided if I'd walked her home from work that night? I should have. I knew Boodjark and his friends lusted after her.

Mokiny cried. He had blamed himself for failing to care sufficiently for his sister. He had carried that burden for many years and it had become heavier over the last six years, since the passing of his parents. Nobody else blamed him. Nobody else in his family knew of his torment.

He recalled how his father had told him and his friends to stay away from Bruce Prentice; that he was *wara* and carried an internal *djinack*. The Wilman nation *karla* people had previously liked young Bruce but Mokiny's father sensed that he was *kaat wara*. His father had been right and Mokiny Jnr hadn't seen it until it was too late.

His thoughts drifted to Mardoo. His only son had an infectious personality and a level of intelligence that would ensure he succeeded in life. Perhaps. There was only one obstacle. Not a problem as far as his kinfolk were concerned but nevertheless, a major hurdle for Mardoo: the colour of his skin.

Mokiny Jnr believed he had the power and a responsibility to help his son take advantage of his education and overcome all obstacles thrown at him. But first he had to deal with his own issues.

He mentally reached for his inner strength, wiped the tears from his cheeks and again took deep breaths. He couldn't go on like this; feeling guilt for not having saved his sister. He would leave the *karla* until he had dealt with his demons. It wasn't unusual for him to wander his *boodja* to seek solace. His family accepted that.

Should I tell Mardoo about the Sorry Time? At eleven years of age, would he understand? Of course he would. He's an intelligent boy, but he doesn't need the burden of such sadness in his life. No, the time isn't right.

Just twenty minutes earlier, Mardoo had talked about his dream, but not in sufficient detail for his father to know the dream was about a scar-faced, evil man. Nor had he shared the detail of other dreams he had experienced in recent years. Dreams that were prophetic. He shared the details with his Aunt Bessie but found it difficult to discuss such matters with his parents, especially his father. His father might react negatively, as he had that morning.

After Mokiny Jnr had growled at his son, Mardoo returned to his sleep-out. He chose not to have breakfast as instructed, but instead rummaged through his chest of drawers and retrieved a clean pair of hidden, charcoal-grey, Falke running socks. He slipped them on, followed by his Adidas runners. He decided not to jog the river track but instead left the *karla* in the same direction as his father.

As Mardoo walked the *djooroot,* he heard a subdued whimpering sound coming from the bush near the large Marri tree. It was almost inaudible. He knew it was a human sound, not a native animal or bird.

Silently and using his best hunting skills, being careful to avoid stepping on dry twigs, Mardoo stealthily crept from the track and peered in the direction of a clearing. Having never before left the *djooroot,* he didn't know the clearing existed. The large tree and thick acacia bushes screened him from view. He saw his father, face buried in his hands. A few feet beyond the stump where his father sat, Mardoo could see a shrine.

He retreated just as silently and left the area. He had one thought: *Now it all makes sense. For my Pa, the Sorry Time must be ongoing.*

Chapter 20

There are some similarities between Mark Twain's 'Huckleberry Finn' and the life of Mardoo and his best friend, Ozzy. Twain's novel dealt with a boy who enjoyed the freedom of country living and a desire to explore life to the maximum; to remove the shackles, the limits society placed on boys of his age.

Mardoo and Ozzy shared the same desire. 'Huckleberry Finn' involved strong overtones of racism. One of Twain's characters was literally shackled to a life of slavery. Mardoo knew his people's past was, in many respects, the same.

Many Australian kids prefer a sobriquet, either self-assigned or more likely a label chosen by their friends. Names they carry with pride in preference to their given names. Mardoo was shorter than Ozzy and was given the name by his local Noongar people soon after birth. It meant 'mouse' in the local Wilman dialect. Ozzy was derived from Oscar, a name he disliked intensely ever since he was teased about it at junior school. He couldn't understand why his parents chose a name that would cause him grief.

Kids liked to allocate nicknames especially if the assigned name was not always to the bearer's liking. In the case of Ozzy, the name was self-allocated. The label was widely used around Cottam Mills. Even his parents now called him by that name.

The two boys were tight friends. Friendship is born at the very moment there is a sudden awareness of likes and dislikes. Likes that are commonly held. Dislikes that may be shared but are not necessarily so. They're less important. In this case, the two boys liked the same types of things. They lived in the same part of town, attended the same school, liked the same sports, liked the same Aussie Rules football team, and had the same values instilled in them from a very early age.

They would hang out together whenever possible. Almost inseparable. "Joined at the hip," Ozzy's father once said. Mardoo would spend time helping his cousin Bessie but if there were no jobs to be done, he could almost always be found with Ozzy. The close buddies spent most of their after-school time and weekends together. They had been buddies for a very long time. Together they played football, cricket, swam, climbed trees, hunted for gilgies, and aimlessly rode their bikes along the many bush tracks surrounding Cottam Mills.

Both were talented and intelligent. They dreamt and talked about their future, what they would do in life once they left school. Ozzy had an expectation of going on to tertiary education, but not so Mardoo. He knew the difficulties his father had experienced with obtaining meaningful employment, simply because he was Indigenous.

"If only we had lived two hundred years ago," said Ozzy. "Our names would be etched in the history books as two of Australia's greatest explorers. Nice to dream," he laughed and then, in a more serious tone, added, "I read a short poem recently, written by an American social activist. I think he's described as a 'social activist' because he campaigned for equal rights for black Americans. That's fair enough, I reckon. I don't know him but I like him already. He wrote about being like a wingless bird if you don't dream of what might be."

Mardoo smiled at his best friend and said, "Sure, it's nice to dream, Oz, but I'm a realist. I sometimes dream about being a lawyer. Doing some good for my people. Lots of pro bono work. If I could, I would."

"Why can't you?"

Mardoo paused, then lifted his t-shirt and pointed, copying the champion Australian Rules footballer, Nicky Winmar, who famously did the same. Proudly displaying the colour of his chest.

"It shouldn't matter, Mardoo. You have a constitutional right to do whatever you want within the bounds of the law." Now it was Ozzy who sounded like a lawyer. "You're smart enough. You'll get the grades. I reckon you're even smarter than some of our teachers."

"Yeah, but if I get into university, there's the problem of the fees."

"You have to dream, Mardoo. How can you fly if you don't?" Ozzy pleadingly asked a rhetorical question, not expecting his friend to respond.

"Yes, there's nothing wrong with dreaming. I understand where you are coming from. If we don't dream we have no vision, no plans. But my dreaming is about my people; my people in ancient times, before *wadjala* came here. My dreaming is about my *boodja*, my land. What has happened to it and what prevents my people from belonging like we once did.

"Don't fret, Ozzy. One day, I'll fly. When it's time to go to the Dreaming."

Chapter 21

The Huckleberry Finn lifestyle was irresistible. The urge to remove the constraints of domestication and overarching societal expectations. Explore life to the maximum. Country life provided that opportunity for the boys.

Thick bush, within the vicinity of the boys' town, invited them. The bush was seriously thick. Scraggy hakea shrubs with prickly points on their leaves would be planted by the local Council in town parks or on the verge of the major highways, but they were native and abundant around Cottam Mills. Numerous different species of Acacia, Eucalyptus, Grevillea, Banksia and Melaleuca. All in abundance, waiting to tear at clothing and bare skin if given the chance.

Trees of different girth and height were also in abundance. Some were very old, others were regrowth after selective logging. Huge stands of virgin forest occurred close to the mighty river that meandered through and around Cottam Mills. Trees were cut to supply supports to underground coalmines, many of which later became open-cut mines. Logging still occurred but on the other side of town from where the boys lived. The timber mills on that side of town cut and shaped logs into planks for jetties or beams for houses.

There was an abundance of massive *balak* (xanthorrhoea plants). *Balak* that grew at the rate of about an inch each year have stood in this bush for hundreds of years.

Long-abandoned foresters' tracks snake through the bush. Many years have passed since the millers used them but, riding their bicycles, they provided the boys access to areas of the forest they loved to explore.

Now, well out of town, they rode with enthusiasm. They followed an old railway track. For a while, Mardoo struggled to maintain the pace Ozzy set on the soft, sandy path. They pedalled past the abandoned Kitty Valley mine about fifteen kilometres from town and linked up with a track that once supported heavy-duty jarrah railway sleepers and the steel lines that sat upon them.

They neared their destination where the track was swallowed by overgrowth. Railway lines appeared to materialise from nowhere, only to disappear again into particularly heavy shrubbery. Compacted earth and a mixture of clay and blue metal had discouraged undergrowth but there was an abundance of prickle bushes seemingly reaching out to scratch at and discourage adventurous bush-intruders.

Marri trees, often called bloodwood or red gum, because they bleed a viscous, blood-red gum when damaged, are abundant in this area. The bark, which peels from the tree easily, looks like a crocodile skin and if the skin is penetrated the tree might ooze its magical substance, known as *mayat* (red-gum sap).

The boys leant their bicycles against a large marri tree conveniently growing adjacent to the old railway formation, avoiding the gum seeping from a wound. This provided Mardoo with an opportunity to share more knowledge of *boodja*. He was always happy to share the information he had acquired over the years, mostly from his Aunt Bessie.

"My ancestors, the Wilman people, who were the traditional custodians of this land, had many uses for the marri tree," Mardoo told his friend. "The blossom would be used to make a sweet drink. Most importantly, the *mayat* had many purposes, including being used for tanning *yongka* skins. It was important for medicinal purposes, too – used as a disinfectant, for magical healing and for diarrhoea."

Mardoo's friend was in awe of the extent of his knowledge about bush tucker and so many other aspects of life on *boodja*.

"Okay, hard work now, Oz," Mardoo said. "On all fours from here."

Head tilted in the direction of his skinny legs, Ozzy stated the obvious in a sombre tone. "Shoulda worn jeans. Tough on the knees."

Adding an exclamation mark to Ozzy's observation, Mardoo grunted loudly before he dropped to his hands and bare knees. He started to crawl.

Mardoo must have the toughest knees in town, thought Ozzy. He just squinted ahead. Didn't even look at where his knees landed.

Ozzy looked at Mardoo and shook his head. He lowered himself gingerly to the earth. They then wriggled their way through the low, thick scrub. Mardoo appeared to know precisely where he was going. His friend couldn't see beyond the entanglement of shrubs ahead. It was difficult to raise their heads, such was the thickness of the low-hanging bush.

My mate knows the bush, thought Ozzy, *and I have so much to learn from him.*

Some patches of scrub were almost impenetrable but the boys pushed on and slowly inched their way through the undergrowth. A thick prickle bush caught Ozzy's shirt, presenting another challenge.

"Bloody hell! I just tore my shirt," he cursed. "Hopefully my mum won't notice that."

Mardoo grunted again and Ozzy chuckled quietly.

Fifty metres or so further on, the railway lines emerged from the scrub and in parallel snaked their way a short distance to a steep embankment bordering the river. Where the riverbank rose steeply to join the scrub, the lines took on a different appearance. Glistening in the late afternoon spring sun, they exuded a certain power and dominance over the terrain.

The boys had a sense of adventure. The old railway bridge was isolated and hidden in the bush. They discovered it the previous summer, when they paddled makeshift canoes some considerable distance downriver. Local kids don't usually venture that far away from the swimming areas closer to town. These boys were different. But this was the first time the boys had searched for the bridge by land. Easy for Mardoo, less so for Ozzy.

At the point where the railway lines emerged from the scrub, they were suspended almost four metres in the air. There was a gap between the land and the top of timber poles that punched down into the riverbank. Flimsy lines of hardened iron appeared to hang precariously, but there was no doubt they were strong enough to carry the weight of two young boys. A few charred railway sleepers hung in the air, inexplicably attached to them, accomplished by the ferocity and erratic imperfection of a bush fire several summers before.

Twisted steel, blackened timber railway sleepers, hardened crust of what looked like volcanic material, and ebony knobs on the vertical poles. The remains of a partially burnt-out bridge that once supported many tons of steam engine and its cargo of coal destined for the coast. For Ditchingham and its power station.

"A fire may have weakened the bridge but not enough to cause a problem for us," said Mardoo.

That was his first comment since leaving the track, over fifty metres back, where they parked their bicycles. An occasional grunt – a Mardoo exclamation mark – had been his only sound.

Other than when imparting his vast knowledge, Mardoo was usually quiet in the bush. He thought a lot but didn't say much. A special relationship with his *boodja*. As if he were absorbing the bush smells, the bush noises, history, strength and ecological system into his soul. His friend didn't usually talk to him when his head was in that space. Ozzy respected his connection with *boodja*.

Cautiously, Mardoo slid onto one of the railway lines. Hands reached forward and grasped the steel. Legs straddled the line. In a sitting position, he drew himself forward and dragged his rear end along the warm line.

"Don't look down," Mardoo urged. "You might come a gutser! Just look straight ahead along the line."

Ozzy waited for Mardoo to reach a more solid part of the old bridge before he followed the same routine. He followed Mardoo's advice and gazed ahead. When Mardoo had made it to the section of bridge that hadn't been destroyed by fire, Ozzy reached forward, pulled and dragged his bum on the steel. Reach, pull, slide... reach, pull, slide. He moved slowly towards the centre of the construction.

Eventually, the boys managed to slide onto a horizontal beam bolted to two larger poles rising from the river. Some stability. Something solid to support them, although with their light frames even a twig would probably suffice. Simultaneously, they stood and edged their way along the well-supported part of the bridge, stepping from sleeper to sleeper. After some twenty-five or so metres, they reached the middle of the river where, under the bridge, there hung a steel construction.

'Our secret spot", said Mardoo. "I doubt anyone knows this place existed."

Between the sleepers they could see two long horizontal logs, either side of the bridge, and fixed in the same direction as the railway lines. The logs were bolted to the side of four vertical poles that had been driven into the riverbed. Attached to the logs, at right angles, was a single, fifty millimetre-wide, two hundred millimetre-deep, milled timber beam. A steel structure was bolted to that beam under the bridge, suspended above the middle of the river.

Not being conscious of safety issues or having an awareness of engineering requirements to support a heavy steel box, they didn't bother to check the timbers or the rusted bolts linking them together. They were immune from mishap. Fearless.

Climbing between the timbers, they dropped into the box. The metal box was, in fact, half a box, open on one side, just over a metre deep, with a wide ledge to sit upon. Legs dangled over the edge, swinging freely above the river.

At this point, the river was quite deep but the boys weren't afraid of falling into the water. They could swim. Perched in the metal structure, about six metres above the river, they didn't fear the depths below them. From there they had a commanding view of the river in both directions. In this isolated backwater, they were in the perfect position to spot any unlikely intruders. Two, or four-legged.

For over an hour, the boys watched the water drift past at a rapid pace directly below their feet. Two pairs of eyes darted left and right and scanned the embankment for *yongka* or wild *doordok* that might venture down to the river's edge for a drink. For a few minutes, Ozzy chatted idly about the things eleven-year-old boys normally chat about. Which footy player he liked to watch. How the Aussies will go in the forthcoming Ashes cricket series. That sort of thing. It was a monologue.

It didn't seem appropriate to talk for too long, especially since Mardoo seemed to be in a different space.

Mardoo had contemplated telling his friend about the truth-telling with his Aunt Bessie. Not the story about Uncle Jimmy. The death of his cousin Yabini had occupied his mind. He was troubled by his *koondarm*. A premonition.

But I don't want to cause alarm. It may be nothing at all.

They sat and admired the beautiful surroundings. The bush aroused their senses. They absorbed the sounds, the rustle of leaves, wind in the trees, and petrichor, the smell of damp ground by the edge of the river. They were enthralled by the sound of running water below them. Almost mesmerising.

Suddenly, "Listen," Mardoo exclaimed, raising his hand to discourage any sound from his friend. "Did you hear that?"

"Only the sound of the bush and the river," replied Ozzy.

"No. There's something else. Something weird. I don't know what it is but... there it is again."

At that precise moment, the Australian tectonic plate moved, pushing north slightly, where it collided with the Philippine tectonic plate. Where they met and collided, rocks were crushed, causing underground tremors. An earthquake. Later that day, the television news bulletins reported the epicentre of this strong earthquake was 270 kilometres away as the crow flies.

Goosebumps crept along Mardoo's arms at the same time as an ethereal wave engulfed his senses. He received the vibes before they felt anything.

That's when it happened. The old railway bridge timbers groaned. Suddenly there was a loud crack, as a weatherworn bolt, supporting the metal structure, gave in to pressure from afar. One side of the box dropped first and then the other was torn away from a timber beam that had formed a crucial part of the bridge. It plummeted into the river, swollen from the heavy rains several days before.

The metal box hit the water first. Fortunately, the angle of its fall meant it sliced straight into the deep. Like an accomplished Olympic diver, it sliced the surface and was swallowed by the depths below. It quickly and smoothly disappeared from sight.

With an awkward splash, Ozzy hit the water. Not an Olympic dive – a huge belly flop. He was quickly carried away by the current. Mardoo concentrated on hitting the water without causing any damage. Arms flailed in survival mode. He made an ungainly entrance to the river and disappeared from sight, largely because of the rapid river flow.

He surfaced about ten metres from his entry point; such was the power of the river. While he wasn't a strong swimmer, he was good enough to swim at an angle across the current in the direction of the riverbank. His head swivelled every which-way, looking for his friend. A usually calm Mardoo was becoming frantic. He couldn't see him.

He reached a log, a fallen tree, with a few branches but no leaves. It was lying partially on the riverbank but mostly in the water. Now waist-deep, he could at last feel the ground below him.

Mud. Slimy mud.

Mardoo scrambled towards the water's edge, mud sucking at his feet. The log had prevented him from being swept downriver. Its rugged knots grazed his legs. His clothes were sodden. He was tired from fighting the current but a combination of fear for his buddy and adrenalin pushed him up the embankment.

Ozzy was not a good swimmer. In these waters, anything could happen. His mind raced. Fear had taken control. *Get a grip, Mardoo.*

"Ozzy!" he yelled as loud as possible. "Ozzy!"

No response. Mardoo continued to call Ozzy's name as he clawed out of the river with the help of reeds firmly embedded on the water's edge. No response. Adrenalin pumped, head swirled with confused, unsettled thoughts. He used as much strength as he could possibly muster and suddenly he was on dry land, standing on a mound. He again called out but still no response.

Further downriver now. Fifty metres or so. He didn't know how he got there.

I kind of floated. Over the water's edge, over the reeds, over the ground. No sense of time. Even no sense of being. My head in a different space. A space where anxiety took over and arms and legs functioned independently of the mind.

How did I get here? How far have I walked? Where's my friend? Where's Ozzy?

Mardoo stood atop a rocky outcrop near the water's edge, downriver, and around a bend from the old bridge. Head swivelled, eyes intently scanned the river and the river edge. He saw movement through some bushes further on. Leaving the outcrop, he pushed through shrubs and just beyond saw the most pleasing sight he believed he had ever seen. Ozzy emerged from the water and coughed vigorously, interspersed with gasping breaths.

The boys sat on a log, gathered their strength and inspected and compared their wounds. Scratched arms and legs: no serious damage. Mostly bruised egos. Not much to be concerned about. They sat in contemplation of what could have been.

Eventually, Ozzy broke the silence. "Do you think the bridge is still standing?" he asked.

"I never saw it collapse," Mardoo replied. "But then, I only saw swirling water. I saw you do a belly flop into the foam. That wasn't a winner. One out of ten, at best."

They both laughed at the description before Ozzy nudged his friend in the ribs and said, "Yeah, I suppose you did a half-pike and a perfect entry."

The pair sat in silence again. Mardoo looked downriver and appeared to be somewhere else. His mind, perhaps his spirit, being carried by the water. Transported out of his comfort zone. Or perhaps the river was his comfort zone. A *beelagu* boy.

"We were saved," Mardoo eventually said, as he gazed into the distance. "*Djanak* tried but didn't take us. *Ngarngungudditj Walgu,* the river serpent, saved us. Guided us to safety."

It was time to go. Before leaving the river, the boys felt smaller tremors. Aftershocks. The movement between rocks caused by stress release between those along the fault line, where the principal earthquake had struck. They would periodically occur for several weeks.

When the movement stopped, the boys ambled slowly away from the water and followed a yongka track flanked by tall marri trees. They hadn't moved far when Mardoo stopped. His senses took in the pungent, musty smell of a *yongka's* frequently used habitat nearby. A place the mob camped. Shoulder muscles tensed in the expectation of seeing kangaroos leap from the scrub but nothing happened. They moved on.

Nearby, there was another kangaroo smell. This time, the foul odour of a dead animal. It was at the edge of the path the boys had followed and was unavoidable.

Ozzy pointed at the rotting carcass and exclaimed, "Maggots! Look at them. If we had a jar, we could collect them for bait. Red-fin perch would love them."

Ozzy's outburst jolted Mardoo to halt. He suddenly experienced the same unearthly sensation he had moments before the steel hideout plummeted into the river. Before the earthquake.

"*Boodjark*," he said quietly, eyes downcast.

"What?"

"Maggots. 'Boodjark' means 'maggots' in Noongar language. They're evil."

He didn't elaborate. He couldn't. He didn't know if maggots were, in fact, evil. It was just a feeling but it left him ill at ease.

Without saying anything further, the boys proceeded along the *yongka* track. The pungency of the dead animal receded but the mob's frequently used track was prominent and easy to follow. They moved more cautiously when Mardoo spotted a narrow, winding furrow that traversed the track. A snake. He closely inspected the groove and concluded there was no need to be overcautious.

"The snake has long gone," he said with firm conviction. Ozzy didn't doubt it: Mardoo said so.

A bronze-winged pigeon took flight at the sound of intruders bumbling deep into the bush. Shards of light shimmered through the tall timber and flashed upon its wings. Breathtakingly beautiful.

The sun was quite low and not visible through the thick bush. Cool, evening air descended and moistened the undergrowth of the river valley. The leaves of native orchids took on a different hue. Bush smells changed to a musty character. Very soon, the light would disappear entirely.

A *kaa kaa* sat high in a marri tree directly above the boys as they hustled back towards their bicycles. It stretched its vocal chords. An abnormally loud call.

Ozzy continued to follow Mardoo, who had been in deep contemplation for the last thirty minutes or so. They eventually located their bicycles.

Ozzy silently recalled a poignant message he had once read. He didn't recall who said it but the message suggested circumstances in life do not make the boy – they do more: they reveal him. The circumstances they experienced that day might help shape their plans for future forays into the bush. They revealed who they were. Country kids who will always want to explore, go beyond the boundaries and if given the chance, escape the constraints of civilisation. Just like Huckleberry Finn.

In the weeks to follow, Mardoo's substance, the awareness of his surroundings and intuitive disposition would become important for his family.

Chapter 22

Four days after the storm, the wind had died and the weather returned to normal conditions for this time of year. Perhaps just a little more humid than one would expect in spring. Perspiration dripped from Boodjark's forehead as he tracked through thick bush in a northwesterly direction. A slow trek. He had plenty of time. His main objective was to avoid capture. He was comfortable with his plan and his strong recollection of bushman's skills, largely taught by his childhood friend, Mokiny.

At the same time, Mardoo and his friend Ozzy had to make two important decisions. Most importantly, they had to allocate nicknames to the newcomers in Ozzy's street. Secondly, it was time to introduce the newbies to a new and satisfying way of life. Teach them new skills.

"The question is, are they willing participants?" Ozzy exclaimed. "Or is this country too tough for them?"

Mardoo was quick to respond. "We'll soon find out. They've been here long enough to decide."

The new boy on the block was Tom. He had a younger sister, Dorothy. Their parents had relocated the family of five, including the grandmother, directly from Nottingham, England. Presumably to escape the cold winters and to give their children a better chance in life, like Ozzy's grandparents had, many years before. That was the conclusion the boys had reached.

"I'm sure our town offers more opportunities than the country they left behind," Ozzy suggested, with pride.

The boys sat on a park bench not far from where they lived. The recently mowed park was partially grassed with a drought and water-tolerant couch that was beginning to change colour with the warmer weather. The park was approximately two hectares in size, rectangular in shape, home to several large jarrah trees, a substantial children's playground and a rudimentary outdoor gymnasium. The boys discussed appropriate nicknames for the relative newcomers. They regarded their own nicknames, acquired many years ago, as legendary. Names long-established in local folklore.

When he was at kindergarten, Ozzy was known as 'Stewy' – an obvious name for a kid whose surname was Stewart. But he preferred the sobriquet he had adopted at an early age.

Although born into a relatively poor family – far from being regal – Ozzy liked to inform anyone who might be interested in his surname that it was derived from the royal clan of Stewart, the most common royal name in Scotland. The boys had decided that alone made Ozzy a legend, part of local folklore.

In his behaviour and socio-economic status, Ozzy was like most of the other kids in town, the main difference being he was more intelligent than most. Mardoo was also intelligent and excelled at school but his education in Indigenous language and culture set him apart from the white kids in Cottam Mills. His broader knowledge should have guaranteed more opportunities in life but he sometimes reminded his friend that the colour of his skin would be a disadvantage. It would count against him when it came to finding employment. To a large extent, he based that view on his father's experience.

"Does your dad ever go for a job interview and hope the interviewer isn't a racist?" Mardoo asked. Ozzy knew Mardoo didn't expect an answer. The silence was self-explanatory.

Discussion returned to the nicknames for Tom and Dorothy. "Marian" was easy to agree upon as her family had emigrated from Nottingham and the story of Robin Hood and Maid Marian came to mind. Sarcastically, Tom was to be allocated the nickname Ace, derived from the fact he regarded himself as an outstanding sportsman, a matter privately disputed by athletic Mardoo and Ozzy.

After several weeks' watching from a distance, Ace and Marian joined the boys in kicking the oval-shaped football in the park. "Marian seemed to grasp the challenge better than you, Ace," Ozzy told him. "Pretty good for such a young girl. And much younger, too." *Ace is not impressed. Whatever.*

The second issue the boys discussed whilst occupying the park bench was the end of the probationary period of three months since the Nottingham family had arrived in town. They had decided a probationary period was necessary to determine if the newbies could stand the rigours of walking the bush tracks. It was time to introduce Marian and Ace to some of the wonders of the land down under.

The local wilderness was thick with shrubs and an abundance of wildflowers. All types of flowering bushes – banksia, bottlebrushes, boronia and many more. Most eye-catching were the stands of old-growth forests. Huge trees that seemingly reached beyond the clouds. Trees that were home to corellas (a white cockatoo), Carnaby's cockatoo, the red-tailed black cockatoo, bronze-winged pigeons, and many other species of birds.

Foresters' tracks weaved through the countryside and provided the boys with reference points from which to explore. They challenged themselves to determine the direction of the compass points, based upon their knowledge of track directions, the location of timber mills, local farms, the types of flora in the area and the position of the sun in the sky. Not surprisingly, Mardoo had the best grasp of the detail.

Intimate knowledge of the bush was their encyclopedia. Not owning watches, the thick bush challenged them to determine the time of day. Agreement was usually reached based upon the length of shadows from the giant trees and the degree to which some of the wildflowers had started closing. Stamens curled in some species of flower during certain times of the day. Mardoo, especially, didn't need a formal encyclopedia. He just knew.

Mardoo usually met the biggest and most exciting challenge with enthusiasm. The challenge of tracking wild animals – *yongka, waitj*, wild *dordok, ngwir*, and even feral cats. His tracking skills reminded Ozzy of Tommy Windiitj. Mardoo had told him about Windiitj.

"He had normal, black fella skills. He originally came from *Kokar* country, where the people spoke *Njaggi Njaggi*. At an early age he was taken to *Wardandi* country, where he grew up. After white fellas occupied our *boodja*, he was recruited to help explorers. He also helped the police. He knew animal and bird tracks, he found water where nobody else could and when all seemed lost, he could read the night sky."

"We can do those things," said Ozzy. "You taught me."

"Yeah, but he could even read the minds of the crims seeking to escape the police. He was the best at his craft."

"I reckon you can do that and more, Mardoo."

There it was again. The unearthly feeling. A strange sensation waved across Mardoo's body followed by goosebumps crawling along his arms. *Was it something I said? Talk of crims escaping the police?*

He changed the subject. "Time to share some of our knowledge with those kids. If they are to become fair-dinkum Aussies, they need to learn basic bush skills."

The group met after lunch at *Warra Wirrin* Park, where the boys met earlier and decided it was time to teach the kids from Nottingham. *Warra Wirrin* Park was to provide an opportunity for their first lesson.

"Have you been curious about the name of this park?" Ozzy asked. "*Warra Wirrin*. An unusual name, yes?"

The Nottingham kids glanced sideways at each other, before Ace responded with a shrug of his skinny shoulders. Marian simply smiled sweetly. It didn't seem important to them.

Mardoo was pleased Ozzy had commenced the lesson with a reference to local Indigenous knowledge. He smiled. *It's better coming from a white kid.*

"It means 'evil spirit' in the Noongar language," Ozzy announced. "It was historically believed that this area was influenced by bad spirits. It's a long-held belief. It may be true. Did you notice Mardoo kicked the footy really well when we played at Yakkan Park, but when we played here he can't kick for nuts?" He laughed loudly.

"At the far end of Yakkan Park, down the embankment, is a small swamp," Mardoo informed the group. "That billabong is the home of freshwater turtles and that's what *yakkan* means."

"That's all, for now," Ozzy said. "The end of your lesson on local Aboriginal names for the moment. Let's go."

In single file, Mardoo leading, the group commenced their ride in a southerly direction. But the procession was quickly brought to a halt at the edge of the park.

"We can't do this without taking a rifle," Ozzy told the group. Noticing the shocked look on Ace's face, he quickly added, "Nothing sinister. Just part of learning about bush living. Wait here. Mardoo and I must go to my grandfather's shop. We won't be long."

Ozzy's grandfather owned a tailor's shop on the edge of the central business district. His grandfather hadn't practised tailoring for a very long time. With the onset of Parkinson's disease, his hands shook too much. Ozzy's cousin Ben, who had ambitions to take over the business, now performed any tailoring jobs required by local folk.

Whilst the tailoring part of the business still earned a good income for the shop, it had become less significant. Firearms and ammunition were also sold there. Tailoring was at the rear of the shop. In the front, behind the counter, was a range of rifles, shotguns and pistols to greet everyone who entered the premises. Ammunition to match the firearms was in boxes hidden from view, below the counter.

Ozzy's grandfather believed him to be a responsible and careful young boy and as a consequence, allowed him to periodically borrow a firearm.

"For security reasons in the bush," he said. "Not that there is any need to be concerned about the safety of your bush sojourns. I know you will be careful. Just make sure the safety clip is always engaged."

The bell dangling from a bracket above the door rattled as Ozzy and Mardoo entered the shop. The front of the shop was empty. Ozzy swung the door a few times to elicit more dinging sounds. No response.

Ben must be out the back, sewing. We'll help ourselves. I'll leave a note for Grandpa.

Ozzy's favourite rifle hadn't been sold. He always left it at the end of the row of firearms, hoping nobody ever saw it. A Browning bolt-action 5.6 mm calibre rifle. Easy to use and light to carry. He felt behind a freestanding cupboard and located the set of firearm-cabinet keys where they were usually hidden, hanging on a nail. He opened the cabinet furthest from the entrance to the shop and removed the rifle. Both boys then stuffed their pockets with ammunition.

"Although I'm sure Grandpa will know where the rifle has gone, a short note under the counter is a good idea," Ozzy whispered, woodenly. "Where I usually leave messages for him."

Within a short time, the pair had rejoined the others at Warra Wirrin Park. They rode south. This area was chosen for the first lesson on bush survival skills because of the abundance of flora and fauna.

At the same time, approximately three hundred kilometres further south, Boodjark was chewing over his good fortune at having excellent knowledge of the bush. He imaginatively gave himself credit for such knowledge. A metaphorical pat on the back. He would never acknowledge the early childhood survival skills Mokiny taught him.

Several kilometres past the southern end of town, where a number of creeks wound through thick bush and fed the river, Mardoo and Ozzy sought what they described as a luxury escape. It was an area of regenerated forest, most of the old trees having been felled by foresters and milled for housing, or exported to England. Many smaller trees were historically used in the underground mines nearby. There were still remnants of old-growth forest in the area, towering above the younger trees with thick shrub at ground level. Magnificent trees providing shelter and breeding areas for a variety of native birds.

They rode slowly to ensure Marian wasn't left behind. Her shorter legs seemingly pumped harder on a small bike.

The bitumen road took them past a popular swimming area and across a long, timber bridge that traversed the mighty Cottam River. At the turn-off to the long-abandoned Kitty Valley Mine, they stopped for a breather. With the Browning strapped across his back, Ozzy felt secure.

They rode on. It wasn't long before the bitumen road ended. Loose gravel made it harder for Marian to keep up, but she did so valiantly. Another few kilometres and Mardoo, still in the lead, turned sharply over the shoulder of the road and dipped onto a sandy foresters' track.

"Now for the serious stuff," Mardoo yelled to his companions.

They crossed a gully that directed a trickle of water from the recent storm over a bed of gravel interspersed with large granite rocks. Ahead there was a clearing where many years before, foresters parked trucks for loading, but first they had to manoeuvre their way past overhanging prickle bushes. The ground in the clearing was so hardened by trucks it never recovered; never re-vegetated as other nearby ground had.

"Let's rest here for a few minutes," Mardoo said as he slid from his bicycle seat onto a log at the edge of the clearing. "Give Marian a chance to recover. First lesson. I just made a monumental mistake for a bushman. What do you think it might have been, Ace?"

Ace again shrugged his skinny shoulders.

"The first thing you must remember is never assume there are no bities under the log." Mardoo emphasised 'bities'.

"Bities?"

"Yeah, bities. Joe blakes and other reptiles. Australia is home to some of the most dangerous snakes in the world. One bite and you're history."

Heads swivel. The Nottingham kids stared at the surrounding ground anxiously, just as there was another tremor growing from deep within the earth, heightening their anxiety. Stress movements in the earth rarely occurred within the region of Cottam Mills but of late they had become a regular occurrence.

Two hundred and seventy kilometres away, Boodjark felt it too as he dug around a clump of sedge grass with a makeshift spade to extract bulbous roots. Bush tucker. He momentarily stopped digging and gazed at a nearby marri tree, watching its top branches shudder with the earth's movement.

"There are many things you need to learn if you are to really take advantage of the opportunity provided by our bush," Ozzy enthusiastically told them. "To really enjoy our country. Mardoo is the best person to teach you, so listen up."

On cue, Mardoo told his students they would need to learn basic bush skills. "You will need to know what is safe and what isn't safe to eat if you are lost in the bush. What to look out for, if lost. You will need to learn how you might be able to use your newfound knowledge of the bush to survive and to find your way home. I will show you how to collect water from the hump of a paper bark tree. Did you know you can also replace your perspiration or quench your thirst by eating raw possum or other animal flesh?"

Neither of the Nottingham kids answered but facial expressions showed they were listening intently. Marian screwed her nose into an unnatural shape.

"You must learn how to appreciate and care for our flora and fauna," Mardoo continued enthusiastically. The master of bushman skills was always conscious of preserving the environment.

"See that sedge grass over there?" Mardoo pointed at the grass standing in clumps in a low-lying area. "If you need bush tucker, dig around the clumps, extract the roots and you have a really tasty and nutritious vegetarian meal." As he spoke, Mardoo shook involuntarily. A small shudder not caused by the tremor but another unearthly sensation.

Why that feeling? Goose bumps too.

"Ozzy brought a rifle, so he'll teach you how to use it. You'll learn where you can find water because that's where you are most likely to put the rifle to good use. Find some tucker."

Ozzy burst into laughter at Mardoo's last comment and pointed in the direction of a line of paper-bark trees.

"Okay, I know. The river is just over there, but they didn't know that," said Mardoo. "Let's walk," he instructed over his shoulder, as he left the clearing on a barely visible track.

After walking for fifteen minutes or so, Mardoo stopped, raised his hand and whispered, "No talking now. Walk as quietly as possible."

He pointed to the ground. "See those marks? *Yongka.* Kangaroo."

"Oh how exciting," Marian exclaimed. "I haven't seen one yet."

"And you won't if you make any noise. And there," he pointed at other markings on the ground, "Wild *dordok.* Pigs."

The group walked on in silence. After ten minutes, the track opened up into another, smaller clearing at the edge of a different creek. Clear water trickled over the gravel bed. Mardoo stopped and in a barely audible whisper suggested to Marian and Ace they should take the opportunity to taste clear, cool spring water.

"It's the best," he whispered. "When you're in the bush and see a billabong or a creek, you should always drink plenty of water. You never know if you'll come across another water source. You mightn't think so with that storm a couple of nights ago but we live on a very dry continent."

Ace was first to move. He edged past some reeds closer to the creek. Suddenly there was a noise on the far side of the clearing. It became ominously louder. The sound of a wild boar grinding its teeth is unmistakable. Aggressively, the boar pawed at the earth and continued to grind its teeth. Foaming at the mouth.

"Climb a tree!" Ozzy yelled as he grabbed a branch on the nearest tree and swung awkwardly upwards. Mardoo disappeared.

Ace faced the boar, Marian nearby. Both frozen with fear.

"Climb!" Ozzy yelled again.

Then the animal emitted a loud growl and charged.

Although a charging animal is quick, everything seemed to happen in slow motion. Ozzy manoeuvred the rifle free of his shoulder, flicked the safety switch and attempted to point it in the direction of the charging beast. The rifle became entangled in another branch.

Circumstances revealed the girl. As the beast plowed through the creek and was about to hit Ace front-on, Marian did the unthinkable. She launched herself sideways and rugby-tackled her brother. A boar tusk caught the side of her dress, tearing it and in the process, flinging her to the ground near a stunned Ace. The boar stopped and turned to repeat the attack.

As he struggled to free the rifle, out of the corner of his eye Ozzy saw Mardoo emerge from behind another tree. He took two steps towards the boar. Nerves of steel. Calmly, he raised his hand and pulled the trigger. The animal was stopped dead in its tracks, a hole in the side of its head, behind its eye at the base of an ear. With a final groan and kick of its rear paws, the massive beast dropped.

"Holey moley!" exclaimed Ozzy, as he climbed down from his tree. "That was close. What a shot! Where did you get that pistol from?"

Mardoo gave his customary cheeky grin. "I borrowed it."

He turned to Ozzy and explained. "When you were writing a note to your grandfather, I decided it wouldn't be a bad idea for backup. I checked to see if it was loaded while you were busy. I didn't think you'd mind."

Simultaneously they turned after hearing a whimper. Marian was crying and shaking in shock. Ace stood, composed himself, brushed dirt from his shorts, and in a very English manner said, "Pull yourself together, girl."

"She probably saved your life, Ace," Ozzy told him sternly. "You should be more gracious and indeed grateful for having a sister with such courage."

"Enough lessons for one day," Mardoo said. "I think you can see how one must always be prepared and take particular note of your surroundings, especially near water. Always be vigilant. Keep your eyes peeled. Become familiar with everything around you and take particular note of where the nearest tree is for climbing," he laughed, gazing at Ozzy.

Awareness of surroundings. Observance. Mardoo wasn't to know, then, how his own sensible application of that practice would soon become important.

Having been contemplating a speech while riding in silence, when the group reached the end of their street, Ace signalled for the others to stop. "I just want to say this. Today I have had the most terrifying experience I'm ever likely to have in my entire life. I really appreciate your friendship and what you did for us today, Mardoo, but I want to make it clear I will never go to that Warra Wirrin Park again. Bad, evil spirits followed us."

You have no idea how true that may be, thought Mardoo, without knowing why he had such a thought.

Chapter 23

The family of Mardoo's close friend, Ozzy, came to Australia from Scotland many years before he was born. Ozzy's grandparents applied for migration to the land down under and because they were farmers their application was immediately successful. But it was conditional. The Government had allocated large tracts of virgin land to aspiring broad-acre farmers on the condition they planted grain crops. They were required to achieve a certain quota of grain, mostly wheat, each year.

But the family couldn't achieve their quota. Years clearing mallee woodland and scrublands was hard, back-breaking work, but still didn't provide the acreage required to meet their quota. Seriously in debt and unable to meet the Government's demands, the banks started circling. Eventually, Ozzy's grandparents simply walked off the land and moved to the city.

Life in the big smoke was also tough for the Stewart family. Work was difficult to find, and the piecemeal and temporary work Ozzy's grandfather received was insufficient to pay the farming debts. Putting food on the table for the family was hard and irregular during the world's financial crisis. As a young boy, Ozzy's father was sent to live with a distant relative in a mining town and set to work. The town was Cottam Mills.

Ozzy never met his father's parents. They were both killed in a traffic accident nine months after leaving the farm. It was a single car accident. Apparently, their car left the road in a wet and winding section of the Snowy Mountains and they plummeted into a ravine. Both were killed instantly.

Mr Stewart never received the education he needed or deserved. But as a proud father, he was determined for Ozzy and his sister to make the most of the opportunity he gave them for a solid education. He was uncompromising in that respect. Whenever his son complained about the subjects he was forced to sit through at school, he raised his hand to end the conversation. There was no need for him to say anything. The signal was enough.

Nevertheless, Ozzy wasn't convinced that all subjects he was compulsorily required to attend would serve him well throughout life. To him, it seemed the teachers deliberately went out of their way to make class as boring as possible.

Perhaps teaching is a job I should aspire to when I grow up. Attempt to make the learning experience more interesting for the next generation.

Fortunately for Ozzy, some classes provided a reprieve from the more mundane. A lesson in scripture was a good example. Although his family wasn't religious, Ozzy and his close friends always liked the scripture lessons. For them, scripture provided the opportunity to whisper about interesting matters not otherwise part of the school curriculum. Things such as football. Chat about the school fights and school love affairs, such as they were. To the boys, those matters broke the boredom. To them, scripture was almost like an extension of the morning recess break from class, except one must stay indoors.

'Smelly' Patrick, the reddish-blond kid who lived around the corner from Ozzy's house, was sitting across the aisle from him in scripture. To the best of Ozzy's knowledge, Smelly didn't have a girlfriend. With a sobriquet like that, how could he? It was bad luck that Ozzy and Mardoo were sitting near him that day.

"Let's allocate Smelly a girlfriend," Ozzy whispered to Mardoo. "Write it on the desk for other kids to see."

Mardoo wasn't into that type of mischief. Unsure if it was a good idea. But he could see from the look in Ozzy's eyes that nothing he would say would deter him. It was relatively harmless, anyway. If it was certain to happen, make it worthwhile. "Who is the ugliest girl in the school?"

For a few minutes the boys contemplated the options. After a short time, Ozzy arrived at a name and dared Mardoo to complete the task. The dare was reluctantly accepted. It was an unusual moment of weakness for Mardoo. He undertook a task normally unthinkable to him. He surreptitiously carved Smelly's name into the top of the desk, a shallow carve with a blue biro. He added Emma's name, the girl whom the boys agreed was the ugliest in the school, if not Cottam Mills. Mardoo pronounced Smelly's undying love and devotion to her: "Smelly Patrick loves Ugly Emma." Arrow through the heart and all.

Unfortunately for Mardoo, the scripture teacher observed the artwork. He didn't stop its progress but instead reported the job to the Deputy Principal. Ace had the measles and wasn't at school that day but hours later, Ozzy told him the teacher had been trying to convince the class that Christians were all about love and forgiveness. "If he were a proper Christian, he would not have reported him. At the very least, he could have dissuaded Mardoo from his endeavour," Ozzy said uneasily, attempting to convince himself. Guilt returned.

The boys were convinced the Deputy Principal was arguably the meanest person in Cottam Mills. They were not familiar with Boodjark. Mardoo knew the story of Yabini but the offender was no longer in town. Incarcerated for a very long time. That left the Deputy Principal. Ozzy told Ace he was, "Probably the 'darkest' person I have met in my short lifetime. If he had children of his own, I would genuinely fear for them but I suspect he's not even married – how could he be? There isn't a woman on this planet stupid enough to be tied to him!"

Towards the end of the scripture class, the Deputy Principal entered the room and paraded the rows. The top of each desk was carefully inspected. Hawk-eyes scanned the room and its contents in expectation of finding something, anything, or anyone out of place. He licked his lips as he walked the aisle.

Something's afoot, thought Ozzy. Trouble. Aptly named 'Face-ache'.

Face-ache spotted the freshly carved markings. He bent over the desk to look more closely and his ruddy pockmarked face turned even redder with anger.

"Did you do this?" he bellowed at Smelly, pointing at the artwork.

Smelly responded within the blink of an eyelid, "No sir. It was him," instantly pointing his index finger at Mardoo.

Mardoo was an honest boy. He meekly said, "Yes sir, t'was me."

He wasn't fearful of a thrashing. He had received many from larger kids at school. Was it simply because of his shyness, his reticence to join in with *wadjala* kids other than Ozzy, or was it to do with his skin colour? He knew he would receive six of the best from Face-ache's weapon of choice:

the cane. The policeman, judge, jury and executioner, swift in his deliberation, ordered him to attend the school office, "Right now!"

Grumpy old Face-ache is renowned for dishing out tough punishment with the cane, Ozzy opined. *I thought the cane was banned. It is in every other school, I'm sure; just not in Cottam Mills because the Parents and Citizens Association, the miners and timber millers, are accepting of that form of punishment.*

One doesn't attend the school office for tea and biscuits with the staff. Mardoo was in for it. He knew he was in for it.

"You're in for it, Mardoo," Smelly whispered in obvious delight.

Mardoo glanced at Smelly but said nothing. Ready for his punishment, he straightened his shoulders and marched out of the classroom. Expecting the worst, as he left the room Ozzy observed Mardoo rubbing his hands over his oily hair in the forlorn hope the oil would lessen the pain – a myth spread widely in the public school system ever since boys plastered their hair with Brylcream decades ago.

Circumstances revealed the boy. All of the attention on Mardoo had become too much for Ozzy. Guilt overrode everything. *I gave Mardoo the dare. It's not his fault but mine. I must put a stop to this madness.*

To everyone's surprise, Ozzy jumped from his seat, rushed past the teacher and out of the classroom. He dashed to the office. He didn't hesitate, charged past the school secretary and thrust open the Deputy Principal's door. Face-ache was visibly shocked at the intrusion. His hand was poised mid-air, bamboo cane in hand.

"Don't do it. It wasn't him," Ozzy yelled as he charged into the room. "It was me!"

Face-ache lowered his hand, unsure. He gathered himself, looked at Mardoo, who remained with his arm extended, hand open to receive the punishment, looked at Ozzy and again at Mardoo.

"Good try, but stupid of you to stick up for him," Face-ache growled, nose upturned as he pointed at Mardoo. "He did it. You know that. I know that. He's Aboriginal, isn't he?"

That remark was too much for Ozzy. The straw that broke the camel's back. "You racist p–" he yelled. Tears started to sting his eyes at that hurtful, racist remark. A brain snap but not one without good reason. He stopped short of calling the Deputy Principal entirely what he believed him to be. A racist pig.

Ozzy reinforced his view with a courageous outburst, "Mardoo's a better person that you'll ever be!"

Face-ache had never been confronted like that before. Bullies don't expect such brazenness. Their behaviour is not usually challenged. He was in a state of shock. He faced Ozzy, mouth agape. Never before had a student addressed him in that manner. Mardoo was also stunned but could see some humour in the situation. A slight, angular grin teetered and then gradually made its way around the corner of his mouth.

Still fuming, Ozzy trembled with anger, not fear as Face-ache probably thought. He walked confidently to Mardoo, placed his hand on his friend's forearm and lowered it. He turned to again face the racist and partially extended his own arm.

Without any hesitation, the Deputy Principal instructed him to extend his arm further. He tapped the back of his upturned hand with the cane signifying he wanted it raised slightly. Then came the sound of a long bamboo cane, a centimetre in diameter, swishing through the air. All six swings found their mark across the palm of Ozzy's hands – left hand, then right hand – blackening the thumbnails.

"I hope you've learnt ya lesson. Now scrub that desk clean. Get your miserable face outa my sight."

You should talk Attila, Ozzy thought, grimacing from the stinging sensation. *A more miserable person I've never seen. You may even be capable of murdering your brother just like the original version of Attila.* At least Face-ache, Attila or whatever he should appropriately be called, had forgotten about Mardoo. *But I hope he never forgets what I told him.*

Mardoo joined Ozzy in what seemed like an eternity of scrubbing. As the boys worked, they discussed the next step. "I'm gonna report Face-ache to the Superintendent for his racist remark. I want him sacked. I hate racism," Ozzy told Mardoo. "A person should not be judged by the colour of their skin but by the content of their character – that's what a smart man once said. Martin Luther King said that."

Mardoo wanted to leave the matter well alone. "It won't make any difference," he argued. "Unfortunately, I hear that sort of comment too often, almost daily. People say those things based solely on the colour of my skin. It shows their ignorance. Some people, including Face-ache, have no idea of the pain it causes. Besides, I did deserve the cane. I did the wrong thing."

After school, Ozzy planned to visit his father who was in hospital, but before doing so he had to explain to his mother how he acquired the blackened nails. At the end of the explanation, he added, "Mardoo is a good person, a very good character. He didn't deserve that slur. Nobody does. I told him so but typical of Mardoo, he still wanted to let sleeping dogs lie."

"Marking the desk was the wrong thing to do but I'm proud of you for being honest and for supporting Mardoo," Ozzy's mother said. "There's no place for racism in our society."

"It's so hurtful, Mum. Mardoo told me he faces it almost every day. Other kids say hurtful things. I think they have been taught racism by their parents," Ozzy offered.

"We all have to call it out, Oz. We've seen it manifested in the worst possible way in our town."

"What do you mean Mum?"

"A happening, long before you were born. A horrible, horrible racist crime. Mardoo's family knows. Perhaps one day, when he is ready, he will tell you about it."

Chapter 24

Ozzy's father looked after the horses at a mine near Cottam Mills. Matthew Stewart was known to his workmates at the *kongal* [south] mine by his position of employment: 'Ostler'. Ozzy explained to Mardoo and Ace, who now often joined the boys in their activities, that an ostler looked after the workhorses that toiled underground. Their task was to pull coal-laden carts to the surface on rails. The ostler's job was to ensure the horses were well fed, fit and healthy, and capable of doing a hard day's work in tough conditions.

The mine, appropriately named Kongal Mine, utilised old-fashioned mining techniques because the coal seam was deep underground, narrow and accessed by similarly narrow adits in unstable ground. Most mines were now either open cut or utilised trucks to transport the material to the surface. The Kongal coal grade was worth pursuing, despite the use of more costly labour-intensive techniques.

In the days since the boys last met, what was usually a straightforward task had resulted in Ostler's hospitalisation. He broke his leg in what Ozzy described as a freak accident but one brought about by his bravery.

"I have to visit my dad. Do you boys want to come with me?"

The boys nodded furiously, not wanting to miss out on the first-hand information about such a serious occurrence.

"It wasn't an ordinary break," Ozzy assured his friends, raising the tension in his voice. "Not, for example, the sort of break you have when you fall from a horse. That's not what happened, of course, because my dad doesn't ride his horses. The break was a fair dinkum smash job."

"Blimey, Ozzy – what happened?" Mardoo asked incredulously. "Anything to do with those earth tremors we keep feeling?"

"Nah. Nothing to do with the earthquake. A mineworker had been tasked with leading one of my dad's best workhorses as it dragged a cart loaded with coal to the surface. Unfortunately, the bloke was inexperienced.

Normally the trolley would be towed directly to the dump area but for some inexplicable reason that didn't happen.

"Near the mouth of the decline, the worker disconnected the cart but he didn't properly apply what Dad called 'the sprag'," Ozzy continued, demonstrating his recently acquired knowledge of mining, or at least, ostlering. "The sprag is the brake shoe attached to the rear axle of the cart. What happened next could have been a disaster for the workers at the mine, for the mining company and the local economy, but instead it was a disaster for my dad."

"Blimey!" Mardoo repeated. "A disaster. Like the New York mining disaster of 1941? They wrote a song about it."

"Nah, surely not that sort of disaster, Oz. That was an underground cave-in," exclaimed Ace. The boys were always keen to demonstrate to each other how well read they were.

"No, but it could have been. Dad was inside the dimly lit tunnel, shovelling coal that had fallen from the trolley. That's not his job but he always dips in and helps with whatever job needs to be done. He is especially mindful of the path his horses must tread and needed to clear the area near the rails."

Ozzy waited for another question from one of the others but they sat riveted on the edge of the park bench, staring at their friend and waiting eagerly for more news. He dramatically said, in the deepest tone he could muster, "There was a rumble from up the line."

Mardoo and Ace, mouths agape, listened intently to the story. Ozzy was a good storyteller. This could be news for the dinner table that night.

Ozzy, now speaking quietly, continued in the most dramatic tone he could muster. "A loaded trolley gathered speed down the chute. Who knows what would have happened if the cart had been allowed to continue its momentum? The only way to prevent the imminent disaster was to throw his shovel into the spokes of the trolley wheels. That's what he did. The tough wooden handle stopped the trolley but not before the metal snapped and was thrown sideways into my dad's leg."

"I reckon your dad was a hero," Ace placed a full stop to the conversation. Mardoo and Ozzy enthusiastically nodded in agreement.

A mother nearby pushed her small girl on a swing. The only sound that could be heard was the high-pitched screech of steel pipe turning against the crossbar with each upward thrust. The conversation appeared to be at an end. The boys merely gazed across the playground. After several minutes of silence, they left the park and walked through the town's central business district in the direction of the Cottam Mills Hospital.

It was a convenient visit for Ace as his grandmother had coincidentally been in the General Ward for a few weeks, under observation. He told his friends he could 'kill two birds with one stone'. Visit his grandmother but not wanting to miss out on the detail of the accident, that visit would be very short. Learning more about Mr Stewart's bravery would be a priority.

"The doctors don't know what's wrong with her," Ace informed the boys as they kicked stones and honkey nuts along the well-worn path through a second park on the edge of the CBD. "Apparently all of the blood and other tests reveal nothing, so they just keep her in the ward, gaze at her medical chart from time to time, and ask if she 'has had her bowels open'." The three laughed at Ace's description.

Upon entering the hospital, the boys were informed by a nurse in the General Ward that Mr Stewart was in the adjoining room to Ace's grandmother. His bed was furthest from the door, near a window that gave him a clear view of red and yellow protea bushes in full bloom. As the boys entered, they noticed there were three other men sharing the room. Onc of them caught the boys' attention when he made a loud groan. As he groaned, he clasped his arms tightly across his chest. Mr Stewart followed the boys' gaze.

"He's got a ring of fire."

"What's a ring of fire, Dad?" Ozzy asked innocently.

"Hemorrhoids."

"What's hemmy roids?"

"Hemorrhoids. Err… a sore bum."

Mardoo asked rhetorically, "Only a sore bum? I don't understand why the groaner would be in hospital for just a sore bum. Weak as water," he concluded with a quiet mumble but loud enough for Ozzy and Ace to hear. They nodded agreement. Both knew that Mardoo was a strong boy. Physically strong and mentally tough. He had to be. They knew how difficult it was for Mardoo to ignore the frequent racist abuse he received from some kids at their school.

Having visited the two patients, the boys decided they had spent enough time in hospital. They chatted for a few moments about how depressing hospitals were, how serious everyone dressed in white seemed to be, how the only person who smiled was the lady pushing the tea trolley, and how long Ozzy's dad expected to be in hospital. It was all about killing time as boys do when bored.

Mardoo decided he had to support Ozzy at this difficult time. That's what friends do and it was the Noongar way to help in a quiet and unobtrusive way, when possible. Their presence at the hospital would give Ozzy courage to face the responsibility of being the only male in the household, while Mr Stewart was recuperating in hospital. They could be relied upon in Ozzy's time of need.

"You don't have to stay, boys," Mr Stewart said. "You must have something else to do, rather than sit with an old guba like me. Why don't you go for a ride? Mardoo might agree to give you lessons about the bush."

That invitation echoed their feelings. They didn't need any more encouragement and after saying their goodbyes and taking one last look at the groaner, they left. A decision was made to fetch their bicycles and again explore the bush on the outskirts of town.

Chapter 25

Doogs is the Aussie name for marbles. Young country boys choose to play doogs when they don't have the time to venture far from home.

Ozzy made an agreement with a boy who lived near his street, across the road from Warra Wirrin Park, and in the direction of Cottam Mills High School. The boy was known as 'Spike'. If Ozzy were to beat him at a game of doogs, best of three, he would secure a loan of Spike's footy boots for the next season. Ozzy didn't have a pair and desperately needed them.

"I doubt the boots fit Spike, anyway. He is a great deal taller and fatter, although he would claim it all to be muscle," Ozzy laughed at that thought, after telling his friends of the doogs competition.

Mardoo replied, "I don't reckon you should play doogs with Spike. He's a sore loser and he has a temper. I wouldn't mess with him."

"Yeah, I know Spike is a bully but I reckon I can handle him. I wouldn't want to cross him, either, if it was avoidable but I'm happy to beat him at doogs, fair and square. Especially if it means I have his footy boots for a year."

"Hmm, maybe," Mardoo replied pensively. "But do you really need the boots? Why don't you play bare-footed like me?"

The boys sat in silence on the bench at their favourite meeting place. Ozzy was still thinking about what Mardoo had just asked, when his friend answered his own question. "I reckon you'll beat Spike at doogs and secure the boots for life. He's as thick as two planks or as my Dad would say, one *yongka* loose in the top paddock. He'll forget to ask for them back."

There are different types of doogs depending on the type of game one is playing. Ozzy liked to play 'circles'. For participants in this version of doogs, there's a gentlemen's agreement that one doesn't use a tombola, the name for a larger than normal-sized doog. The aim is to knock one's own doogs out of a circle drawn on a patch of sand by flicking another doog off one's pointer finger with one's thumb. The first person to knock his or her doogs out of the circle is the winner. The prize? The winner keeps all the doogs left inside the circle.

Using a tombola is acceptable when playing closest-to-the-line. Two lines are drawn in the sand, about ten feet apart. The idea is to stand behind one line and drop one's doog as close as possible to the other. Closest wins. Ace liked to use a peewee because, being the smallest doog, it would sometimes flick across the ground and fall into the furrow of the target line. That happened if the line was deep and the ground was reasonably firm.

Older and bigger boys in Cottam Mills, trying to prove something to the world, would often use a tombola playing circles. They mistakenly believed it gave them an advantage. Perhaps it was more about creating a macho image or boosting a macho self-image.

It was the day of the big doogs championship. It was also the fifth day since Boodjark had escaped prison. News of his escape hadn't left the southern region, where the Kolbang Prison Farm was located. Not wanting to alarm the populace, the Superintendent had managed to contain the news to the prison officers and the local police but it was sure to leak to the media at some time. Probably sooner rather than later, but the Superintendent wanted a head start before outside interference.

The death of an inmate required thorough investigation. It was unlikely to have been the result of an accident or some unforeseen circumstance, especially since the dead prisoner appeared to have died from a severed aorta. An autopsy was required and that would take a few days. Perhaps that would give the police sufficient time to hunt the escapee without the nuisance of chasing down false sightings or other leads from the public at large.

An irresistible inference suggested the inmate's death was a murder committed by the escapee. From an initial forensic examination, it was thought the two events roughly coincided in time. It was unlikely to be a coincidence but the authorities had to first rule out death by misadventure by another prisoner. In the meantime, the prison was in lockdown and the inmates were required to remain in their cells, allowed out only for exercise and meals. Normal farm activities had been temporarily suspended.

Massively important matters occupied the minds of the combatants in Cottam Mills. It was agreed the big doogs championship would be played on a sand patch at the edge of Warra Wirrin Park. 'Bad spirits' Park was neutral territory.

Spike drew a circle on the sandy ground. More of an oval, but Ozzy chose not to draw it to his adversary's attention. *Best not to question Spike, especially today.*

To decide who went first, the pair played a game of paper, scissors, rock. The hard and fast rule was that the participants must simultaneously indicate which of the three they choose. On the count of three, Ozzy extended his arm and pointed his forefinger and middle finger forward in the shape of a pair of scissors. Spike paused, waited just a second to see which of paper, scissors or rock Ozzy chose and then threw out his open right hand to signify paper.

The cheat, thought Mardoo from Ozzy's 'corner'. *I knew he was stupid. He wanted to see which item Oz chose before he decided. But he still got it wrong. He needed more than a second. A clenched fist to signal 'rock' would have been smarter. Rocks grind scissors. Scissors cut paper. Ozzy wins.*

First to start, within a short space of time Ozzy had most of his doogs outside the circle. He didn't look up lest Spike thought he was gloating.

"You're on a roll! You're killing him!" The proud voice of Mardoo.

The street's new boy had become more observant in recent days, especially since the near encounter with a *dordok*. He saw action on the sand patch nearby and ambled along the street to check it out. When he saw the doogs carnage, Ace quietly clapped his hands together.

Spike's glare was murderous.

Ozzy heard the arrival of another spectator and took the opportunity to glance at Spike. He could see a dark cloud emerge from below his eyes, climb towards his forehead, reddening as it rose.

Is that steam coming from his ears? Don't look. Head down. But Ozzy's concentration and rhythm had been broken and he missed the second-last shot.

Still glaring at Ace, Spike moved to the narrow part of the oblong "circle" and dropped his doogs. From there, he had less distance to shoot them from the ring. He then reached into his cloth doog bag and extracted a tombola.

"That's cheating, Spike," said a usually quiet and timid Ace. "I'm no expert at marbles but even where I come from, one can't use a tombola to play circles."

Spike's glare darkened further. He yelled, "Shuddup! Keep out of this or you'll regret it, you little squirt."

Ace seemed to grow in stature and confidence in the presence of Ozzy and Mardoo but he didn't respond, thinking, *discretion is the better part of valour.*

The tombola was put to work. If Spike was any good at marbles, this was his best opportunity to clean out the circle. But he fumbled badly, turned again to Ace as if it was his fault and uttered in a threatening tone, "Get the hell out of here."

Ace shrugged and started to walk away, stumbled and fell over.

Spike laughed but laughter quickly changed to a menacing stare. Meanwhile, Ozzy shot the last two doogs from the circle. First game to Ozzy in the best of three.

"We take it in turns to go first." Spike changed the rules to his benefit. Another rule change; he pushed past Ozzy and collected his doogs from the ring, announcing, "We are playing for the use of the boots only. You don't get to keep my doogs, short-arse!"

I want the boots. I don't care about your doogs, I have enough, anyway.

"What happened to my tombola? You didn't pick it up, did you?"

Both Mardoo and Ozzy spent a few minutes attempting to convince Spike that the latter didn't steal his tombola; it had probably spun away into the nearby bush.

Did Ace pick it up when he stumbled, thought Mardoo.

The boys played on but there really wasn't any contest. Spike was done like a dinner, to use one of Mokiny's expressions. At the end of the championship, a competition that wouldn't be bragged about at school, the boys went directly to Spike's house and collected the boots. Spike shuffled along the street, either deep in thought or sulking. He was a humourless, poor loser and was possibly plotting revenge.

***

Although each kid in the tightly knit group had a bicycle, they still walked the roughly three kilometres to school. They were realists. One could never be sure that one's little luxury would not "walk" away from school in someone else's possession. Should that occur, the usual manner of collecting said property was by fighting for it.

Cottam Mills children usually decided there was no point in seeking help from the local constabulary. First, one would be branded a "dobber" – almost as bad as being called a coward – and second, the boys thought the cops didn't seem all that effective in dealing with what they considered 'insignificant matters'. "Too much unnecessary paperwork," they would say, "And we're understaffed."

The boys always walked home from school together and now Ace joined them. They all lived close together, along the road and around the corner from the home of the International Doogs Tournament.

They would usually take a short cut down a laneway, behind a row of houses near Smithy's shop. The lane once provided ease of access for the night carts to the toilets at the rear of the quarter-acre housing lots. Since night carts were no longer required to empty 'thunder boxes', as sewerage had been introduced, the laneway now provided access to garages and sheds at the rear of the properties.

The lanes widened where a garage was located. In one particular location there were two garages directly opposite one another. Here, the lane doubled in width. As the boys walked home they came across a large gathering of kids in that particular spot. About twenty or so fellow students milled around. *Most unusual*, thought Ozzy. *Indeed, it looks a little ominous.*

Every school and every town has its share of bullies. Cottam Mills High School seemed to have exceeded its quota. Some stood out more than others. The renowned Spike was one. He stood expectantly in the centre of the widened lane, fists clenched. The widened lane and crowd appeared to have created a makeshift boxing ring.

"C'mon, gutless. Put up your fists!" Spike taunted, apparently directed at Ozzy.

Mardoo warned me not to play doogs with him. Poor loser.

Suddenly matters took a surprising turn. Up until this point in time, it couldn't be said that any of the kids knew Ace particularly well. Ozzy and

Mardoo knew him to be an intelligent, quietly spoken, and tolerant young bloke with a funny accent. But they didn't know him to be suicidal.

Spike stood about four hundred and sixty millimetres taller than either Ace or Ozzy. He was older, heavier, bigger, and stronger and clearly, in the minds of their school colleagues, neither boy would be a match for the bully. But appearances can sometimes be deceiving.

"Spike, Spike, Spike…" The loud, blood-curdling chant from the spectators started. Ozzy dropped his school bag in anticipation of an onslaught. He wouldn't run from a challenge and be branded a coward. A fool, yes, but a coward, definitely not. He decided he would rather die. He thought he was probably about to.

The chant became deafening. That's all he could hear. Ozzy was hoping the rumble would be heard by the School Principal, the police, a doctor, a paramedic in an ambulance, *Yes the ambulance… Where's the ambulance?* He raised his fists. *Better to die with fists up than down.*

I'm not spineless. Show some backbone. And then reality returned. *Who am I kidding?*

Circumstances reveal the boy. Ace was definitely suicidal. He stepped forward in front of Ozzy. Between Rocky Marciano and Ozzy.

"It's me you want. Not my little friend," he declared in what he might describe as the 'Queen's English'.

"Well, I'll be a monkey's uncle. The Pommy has spoken!" laughed Spike. "You're right. He's only knee-high to a grasshopper. But you're no bigger. I think I'll do both of you."

The chant continued. "Spike, Spike, Spike…" Fists clenched, Spike smirked at Ace. At first he didn't move; just stood still and smirked. Seemingly absorbed by the adulation from the crowd of kids. Then without warning he threw a round-arm punch. Ace ducked. The attempted punch missed its mark by at least thirty centimetres.

Whoa, Ace was quick. I'm glad that didn't connect – it would have killed him, thought Mardoo.

Deft footwork also caused a straight left to miss its target, but Ace's counter-punch did not. A right jab to the midriff surprised the aggressor but the biggest surprise was to follow. Diminutive Ace pushed Spike back across the makeshift boxing ring and with both hands firmly gripping the latter's shirt, lifted him off the ground and banged him hard against a heavy garage door.

The crowd looked on in astonishment as Spike was repeatedly thrown against the woodwork. Eventually, Ace released his grip on Spike's shirt and he crumbled to the ground. Deprived of any combativeness.

The chant had stopped. Nobody moved. The crowd of mostly boys just stood and stared at the hapless bully, who had the wind and the fight knocked out of him. He appeared unconscious but was probably only embarrassed and remained on the ground, chin lowered to his chest, back to the wall.

Ace and his two friends left the scene. As they strolled away, Ace reached into his pocket. "I think this is what he wanted," he smiled, as he tossed the tombola into the air.

That day almost confirmed Ace's position as one of the locals. He still lacked knowledge of the bush – that was a work in progress – and he lacked prowess at Australian Rules football but his surprising physicality may be important in Cottam Mills.

Part Four

The Last Judgment

Chapter 26

The storm had subsided. Rain-bearing clouds had slowly travelled up-country during the night, in the direction of Cottam Mills. Towards Bessie's house and Mardoo's *karla*.

Kolbang Prison Farm was very quiet, relatively still and dark, save for the dim lights on some walkways. A glow could be seen through the high windows in the mess hall, given off by large, drink refrigerators. Another glow came from the ablutions block. That was it. Almost total darkness. There was no moon to be seen and clouds hid the stars.

Over recent months, Boodjark had carefully planned the walk. How he would walk out of the minimum-security Prison Farm earlier than expected. It would happen after the obligatory, second muster check on a dark night. Timing was everything. Phases of the moon, the roster for prison officers and night-time toilet visits by other offenders had to be considered and aligned.

After lights-out, prison officers were required to undertake two musters – one before and another after midnight. It was a head count; not that it was considered essential by some of the older officers, who had served at the farm for many years. After doing time at a medium-security prison, the offenders were considered sufficiently trustworthy to be sent to the minimum-security facility. There were no locks on their bedroom doors. No high fences topped with razor wire around the compound. Nobody would escape Kolbang Prison Farm. It was surrounded by trust.

Over the years, a story constantly circulated at Kolbang about an offender who had attempted an escape in the early years of the Farm. It probably wasn't true but to encourage offenders to keep the trust, the prison officers perpetuated the myth. The story wasn't part of the Sentence Management Manual but it could have been. It was an important tool in offender management.

"A prisoner with gate-fever had attempted an escape," they would tell newcomers. "Don't think you'll ever be returned to Minimum if you decide to do the same. You'll go straight to Palmyra Prison and will regret it for the rest of your life."

'Gate-fever' was a term used by prison officers to describe an inmate's fear of being released. A fear of the unknown world outside. Insecure, probably unemployable, unsure of himself, and not having the certainty that existed inside the boundaries of prison life. Someone with gate-fever would commonly reoffend in order to be returned to prison.

In the case of the absconding offender, many years before, according to the story, he had been sent back to the State's main maximum-security prison.

"Life became a living hell and there was no respite," new arrivals were always told. "Apart from the added years to his sentence, the other offenders punished him for failing. They always fail, you know." That was the story.

Gate-fever was more common amongst the long-termers and in the larger medium-security prisons. The prison officers at Kolbang considered it highly unlikely to be a problem because of the trust and the category of prisoner at the farm, but musters – a head count – was still part of the established routine. Both day and night.

Although the night-time checks were meant to be at irregular intervals, to ensure offenders wouldn't become accustomed to the routine of checks, the rule relied upon strict adherence to the prison officers' Local Orders. Most would dutifully follow the protocols, but there was the occasional lacklustre officer. Usually an older, sometimes overweight, man, less concerned about security and too sedentary to be bothered leaving the comfort of his chair for checking.

Boodjark had paid particular attention to the pattern of rosters over several months. He knew which officers were assiduous, motivated by ambition to climb the ladder in the system. Those who would strictly follow protocol and might check at odd times. He wouldn't 'walk' when those officers were on duty. He knew which officers would always check between midnight and 0100 hours, purportedly complying with the rules, and leaving him plenty of time to absent himself.

At night, there were two prison officers who shared the duties. A senior officer would be positioned in the administration building and a junior officer located in a gatehouse near the entrance to the facility. They would alternately undertake periodic foot patrols and offender counts. The senior officer was responsible for initiating the checks, sometimes but not always undertaken by the junior officer from the gatehouse. The timing depended upon which programme was being broadcast on the television in the comfort of the administration building.

There was no need to be too concerned. Nobody ever walked out of Kolbang Prison Farm, despite the Noongar meaning of the word '*kolbang*'. Go forward. The name was not chosen for its location but rather, to encourage offenders to never look back.

The offenders had separate rooms. Open the only door to the room and the prisoner would step onto a grey, cracked and well-worn concrete walkway that led to the ablutions block. There, the path took a sharp turn in the direction of the mess hall. The walkway surrounded a grassed area. The ablutions block was located approximately thirty metres from the closest accommodation block and about fifty metres from the other block where Boodjark's room was located.

Movement between the individual rooms and the ablutions block was common at night. It had become noticeable to Boodjark that most offenders, especially the older men, would generally visit the toilet about four hours after lights out at 2100 hours. After the second muster and after most of the men had exercised their need to visit the toilet – to empty their bladder – that would be the best time to escape. Soon after 0100 hours.

It would mean a dark night and the right prison officer on duty to coincide with that night. Boodjark waited for such a night. It had arrived.

Before liberty beckoned, before he proceeded to the first step in his desire for revenge against the woman who had taken his freedom, Boodjark had what he considered to be a final essential job to undertake. A quick visit to another offender's room.

He would relish an opportunity to exact revenge against a prisoner he despised. Revenge for being taunted and being called a name he hated. Scarface. Then he would permanently depart Kolbang. Additionally, his plan would create chaos, distract attention from his absence and take manpower away from a search.

Job done, Boodjark had to make a quick escape before the sun rose and his fellow inmates started to rise soon thereafter. That would usually be at about 0600 hours. He had a minimum of five hours to get well away from Kolbang before the next body count. Put some distance between him and the prison before his absence was discovered.

The prison greens had to be dispensed with. His clothes were splattered with blood. Not Boodjark's. He cast his eyes down at his green tracksuit pants where he had wiped the blood from his knife. He touched the pocket. Felt the blade. Used once to good effect. Another soon. Boodjark smiled at that thought. The blood of a coward. The blood of an informer and friend of the screws. Blood that belonged to a new, albeit dead, Scarface.

He would need to look like John Citizen as he made his way north, past populated areas where he may be seen. Wearing prison greens, especially clothes splattered in blood, would definitely not be a good idea.

He needed to gain access to the appropriate storage facility. There were two. One was located in the main admin block, where security was tight. The other contained clothing for those offenders who were permitted what was described in the system as 'Home Leave'. Offenders permitted regular unsupervised home leave for up to thirty-six hours before eventually being permanently released would store their clothes for their day's liberty in a small building behind the mess hall.

The less secure, temporary storeroom was externally locked with a heavy-duty hasp barrel bolt. Sometimes. Most of the time but not always. While the barrel attached to the door would be slid into the fixed fastener on the timber doorframe, it wouldn't always be padlocked. Either way – barrel fixed into position or not padlocked – it wouldn't prove to be an impediment to entry. In his youth, many months of practice at manipulating locks had made certain of that.

Having convinced a senior officer that all doors throughout the complex were in need of maintenance, over the previous week Boodjark had made sure the hinges on all offender's room doors were well oiled. He also took the opportunity to oil the hinges on the storeroom door.

After the visit to Shorty's room, he had returned to his own quarters to clean blood from his hands and arms. He now stepped outside his room and lightly onto the walkway that skirted the accommodation block. He moved quickly and quietly.

At the ablution block, he held the door open and nodded to another inmate leaving the block. He waited a few seconds until the older man had rounded the corner. He didn't enter. Instead, he crossed the grey, concrete path onto the grass, where his movement would not be heard, and walked quickly to the building in which the 'Home Leavers' clothes were stored.

Manipulating the lock to enter the storeroom was easy. Before he committed the crime that landed him in a juvenile prison, Boodjark and his delinquent friends had a regular competition. They competed at lock picking and had mastered the art. Boodjark usually won with his deft hands.

Part of his preparation for the escape from Kolbang was to surreptitiously examine the types of locks used in the complex. The storeroom lock was an old pin-and-tumbler. Easy pickings. He used a flathead screwdriver he had secured from the workshop as a tension wrench and applied pressure in the keyhole, while using jumbo paperclips, collected over recent months, to lift the pins. He had twisted and reshaped the heavy-duty clips to meet his needs.

It was dark inside the room but Boodjark chose not to turn the light on. There were no windows but he would play it safe. He had matches to provide sufficient light to find clothes belonging to a regular 'Home Leaver' that would fit him. He expected it would take some time to find the right clothes but time was on his side. The second body count had been completed at a quarter past midnight. He fumbled in the semi-dark.

Being only slightly above average height and a similar size to his friend Bluey, he decided those clothes would be best. There was a row of ten, brown, heavy cotton clothing bags that had been manufactured at a textile workshop in another prison. They were hooked onto an aluminium rail by a clothes hanger. The rail was about 30 mm in diameter and two metres long, supported between the walls. A large brown label bearing the prisoner's name was pinned to each bag.

He moved from hanger to hanger, searching for Bluey's name. He knew Bluey was regularly on Home Leave. His clothes would fit.

What's his name? Not 'Bluey'. Damn it, what's Bluey's real name?

Then it came to him. Peter McCardle. He found McCardle's bag, second last in line. He quickly emptied the bag onto the floor and dressed in a dark blue polo shirt bearing a logo that read 'Gant'. The dark blue Gazman, lightweight, stretch jeans were also a perfect fit. The clothes had a distinctive, pungent smell of camphor. Several mothballs fell onto the concrete floor when he emptied the bag. He quickly rummaged on the floor to retrieve them and returned them to the bag.

No need to change underwear, socks, or his joggers, but he would take Bluey's Adidas joggers with him. He pocketed the knife and screwdriver. Without any care for neatness, he shoved his prison issued clothes into the cotton bag, zipped and returned it to the rail. His bloody prison greens would be found in two weeks.

Dark clothes. *Thanks, Bluey,* he thought. *You were such a good mate.*

Boodjark slowly opened the storeroom door. Enough ambient light drifted into the room for him to see a small bag on a table near the door. It was a soft, green pack bag with a red circle in the middle highlighted by a white cross.

A first-aid kit. Never thought about one of these. Might be handy. How lucky am I?

His eyes moved quickly and scanned the area outside. There was no one to be seen. He slipped through the slightly ajar door, slid the latch across, and placed the lever flap over the fixture to which the padlock would be secured. Satisfied everything was the same as it was when he entered, he took a last look in the direction of his room and, hunched over, he hightailed it from the scene, carrying joggers and the first-aid kit.

He moved in a southerly direction away from the front gatehouse and the admin building. He would ultimately change and move in a northerly direction but first needed to be well clear of the farm area. He planned to move in a direction not expected by the authorities.

Heading south he would be swallowed by the bush and the dark of night.

That's it, he thought. *No intention of returning, no matter what. I'll die first.*

***

At that precise time, in Cottam Mills, Mardoo woke from a restless sleep. He looked at his bedside clock. Thirty minutes after midnight. He had a bad *koondarm*. He had dreamt of a man with a scar the length of his face, dressed entirely in black, walking the streets of his town.

His immediate thought was: *What does that mean? I don't understand dreams. What is the meaning of that epiphany? Is evil coming to Cottam Mills? Shall I ask Pa or Aunt Bessie about dreams? Perhaps my aunty, but first I must ask her about Uncle Jimmy.*

The last thought even surprised Mardoo. He had no reason to think about his cousin's late husband but now he knew he had to learn more about his family. 'Aunt' Bessie would tell him.

There is so much sadness. I can see it in my Pa and Aunt Bessie. There is so much I don't know about my family.

The early part of the night had been difficult for Bessie, too. A night of *kep boolarang, malkar* and *kilang*. It had kept her awake for several hours but, as usual, so too had the thoughts of her late husband and the burden he had carried.

Her thoughts drifted to the night, sixteen years before, and the bright star in her family, Yabini. She was engulfed with sadness and started to cry.

Buster was a light sleeper. He heard his owner and stood, ears raised, alert. He bounded across the room and leapt onto Bessie's bed. He licked her face, lapping the tears away. Bessie gave her dog a cuddle.

"You're a sensitive, beautiful dog," she said. "Now go back to your cushions. I'm okay now. Thanks, Buster."

Bessie's last thought before she finally drifted off to sleep was she would spend the next day in her garden, weather permitting. Gardening was a positive distraction and always gave her peace of mind.

Chapter 27

"On the count!"

At 0630 hours every morning, the duty senior officer would yell the instruction to the offenders. An order to step outside and stand on the walkway in front of their room ready to be counted. "On the count" was enough. Everyone knew what the simple instruction meant. It was important to immediately act as instructed and step outside, even though for Kolbang Prison Farm it was a mere formality.

By 0630 hours, some offenders had already been out of bed for well over half an hour, completed their morning ablutions and returned to their room to await the call for the body count. It was rare for anyone to sleep beyond 0600 hours at this time of year.

Duty Senior Officer Fraser yelled the instruction again. "On the count." Fraser stood in front of the mess hall and cast his eyes along the two rows of rooms. He counted but could see there was a gap in the line. One inmate was still in bed. On the first count, he hadn't noticed the second gap in the line as the two offenders either side of Boodjark's room had suspected something was wrong and closed the space, talking to each other. Mingling meant there could be three in the group with the third offender being obscured.

Fraser turned to his subordinate. "Go and give Shorty a shake," he instructed. "Unusual for him to sleep in."

"On the count," yelled Fraser again. "Stand to the front of your door." Boodjark's neighbours separated and returned to the front of their rooms. Fraser counted. He yelled another instruction to the prison officer but it wasn't heard. The instruction was to check Boodjark's room, too.

Ashen-faced, the officer stumbled out of Shorty's room in a panic. He yelled to his senior colleague as he hurdled a bush in front of Shorty's room and started to run across the grass. "Boss, Sh... Sh... Shorty's dead," he stammered.

"What are you talking about?" Fraser barked.

Having regained some composure befitting a prison officer, the junior man ran to Fraser and in a rasping voice repeated, "Shorty's dead, sir. In his bed. There's blood everywhere."

"Did you feel his pulse?"

"No, but I'm sure he's dead. Too much blood. His throat appears to have been slashed."

"Get on the radio. Call a code-red medical emergency. Tell the gatehouse we need an ambulance. Priority one. I'll phone the Super. We probably have a DIC."

The younger prison officer had taken deep breaths and fully regained his composure. "DIC?" he asked, not familiar with the term at Kolbang

"Death in Custody. But it's not for us to say. That's a medical issue. Now get onto it."

Fraser turned to the remaining prisoners, some of whom looked puzzled by the unusual and sudden activity, whilst a few others glanced at each other knowingly. He yelled, "Everyone back inside. Close your doors and await further instructions."

He walked briskly to the one door that hadn't opened upon his command. Boodjark's room. He opened the door and yelled "Prentice. Boodjark!" at the bundle of towels below the blankets. He quickly entered the room and lifted the top blanket to see towels rolled in the rough shape of an adult lying in a near foetal position.

"Sssshhit!"

Fraser stepped from the room as Bluey in the adjoining room opened his door slightly and said, "I think he might be in the ablution block, Mr Fraser. He complained of having diarrhoea last night. Gastro. Probably food poisoning."

"Close your door and stay inside," Fraser growled. "Don't bullshit to me!"

He believed Boodjark's friend had told a trumped-up story in an attempt to buy him time. That thought was a safe and accurate assumption. There was no time to waste. It was an irresistible inference that Boodjark had reoffended and absconded but Fraser still needed to check the toilets, just in case Bluey was telling the truth for a change.

He moved quickly towards the ablution block and as he made his way there, he alerted the other prison officers on site, by radio, of a possible escape. "Code-red echo," he informed them. "An emergency count!"

Within minutes they had left their work areas to put into practice the procedure outlined in their Emergency Management Plan.

The procedure practiced but never before put into action was for all officers to assemble in the large meeting room of the administration centre, dressed in what some euphemistically called "riot gear". It was highly unlikely offenders at Kolbang would create a threat to the officers but they couldn't take the risk.

The available officers congregated at the admin centre. SO Fraser directed another officer to find the bag of personal protection equipment in the storeroom at the rear of the building. Soon after, his subordinate returned with a large canvas bag. It was covered in dust and he initially struggled to free the zip. Inside, he found some arm and shoulder pads, gloves, out-of-date pepper sprays, handcuffs and batons. Those items were distributed amongst the prison officers who wanted them. But most simply wanted to get to work on the search.

Whilst waiting for the Superintendent to arrive, Fraser located a box of solid brass monobloc padlocks. He distributed them between two officers and instructed them to padlock the offenders' rooms. He couldn't risk any others absconding, any chaos or any interference in the search of the farm that would follow. The two officers were instructed to advise the offenders that locking them in their room would be a temporary measure and only procedural. They must be reassured there was no breach of trust towards the remaining inmates. Everything would return to normal within hours.

Superintendent Jacinta Millman's arrival at Kolbang calmed the anxious prison officers. Millman had been a worthy appointment to the position of Superintendent four years earlier and was highly regarded as a leader in what had traditionally been a male-dominated occupation. Millman was an intelligent and capable woman. At fifty-two years of age, she had resisted what some of her male colleagues laughingly called a 'middle-aged spread'. By contrast to some of the younger officers who were clearly less fit, Millman was athletic. She jogged ten kilometres each day and followed a healthy diet.

Upon her arrival, Fraser immediately briefed Millman on what had transpired over the previous forty-five minutes. "I know we have to wait confirmation from the ambo but there's no doubt in my mind that Shorty is dead. He had a jagged knife mark across his face and his throat had been cut. He's not breathing and there was no pulse. His room has been treated as a crime scene. I left it untouched. I'm not sure there was anything else I could have done," he said.

"Your response was very good, Jeremy," Millman reassured him. "You correctly followed procedure. On my way over here, I alerted the Abannerup police. Their forensic people will be here as soon as possible. If someone is missing, we cannot assume that person was responsible for the offender's death. That is a matter for the police to determine. But what we must do is find the missing offender as a priority."

"Where do we start? Where would an offender likely go? We're a long way from major towns. What is his motivation? Do we alert the public to a possible escape?" A prison officer rattled off a series of rapid-fire questions.

"I'm advised by the police inspector that we mustn't alarm the community at large. There will not be any immediate announcement. Our media people at Head Office, in consultation with the police Regional Superintendent, will manage any public comments. Jeremy will take control of the search of all buildings and the farm as a whole. The area will be divided into grids for the search. If you see anything that may have been used as a weapon, do not touch it. Communicate by radio. Work in pairs."

Millman glanced at the officer who had asked the series of questions and added, "Any other questions?" Heads shook in the negative.

"Thank you, gentlemen. I'll leave you in Jeremy's capable hands for the moment."

Millman left the gathering and went to her office. It was necessary to inform the Inspector of Custodial Services, and the Commissioner of Corrective Services and to meet the police upon their arrival. She hoped they would attend Kolbang expeditiously.

Fraser assigned search areas to his colleagues. There were numerous buildings to search within the immediate vicinity of the accommodation and Administration blocks, including typical farm sheds, recreational facilities, greenhouses and plant nurseries. There were prison-farm and private vehicles parked in sheds and at car parks on the perimeter of the complex. They needed to be checked as a priority.

To the north, in the direction of the main road that passed the farm, was a wide strip of bush. The officers agreed with Fraser's assumption that any escapee would likely go there. It was logical that he would either steal a car in the prison grounds and head in that direction, or attempt to stop a passing vehicle. At that time of the day, there was a great deal of vehicular movement on the highway and it probably wouldn't be a problem to hitch a ride with a truck. The thick bush would provide a suitable hiding place until a vehicle approached.

After a short discussion about an escapee's options and several questions about priority areas upon which to focus, Fraser reinforced Superintendent Millman's instruction about working closely in pairs. "Importantly," he said, "ensure you don't touch anything that might be police evidence. Get to work and report in by radio every fifteen minutes."

For over five hours Boodjark had been getting to work, too. Comfortably dressed and appropriately attired in lightweight running shoes, he was able to move quickly. He worked to the south; away from the direction the screws would expect him to travel. He kept to firm ground that would unlikely show footprints. Being light of weight helped.

Away from the complex of buildings, Boodjark had walked quickly along the edge of a gravel track, past a small dam alongside which was a shed that contained two, almost new Suzuki all-terrain quad bikes. One of them had a key in the ignition. Taking a bike wasn't part of his plan. *Too noisy. Leave a track to follow,* he thought and had continued on foot.

He had followed a narrow line of trees past a football ground. Beyond that there was an open area but in the dark of night he couldn't be seen and he crossed it with confidence that he was invisible.

Two kilometres on the southern side of the farm, the narrow gravel road reached a T-junction. Boodjark turned in an easterly direction and traversed a thickly bushed area before doubling back through the shrub in a westerly direction. His footprints, if discovered, would reveal he was heading east.

The bush was perfect for his plan. He knew the bush better than most. Certainly better than prison officers who were former farmers, police officers, military personnel, or simply career people from the city. Probably not accustomed to the bush.

***

Mardoo rose early at his *karla* on the edge of Cottam Mills. A restless night had been further interrupted by his father making a vegemite sandwich and boiling the kettle for a cup of tea in the middle of the night. Obviously, Mokiny couldn't sleep either. The walls in the Trunning shack were corrugated iron and every sound could be heard in adjacent rooms. The fact his father was noisy didn't help.

Eventually, Mardoo had drifted to sleep but awoke in perspiration after a *koondarm*. He could recall only glimpses of it and didn't understand its meaning. But it worried him. He needed to talk to his Aunty Bessie.

Chapter 28

At first, the walk from Kolbang Prison Farm was slow. After passing the football ground, Boodjark was careful to ensure he didn't leave any clearly visible footprints. The darkness meant he had to be extra careful not to slip on the gravel and leave scuff marks.

There was also the occasional depression in the surface of the track, where water from the storm had pooled. On three occasions he stepped onto the edge of a puddle, sufficiently immersed in the water to dampen the sole of his running shoes and possibly leave an imprint on the track.

After he stepped onto moist ground, Boodjark meandered his way forward, leaving the track and walking into the bush. That process slowed his progression but would undoubtedly make it more difficult for others to follow his footsteps.

He'd had been walking for just over an hour, when he detected the unmistakable smell of Tasmanian Blue Gums. The smell overwhelmed his senses. There was a softwood tree farm at the southwest edge of the 2,600-hectare prison farm. Until reaching the plantation, the only smell was petrichor. The thick undergrowth and accumulation of tree branches and leaves over recent years, since the area's last prescribed burn, meant the earthy bush smell, following rain, was particularly strong. But petrichor subsided with the overpowering smell of the gum trees.

"Cat's piss," Boodjark muttered quietly. "Blue gums smell like cat's piss. How can anyone work in a job like that, harvesting those bloody smelly trees?"

He decided he shouldn't vocalise his thoughts. *No noise, Boodjark, there could be harvesters camping nearby. Probably not but best be careful.*

North-south. Those trees are planted in a north-south direction.

When planning his escape, he took note of the lay of the land around the Prison Farm. He recalled the direction of the tree rows when working on the farm's southern-most perimeter fence.

Following the tree line to the north would be easiest but too predictable. If my memory serves me right, in about two kilometres I'll be in thick, native State forest. They'll never get me there.

On the side of the track he was following, there was a large, fallen pine tree, where the track turned north to circle the tree farm. Boodjark sat on the tree stump, placed the first-aid kit next to him, and removed his Asics running shoes. He tied the laces of the two shoes together and linked them with the first-aid kit's straps for ease of carrying. He placed them to the side, on the stump, and slipped into Bluey's Adidas joggers. This would serve two purposes. He would be wearing dry shoes and if trackers had identified the tread on his Asics, the new tread would create confusion.

Tired. When I'm into the State forest, I'll find a place to sleep for an hour. Recharge the batteries. I can't afford any longer than an hour.

I reckon the body count won't be for another four hours. There'll be two missing from the muster. When they discover their brown-noser informant is dead, the screws will be upset. They'll discover a vacancy in room 15. Then they'll need to call everyone in, organise a search, and get the cops involved. That gives me at least another hour from muster. Hmmm, let's say half an hour to be safe. Three and a half hours on the move.

As he moved away from the log, Boodjark stepped on a thin layer of pine needles deposited from the horizontal log. His right foot penetrated the surface: it was covering a rabbit warren. As he fell, his right arm was caught by a protruding branch and left a scratch about ten centimetres long. It wasn't deep but caused a stinging sensation. In a spontaneous reaction Boodjark grabbed at the area, felt the scratch and the sticky warmth of blood.

Again Boodjark sat on the tree stump; this time to attend to his superficial wound. He didn't need traces of blood following in his wake. In the darkness, he could just make out an assortment of sticky-edged plasters of various sizes in the first-aid kit. He chose the largest and applied it to the wound, returning the dressing's tags to the bag.

Bloody rabbits. Need to be careful. There'll be more rabbit holes on the edge of the plantation.

Boodjark managed to pass through the softwood plantation without further mishap. In the thick State forest he followed a narrow path that conveniently tracked in a northwesterly direction. The exceptionally strong, astringent, at times musty, smell of a mob of kangaroos or wallabies revealed a secluded place where the animals slept. The track he followed was created by the macropods.

Well into the State forest, at the side of the track, Boodjark came across a rocky granite outcrop. Straddling the edge of the large rocks was a fallen tree, creating a hollow shelter in the ground and providing the perfect spot to rest.

Disturbed by the sounds of the bush, Boodjark jolted upright. He had slept fitfully for almost an hour, interrupted by gusts of wind, the groaning of tree branches overhead and the sounds of kangaroos moving cautiously nearby. The *yongka* followed the well-worn track from their lairs through the State forest to grassed areas at the edge of the Prison Farm. There, in the early hours of the morning, well before sunrise, they would daily take their nourishment from vast patches of meadow grass and tall fescue grasses. Both were abundant in the heavy, moist soil of the area.

Boodjark had carefully planned his escape to include diversionary tactics aimed at confusing trackers and buying time. Time would create distance between the hunters and the hunted. He hadn't thought the *yongkas* might help but help they would. They helped when the mob trampled on the track, erasing any traces of a male human passing through the area.

They helped with their pungent body odour that would make it difficult for any tracker dog to detect human smell. Their refined olfactory system was probably not refined enough, capable of separating the powerful odour of the kangaroo from the more delicate smell of man.

There was nothing elaborate about Boodjark's escape plan. It involved a series of simple steps to create potential confusion. Most importantly, it would cause the authorities to use their resources inappropriately. Akin to chasing a rabbit down the wrong hole.

He had changed into civilian clothes that didn't belong to him. The clothes would carry Bluey's body odour and a tracker dog would not be looking for Boodjark's friend. It would be searching for the same smell as Boodjark's bed linen, a smell expected to be on his prison clothes. Clothes that wouldn't be found until Bluey was again ready to take home-leave, in about two weeks' time.

They didn't expect him to leave by foot but instead he would be expected to steal a car from the pool of vehicles at the Prison Farm. He didn't. They would expect his departure to be in the direction of the main road that passed on the northern side of Kolbang. He went south. He would, no doubt, head towards the nearest town. But he walked in the opposite direction. He changed into Bluey's shoes. And now he had the *yongkas* assist him.

The coup de grâce that made him laugh, when he thought of it, would be to send the police to a mining town about eight hundred kilometres away.

Chapter 29

"Where are you headin', mate?" the truck driver asked, after lowering the passenger side window.

"Headin' east. Thanks for stopping."

"I'm not going far. I can give you a lift to a winery about thirty kilometres from here. I've got a delivery and then headin' back this way. Best I can do, mate. At least it's somethin', I s'pose."

The final deception. The coup de grâce. Over the last twelve months, when working on the northern perimeter of the Prison Farm, Boodjark had taken particular notice of vehicular movements on the road passing the entrance. On two occasions he even crept out of his room at night, moved surreptitiously past the gatehouse, crossed a paddock and waited amongst the trees, near the farm entrance, to observe traffic.

Medium and occasionally heavy-duty box trucks would travel from west to east and the same truck would return anywhere between two and four hours later. There seemed to be a regular pattern of deliveries by trucks of various sizes either to Abannerup or to a commercial enterprise between Kolbang and the regional town. That type of vehicular movement was constant, even at night.

Boodjark was confident his absence from the farm wouldn't be discovered for at least two hours but he nevertheless stood, secluded behind a tree, near the side of the road. When the lights of a vehicle approached, he stepped out and extended his arm, thumb raised to passing vehicles. Hoping to thumb a lift but in the middle of the night the traffic was light. Two sedans passed, one slowed but the driver changed his or her mind and again accelerated.

He watched as the glow of two spotlights appeared in the distance, around a bend in the road. Only seconds passed before the bright lights came within full view and illuminated the road for at least a kilometre ahead. Boodjark again stepped from behind the tree and walked casually along the shoulder of the road with arm elevated to catch attention.

As expected, a box truck, a medium-sized commercial vehicle, slowed as it neared the hitchhiker. With a cabin separated from the cargo section and not having a sleeping compartment, the truck was designed for relatively short runs of a few hundred kilometres. From his observations, Boodjark guessed this to be a truck making only a short run to a commercial enterprise nearby. Perfect for his plan. Probably a winery, common in this region. He had watched the movement and timed the return trip of such trucks.

"As I said, I'm not goin' far," the driver repeated, "but jump in."

Boodjark opened the cabin door and was greeted by a rush of warm air. He climbed in, nestled against the back of the black, well-worn leather seat and fastened his seatbelt. Even though it wasn't a cold night, the driver had the truck's heater blasting warm air at twenty-five degrees directly at the passenger's seat. Boodjark wiped his brow as a rivulet of perspiration quickly formed.

"Sorry, mate," the driver said, as he redirected the air vent between the two of them. "You've been walking and you don't need the hot air straight at your face." He chuckled.

Boodjark grunted and attempted a smile in response but it didn't emerge.

"My name's Tom. Tom Warner." The driver extended his arm to shake his passenger's hand. Boodjark looked at the hand as if deciding whether a handshake was normal before he slowly responded appropriately. Callused hands gave a short but firm grip.

"I'm delivering a load of empty bottles to Blissful Mountain Winery. I'm gonna be early but I'll take a nap before they open the cellar storeroom at six. Then I return to the big smoke with cartons of their grog. Sorry I can't take you further, mate."

Boodjark remained silent and gazed ahead beyond the light mist that had crept into the valley.

A strange man to be hitchhiking at this time of day, Warner thought. *The silent type. Didn't offer a name.*

"Where ya headin'?" Warner asked again, head pivoted and eyes quickly averted from the road to the passenger.

Pregnant silence.

"Where ya headin', mate?" he repeated but louder, in case his passenger was hard of hearing.

Boodjark had heard but intended Warner to think him reluctant to state his destination. It was all part of the plan. He didn't respond immediately and then, as if the question had just landed in his in-tray labelled for 'urgent attention', he hastily shot upright and said, "Family trouble. Gotta visit a cousin. Borrowed my car and pranged it. Miserable bastard's in 'ospital. Can't return it."

Warner noticed his passenger didn't make eye contact. His probing eyes sought out his passenger's. Sensing this, Boodjark quite deliberately looked away, head dropping further and inclined to the roadside. His eyes followed the moving tree line next to the highway. A calculated move to encourage belief that he was hiding something – his identity.

The road ahead in the truck's headlights had an almost magnetic attraction and Boodjark soon returned his gaze along the highway. Warner again glanced at his passenger, who was wearing a baseball cap bearing a Jack Daniels emblem. In another deliberate move, Boodjark slowly pulled the cap lower over his forehead, casting a shadow over his face, but not before the driver noticed dark, tired lines and puffiness under his eyes. He also noticed the scar.

"Is your cousin okay? Much damage to your car?"

"Nah. Not much damage."

"Your cousin?"

"Don't care. Paddy is an idiot. A humourless, stone-faced bloke."

Stone-faced. That's ironic coming from a colder person I've never met.

Warner was surprised when the passenger continued without any further prompting. "Yeah, stone-faced. Paddy never utters a word. Just sits on his seat at the corner near the pub. Gazes all day at people walking by. Doesn't move." Boodjark chuckled quietly, just loud enough for Warner to hear. Part of his plan.

Now there's a hint. "Are you headin' to the goldfields?"

Silence.

Nothing further was said over the journey. Not a word. Fifteen kilometres past the turn off to Kolbang Prison Farm, a sign indicated

"Blissful Mountain Winery. Deliveries". Warner turned the truck into the driveway, drove about twenty metres and stopped.

"This is the best I can do, buddy. I'm not going any further. Heading back the other way in a few hours. This road is fairly busy so you shouldn't have a problem gettin' a ride. Good luck."

Boodjark climbed down from the cabin and uttered one word as he closed the door, "Thanks."

***

When Warner later became aware of the prison escape he contacted the Crime Stoppers hotline.

"How can you be sure the hitchhiker was the escapee?" asked the Police telephone operator.

Impatiently, "I already said he was thumbing a lift not far from the Kolbang Prison Farm. Fitted the advertised description perfectly. Right height, right hair colour... right everything. Had a scar on his right cheek, too."

"Hold the line please, Mr Warner, and I'll have another officer talk to you."

Warner listened to a clacking sound as fingers brushed a keyboard. There were other background sounds, people talking, one side of a telephone discussion... then silence. After a few moments a new male voice greeted him. A deeper tone.

"Hello, Mr Warner, Sergeant Hockley here."

"Call me Tom."

"Mr Warner... er, Tom, is your residential address where you are currently located? Our GPS places you in Clifton Street, Sandford. Is that correct? What number on Clifton?"

Without waiting for an unnecessary confirmation Hockley continued, "We shall send a police officer to your home in the next thirty minutes or so to get a full statement. In the meantime, can you answer a few questions for me? Firstly, did your hitchhiker say where he was going?"

"Yes. He was reluctant to talk but I persevered. I asked him several times about the reason for hitching a ride at such an early hour–"

Hockley impatiently interrupted. "Where was he going, Tom?"

"The goldfields. He was heading for Silkspear." Silkspear, geographical coordinates approximately 30° 44' 56.0040" S, 121° 27' 57.0096" E.

"Did he specifically say 'Silkspear'?"

"No he didn't but perhaps I should've been a detective and not a trucky. I—"

Hockley cut him short again. "How can you be certain he was travelling to Silkspear if he didn't mention the town?"

"As I said, I should have been a detective? He spoke of his cousin. Called 'im Paddy. Said he sits stone-faced all day on a corner near a pub. What does that tell you, Sergeant?"

Hockley didn't answer.

"It tells me he didn't want to mention the name of the town but was having a private little joke. He chuckled when he said it. There's a statue of Paddy, the bloke who discovered gold, in the main street of Silkspear. On the corner in front of the pub. Just where the escapee said his cousin sits all day. Stonefaced... Statue. Got it?"

Hockley remained silent for a moment. His thoughts were interrupted by Warner. "Are you still there, Sergeant?"

"Yes, I'm here. I was thinking about your... er... detective skills. You might be right. He didn't want to disclose his destination despite your repeated questioning," Hockley said with a hint of sarcasm. "Tom, do you have any insight into why he would even tell you as much as he did? Tell you about his cousin Paddy, the statue?"

"Because he's a smart-arse, that's why. He couldn't help himself. Yeah, a real smart arse. He was evasive. Reluctant to talk but I got it out of 'im," Warner said, beaming with pride and self-importance. "I told ya he tried to hide his face, didn't I. Wouldn't look at me. Wouldn't engage in conversation. Unusual for a hitchhiker. But I noticed the scar, Detective. That bloke had been in fights, probably while he was in prison. He looked like a crim!"

The telephone conversation ended with Sergeant Hockley reiterating that a police officer would visit Warner within a short time to take a full statement. A statement that may be used as evidence. The information provided in the telephone link would be quickly assessed by police officers involved in the search. The focus of the search would shift.

Warner made the final comment. "I tell ya, the bloke's no idiot but he is a smart-arse. One last thing, Sergeant – is there a cut-off age for recruitment of detectives?"

Chapter 30

Warner's delivery truck moved slowly along the driveway lined with poplar trees. Boodjark also moved slowly, back towards the main road. When he reached the shoulder of the main road, he stopped to watch the truck recede towards a building one hundred metres away, adjacent to several large aluminium tanks on stilts. Tanks used in the processing of wine.

As the truck approached the building, Boodjark saw a dog emerge from behind one of the poplar trees and stand in the middle of the driveway after the truck had passed. Ears erect, the dog didn't move. It stared in Boodjark's direction.

A guard dog. Can't tell what sort. Probably a Doberman. About that size.

With a shrug of his shoulders, Boodjark turned and walked in an easterly direction. In the direction he had led Warner to believe he was heading. When he was out of sight from the truck, he crossed the road.

Opposite the winery, the bush was thick with native shrubs. Acacia, banksia, native cycads. All a healthy and substantial undergrowth to large eucalypt trees. He walked into the bush. Disappeared from sight to the truck driver who had given him a lift and seemingly swallowed his story about his destination, and to any passing traffic. But he didn't disappear from the dog's sight.

Twenty metres into the bush, Boodjark wrestled past some thick shrubbery and turned again, this time towards the west. In the direction of the Prison Farm. Another twenty or so metres on he stopped, crouched and peered between bushes at the winery.

The delivery truck had activated a sensor. A vibration movement was detected and combined with ultrasonic waves that pulsed as the truck moved into the sensor's field. A complex set of electronic components sent a message wirelessly to a floodlight. Upon receiving the input, the light activated and drowned the area in brightness. The equivalent of a bright summer's day.

He could see the truck, now standing silently in front of 'Deliveries and Dispatch'. He could see the dog. It hadn't moved and still gazed along the driveway in the direction of the winery's entrance and the bush beyond.

Boodjark didn't move, either. He hunched down on his heals. Motionless. As motionless as his "cousin" Paddy in Silkspear. He had to wait for the light to switch off at which point, he assumed, the dog would return to its place of rest. Eventually the light extinguished but then he heard the truck door slam shut. The driver had exited the vehicle to stretch his legs and the light was again stimulated. Boodjark sighed in frustration but knew he had to be patient. Surprisingly, the dog hadn't moved.

Bloody, stupid animal, he thought. *Surely it can't be worried about a potential intruder it can't see. I'm sure it can't see me. Or can it?*

In the still of the night, he could hear the faint sound of water hitting the ground. He caught a glimpse of the driver standing near one of the poplar trees, head bent down and his right hand at about waist height in front of him.

He's taking a leak. The stupid dog is still standing in the driveway.

Then there was the sound of the truck door closing, followed soon after by the floodlight burning down. Time to move.

As quietly as possible, he walked through the shrubbery in a south-westerly direction. From studying maps of the area on the Internet in the prison library, he memorised the lay of the land and knew he would eventually reach the eastern boundary of Kolbang Prison Farm. After battling the undergrowth and terrain in the dark for over an hour, he reached the fence line. He followed it south. He would again circle the farm but this time stay well into the bush before heading west.

Chapter 31

Convinced he had created sufficient confusion and possibly even chaos amongst the screws and the police, Boodjark proceeded in a more relaxed frame of mind. He could turn his attention to navigating his way to Cottam Mills. It would be a long trek but at the end of it he would have retribution. A day of reckoning for the black woman he believed was, alone, responsible for his incarceration. Never mind the fact he took a life. In his mind, that life was worthless, anyway.

At last, the shackles of depression would be removed. At last, he would have freedom.

As he navigated his way through the shrubbery and past tall, old-growth forest, Boodjark considered the steps he would take in his old town to achieve retribution. *I'll watch her house. Watch her movements. Kidnap... torture. Perhaps. She deserves to die, the black bitch.*

***

The Cottam River wound its way around the edge of town and it was in the southern-most housing area where Boodjark's target Bessie, lived. Not far from Mardoo's *karla*. Boodjark knew the area well.

Further south, an area with which Boodjark was intimately familiar, Mardoo and his friends loved to explore the bush, the riverbanks, and foresters' tracks near where *Ngarngungudditj Walgu* rested. In the foreseeable future, Boodjark would emerge from that same area, south of the town. The area he knew extremely well from his friendship with Mardoo's father in his early years of living in Cottam Mills.

The day after Boodjark's escape, it was the boy's proposed destination on a beautiful, cloudless *dirdong* day.

Wild animals were plentiful throughout the district. The three boys challenged each other over their markings, Ace having studied a book entitled "Australian Flora and Fauna". They took pride in knowing the footprints and mostly agreed on the type of animal but often disagreed on how fresh they were. Not surprisingly, Mardoo was always best at determining how recent a *yongka*, a *kwoka* (wallaby), a *waitj* (emu), wild *doordok* (pigs), or a *djooditj* (wild cat) had passed by.

His friends were often in awe at how accurate he was, when they eventually crept through undergrowth to find a flock of emus, just as Mardoo had predicted. They never got near the *yongkas* or other animals but *waitj* don't take flight of course. They can't. They have wings and feathers but can't fly.

"According to the book I've been reading, they run pretty damn quick though," Ace stated the obvious.

"If we get close to a flock, we have to be vigilant," Mardoo instructed.

As they wheeled their bicycles slowly through the bush, they inevitably debated the types of reptile that left behind an indent as it slithered along the grey, sandy track some time in the last twenty-four hours. Usually a *dileri* (bluetongue lizard) or a *yoorn* (bobtail goanna) is easy to identify. It was also easy to identify the track left by a *ka-dar* (racehorse goanna) and that made by a *yoolart* (skink) but not necessarily a snake.

"That's not a racehorse goanna, it's a different type of reptile. Maybe a skink," Ozzy told his friends pensively, pointing at the track in front of them.

"Did you know 'racehorse goanna' is not its proper name? It's actually a Sand Monitor," Ace said earnestly.

Since his first excursion into the bush, Ace had been studying a second book entitled "Reptiles of Australia". Mardoo's warning to him about deadly snakes being plentiful in the Australian bush had prompted him to become more aware of the types of creatures he might encounter.

Mardoo smiled. A few days ago he had told his friends the Noongar names for the various reptiles but it clearly hadn't been fully absorbed into their memory banks. "Call it a racehorse, a sand monitor or whatever you want, but I'm sticking with the Noongar word, *ka-dar*," he said quietly.

Silence. Embarrassed foot-shuffling before Ozzy finally said, "I made a statement with a rhetorical question. To me, it's a racehorse goanna. It runs really fast. Unbelievably fast, hence the name."

Ace ignored the comment. Having spent time in the school library, he continued with his recently acquired knowledge on reptiles, "Did you know that if a Sand Monitor… er… *ka-dar* is running towards you and you are standing dead still, it might think you're a tree and scale you to sit on your head?"

"I don't plan to stand still if I see one of those things coming my way," Ozzy replied. "Besides, I reckon the racehorse is more likely to think we're saplings."

The boys laughed at the imagery before Mardoo squatted over the grey sand and examined some markings that appeared reasonably fresh. Animal markings provided a challenge to Ozzy and Ace but not so Mardoo. He enjoyed sharing his knowledge with his *wadjala* friends. He even claimed to be able to tell if a snake track belonged to a dugite, a tiger snake or a brown snake, as preposterous a suggestion that may be.

Mardoo pointed at the meandering indent in the sand. "A dugite," he said. "A large one."

"You're full of it, Mardoo," Ozzy asserted, nudging him as he spoke.

Ace joined in and suggested Mardoo has been reading too many comic books. "Next you'll be saying the Phantom was here last week," he laughed.

"Well, as a matter of fact he was," Mardoo replied earnestly.

Friendly banter would never threaten or reduce their friendship. They knew they could give each other a bit of stick and no offence would be taken.

Being an old mining town, there were always exciting things for the boys to occupy their weekends. Their parents would likely regard some of their activities as foolhardy, even dangerous, but the boys would never be deterred by a difficult challenge. Near exhausted mines, there were abandoned buildings to explore. Disused gantries to climb. Rocks and rocky outcrops to paw over. They never got bored and no obstacle was too big for them to meet.

Three kilometres along the foresters' track, the undergrowth thickened as the canopy of large trees disappeared. There, the sun could more readily penetrate forest, satisfying the shrubs' need for energy absorption. There was some marri and jarrah regrowth but those trees were fewer. Much of the forest had been cut for use in the former Kitty Valley mine, about three hundred metres beyond what had been a heavily-forested area.

The boys made their way along the track, a different track from the one they had walked recently, occasionally stopping to observe and identify an animal or reptile mark. They headed in the direction of the old mine site.

While they had previously explored around and inside the old ramshackle buildings that comprised abandoned offices, crib rooms, locker and shower rooms, the boys had never ventured near the old mine workings. They could gain access to the rustic buildings but not the old mine itself. There were numerous signs positioned at strategic locations to remind visitors of the dangers beyond the boundary fence.

A large chicken-wire fence with barbed wire on top surrounded the mine proper. There were signs attached to the fence and a more serious warning attached to the main vehicle gate. That sign had a picture of a black stick figure surrounded by a red circle, and a red line through it. Beneath the picture the bold capitalized warning read, "NO ENTRY" and in smaller print underneath, "Authorized persons only."

The boys parked their bikes against one of the freestanding signs several metres from the entrance to the site. They stood in silence and alternately gazed at the mine's headframe beyond the fence, and the buildings nearby. The headframe was constructed from heavy jarrah timber. Four uprights, evenly spaced four metres apart, rose at an angle twelve metres to a gantry head that once supported a winch and wire rope for hauling coal from a shaft.

The buildings were mainly constructed of large hand-made limestone bricks. Most were windowless. Pieces of glass glistened in the sun at the base of buildings where casement windows had once existed.

"You know, lads," Ozzy broke the silence. "This mine would have been a hive of activity many years ago when coal was in such huge demand. Especially when it was used at the old power station in Ditchingham."

His friends nodded in unison.

"Now look at it. Nobody ever comes here, not even old miners or tourists. Come to think about it," Ozzy opined, "this would be a perfect place for a criminal to hide from the police."

Ace chimed in. "You're right, Oz. If someone committed a crime in our town and escaped a police cordon, this would be the ideal hideout. I can't imagine a crime worthy of police attention, though. Perhaps scumbag Spike would be the only person likely to commit such a crime."

"Can you imagine some of our local, overweight constabulary climbing over the rubble here, or going into the darkness of the mine? It wouldn't happen," Ozzy offered.

Both Ozzy and Ace laughed quietly at the former's description. Mardoo remained silent. His thoughts were elsewhere. He thought of the recent discussion with his Aunt Bessie. The truth telling. *There was a heinous, racist crime committed in our town before we were born. I have an uneasy feeling we haven't heard the last of it.*

Puzzled, Ozzy and Ace noticed Mardoo's unusual body posture. Shoulders slumped, torso twisted away from them. Mardoo sensed he was being watched and looked away, but not before his friends had noticed glistened eyes from the welling of tears. The boys didn't know why but they would soon understand the reason.

Ozzy changed the subject. A well-worn path near the entrance gate had caught his attention and provided the opportunity to change direction. "There's a hole in the fence," he said. "It can't be that dangerous, if people enter through that hole. Are we authorized?" And without waiting for an answer, "I think we are because we're locals. Let's take a look."

Mardoo and Ace hesitated. Mardoo wiped underneath his eyes and glanced at Ace. He looked at the sign, looked at the hole, and decided Ozzy was right. "We're authorized."

In a half-crouch, they entered the compound through the hole in the fence. Tentatively at first. Inside, not seeing any imminent danger, they moved less cautiously towards the mine adit. The entrance to what the boys mistakenly thought was the main decline was situated twenty metres from the headframe standing aloof over a shaft. Old, soft timber boards had been nailed to poles, presumably in an attempt by the Department of Mines to prevent entrance to the mine decline. Some had aged and weathered badly. Several had been deliberately broken.

Ozzy pointed to pine boards on the ground, near where they had been removed from the timber frame. "It's obvious someone has been inside," he said. "Probably some other kids from town. So why shouldn't we?"

The question hung in the air. No response. But then, it didn't warrant an answer. The boys edged their way past the partial barrier into the tunnel, tentatively walked several metres forward and stopped.

"Shall we explore further?" Ace asked, with a hint of uncertainty in his voice. "It's really dark."

His mates decided the question didn't warrant an answer. They moved forward, down a gradual slope. Suddenly the ground seemed to move from under their feet. It didn't collapse, but they slid uncontrollably at a rapid pace down the slope, which had become a steep, smooth surface.

When the three hit a solid wall at the bottom of the drive, fine powder puffed into the air as they come to a sudden stop. Feet and arms were chafed and there was a trickle of blood here and there, although they couldn't see the damage. It was too dark.

Mardoo groaned a little and then asked, "Are you guys okay? I'm a little sore, nuthin else."

"I reckon I might have lost some bark off my arms, but at least I'm vertical," Ozzy replied, as he rose to his feet.

"Yep. Same… same but all good," said Ace, brushing soil from his legs.

A sliver of light from above was just enough for the boys to see it would be extremely difficult, if not impossible, to climb back up the slope. Not only was it very steep, it was also worn smooth. The surface shone the length of the sliver. There appeared to be absolutely no chance of gaining a foothold but they had to try. They spent the next few minutes attempting to climb but to no avail.

"How in the hell are we gonna get out of here?" Ace sounded alarmed. "Nobody knows where we are. One of us should've stayed on top, then we could get help."

"My Pa's in hospital. He can't help," exclaimed Ozzy.

"And my old man's in a grumpy mood. I wouldn't want to hear his negative observations today," said Mardoo. He had a brief vision of Mokiny Jnr seated on a tree stump near the *karla*, elbows on knees and hands covering his face. Mardoo immediately had a sense of guilt for his comment.

"Doesn't matter. Nobody knows where we are," repeated Ace, sounding increasingly alarmed.

"My pocket knife," exclaimed Mardoo. "I've got a pocket knife. We can use that to carve some steps, or at least footholds and grips."

For the next thirty minutes or so – it was hard to tell how long – time passed slowly as the boys took turns to chip at the incline. Progress was slow. In fact, virtually no progress was made at all. They remained at the bottom of the slide.

Ace was again becoming agitated. "Starve. We might starve."

That comment sent a shiver down Ozzy's spine. *I don't fancy death by starvation in a dark and lonely sarcophagus.*

"We must stay calm," Mardoo told his friends, although his voice couldn't disguise a hint of concern. "We need to think. Let's not panic."

Suddenly there was an unusual whining, cat-like sound from deep within the tunnel.

"Sheeeet!" whispered Ozzy. "What in the hell was that?"

The noise echoed along the tunnel again. Ace opened his mouth to speak but there was no sound. Fear made it impossible to talk. His throat felt like it was wrapped in a tourniquet. Tightening. His Adam's apple was pushed to the back of his throat and prevented any coherent sound from escaping. It was hard to breathe.

Mardoo managed to again rasp out his previous instruction, "We must stay calm." But he was trying to convince himself.

"Hear it? There's that noise again," exclaimed Ace, finding voice. "An animal running. It sounds like a dog; maybe a possum."

The darkness in the tunnel consumed everything. The walls, the ceiling swallowed any noise. The sound of anxious boys breathing deeply disappeared. Everything.

In the darkness, it was impossible to tell the distance but suddenly an animal appeared, about seven metres away. A ghostly image. Nothing else was visible, too dark. Only the image mysteriously shone through the darkness. The animal stood perfectly still and looked at the three boys huddled against the mine wall. They were doing their best to blend into the coalface and look invisible.

"That's a chuditch," whispered Mardoo, as he regained some composure. "It looks a bit like a cat, about the same size."

"Except it's the wrong colour and it's bigger. It can't be a chuditch," Ozzy replied nervously. "And look at the tail. Its stiff and not fluffy like a chuditch's."

Mardoo privately agreed. Actually, it does look bigger than a chuditch. About the same size as Aunt Bessie's Buster. Perhaps it's a young dingo.

It's strange how weird and seemingly irrelevant thoughts sometimes flash across one's mind in times of crisis. And this was a crisis. Mardoo remembered his father, the *kabap* (witch doctor), once saying that matter is non-destructive. It doesn't die, it doesn't disappear. It just morphs or takes a different form. He never doubted his father's wisdom.

Could this creature be a dingo? No, it doesn't have a dingo's head. Could it be a Tasmanian tiger? He concluded it could be, perhaps having morphed from something else because the island animal never ventured to this part of the mainland.

"That's a Tasmanian tiger," Mardoo whispered through clenched teeth. "Look at the stripes across its back."

His expression wasn't visible but Mardoo could sense Ozzy's disbelief. After a short moment he responded, "Not possible. Tassie tigers are extinct."

"I know, but maybe there is one left. Or maybe it's a chuditch or a feral cat morphed into one."

Then the animal – or the glowing image – turned and trotted along the drive, almost in slow motion. It stopped a further three metres away and looked back in the direction of the boys. They didn't move. Frozen to the spot.

Circumstances reveal the boy.

"Let's go," Mardoo exclaimed. "We can't wait here. Let's follow it. If that thing is real, there must be an exit back there somewhere. If this tunnel holds its lair, it must go outside to hunt. There has to be another exit."

They edged their way along the tunnel, unable to see. They managed their way forward, shuffling feet, feeling and sliding hands along the rough mine wall. Mardoo was in the lead, keeping his eyes glued to the image that trotted ahead. Ozzy and Ace in single file behind him.

It was impossible to know for how long they walked. It was difficult to assess and made even more uncertain by regular stops. The image stopped periodically, seemingly to ensure the boys followed. The walk seemed longer than it probably was. Like an eternity, because it was pitch black. There wasn't the slightest hint of light but even if there was, coal doesn't reflect light. Sound and light are absorbed.

As the boys scratched their way forward in the darkness, Mardoo noticed a very slight further decline before it rose in an almost imperceptible incline. He had a strong connection to the land and could sense irregularities. At one stage the tunnel floor became harder and rocks protruded above the ground. Mardoo stumbled and fell.

"Are you all right, buddy?" Ozzy asked.

Whilst he couldn't see him, Ozzy knew Mardoo was clambering to his feet. He gave a snorting sound and then sneezed.

"Shhh," a concerned, almost frightened Ace whispered.

As he stumbled, Mardoo had detected an unpleasant odour that caused his loud reaction. "Did you get that strange smell? Not an animal I know."

"Yeah, a Tassie tiger," Ace said acerbically. "They apparently had a strange smell." He didn't know it but Ace's sarcastic comment was actually correct.

Then came the whining cat-like sound again. Further away now.

The boys hustled on and followed the wall around a bend to the right. They could no longer see the image but followed the sound. As they rounded a second bend, where the tunnel broke to the left, dim light was visible against the wall. Suddenly there was an opening ahead at their level and light streamed into the tunnel. The ghost-like animal stood near the opening and looked back in their direction. The animal wasn't silhouetted, as it should be against the bright light. The light appeared to pass right through it.

Then it was gone. It just disappeared. Seemingly vapourised.

***

The next morning, the boys again visited Mr Stewart in hospital. They were determined to pick the ostler's brains.

After the initial pleasantries and surreptitious glances in the direction of the groaner across the room, Ozzy started the conversation. "That mine you once worked at, Dad, before you worked at Kongal Mine… the mine called 'Kitty Valley'. Why was it called that? How did it get its name?"

"Legend has it that a Tasmanian tiger was once sighted there. Some mineworkers said it was a chuditch. Who knows? They say that a cave-in killed a cat's lair not long after mining commenced. Whether the so-called cat was a chuditch or a Tasmanian tiger, we'll never know. The animal was buried and never seen again. That's the legend. But it can't be true of course. Tasmanian Tigers are extinct. It was probably a dingo."

"It was a Tasmanian tiger," Mardoo emphatically suggested."

Mr Stewart sniggered deprecatingly.

Undeterred, Mardoo confidently reasserted his opinion. "Yes, definitely a Tassie tiger, Mr S."

Ozzy frowned at his father. Knitted brow revealed that he didn't appreciate Ostler's dismissive manner. The boys knew Mardoo had an uncanny awareness of his *boodja*. They knew Mardoo had an incredible degree of intuition. A subconscious, instinctive reasoning. They understood he inherited powers the *wadjala* boys didn't have, couldn't have, and others would never understand. He had the genes of his *kabap* father.

"Mardoo may be his nickname because of his size, but his stature and incredible wisdom about our country is unsurpassed in my eyes," Ozzy said icily.

He glared at his father and defiantly added, "If Mardoo said it was a Tasmanian tiger, it was. Simple."

Chapter 32

A ball of light had emerged above the tree line to the east. The expected warmth of the day would soon transform the glistening leaves to dullness. The storm had left a cascade of tree branches and other debris sprawled unevenly across the forest floor. Boodjark had stumbled his way forward but there was now enough light to more easily manoeuvre a path through the countryside.

It would be a silent walk: unbeknown to him, a walk tracked by an unusual beast.

Now that he was in the clear, having made ground and distance from the highway, Boodjark was more relaxed. Hot, but less tense. The only tension he felt was in the arm he had scratched during the night. The plaster he had applied seemed to grip harder. The area around the wound had tightened with a slight swelling. But he had enough sticky plaster in the first aid kit to change the dressing in due course.

There was still a considerable distance to hike before Boodjark would feel totally comfortable about making camp. The plan had always been to head in the direction of the coast, well south of the Kolbang Prison Farm, before turning to the west. He would make camp at Lake Kooyarup (coordinates approximately 34.5108° S, 116.6747° E). Had he not cleverly created the impression he was heading to Silkspear, an irresistible conclusion for the police, an Aboriginal tracker, the canine squad or police rotary or fixed-wing aircraft would likely hunt him.

His subterfuge made it unlikely the dog squad would be useful if employed. He had discarded his own clothes and the sniffer handlers wouldn't know he wore Bluey's clothes for at least another two weeks. Aircraft wouldn't be used for a search when the absconder was almost certainly heading by vehicle to Silkspear. That left the Aboriginal tracker but Boodjark had overheard a conversation two months earlier.

"I need three volunteers tomorrow morning," the prison officer yelled like a regimental sergeant major at an Army training barracks. "You, Billy, you and you," index finger arrogantly jabbing the air in the direction of three Indigenous inmates.

The three First Nations people were having their evening meal in the Mess Hall when the prison officer yelled his instruction. They glanced at each other suspiciously.

"What for, boss?" Billy asked. "Whadya want us to do, boss?"

"You've got a job to do at Lake Kooyarup. It'll be a good break from your routine. An opportunity to get out and have some fresh air. You might even catch some tucker. 'Kooyarup' means 'place of frogs', doesn't it? I know you're not French but you blacks would like frogs, wouldn't ya?" he laughed at his own weak joke. It didn't arouse the same response in others.

"We need to do some work on the public Observatory. Maintenance on the boardwalk, the picnic tables, and then a general cleanup around the shelter. Should take all day. Maybe two. Depends how much needs to be done. We'll find out when we get there. We'll leave after breakfast in the morning."

Boodjark watched from another table, where he always dined with Bluey. He never spoke to First Nations people, ironically believing he was a better class of crim but like other offenders there, his eyes and ears were attuned to any opportunity for information that could give him an advantage over others, including the screws.

Billy and his friends were horror-stricken. Jarred by the instruction, it took a few moments before Billy was able to respond. When he did, his comment was genuine. "S ... s ... sorry, boss." Billy stuttered, eyes downcast. "But we can't do that, boss."

There are many small lakes connected by creeks on the eastern side – the Kolbang Prison Farm side – of the large Lake Kooyarup. The mythological story repeated by some local Indigenous people is that one of those lakes swallowed a group of Noongar people from the Minang mob. The truth has never been discovered but what is known is that there have been numerous earthquakes in the area and there are also patches of quicksand. Those may have contributed to their vanishing in some mysterious way, but the story of the disappearance had grown over the years.

"Whadya mean, you can't do that? It wasn't a request," the prison officer barked.

"That place evil. Bad spirits, *djinack*. Blackfellas disappeared. Blackfellas can't go there. Very bad. Sorry, boss. Maybe a *wadjala* be best to volunteer, boss," Billy rambled almost incoherently.

The prison officer initially detected the genuine alarm in Billy's voice and then followed by a hint of sarcasm with the last comment. But he decided to let it slide. He made the decision not to force the matter. The Superintendent had demanded officers to be respectful of Indigenous culture and to avoid confrontation.

"Okay. Any volunteers amongst you white fellas?"

Several hands shot up, including Boodjark's. A stroke of luck. An unexpected visit to Lake Kooyarup would be hugely beneficial.

He had walked for over four hours. Despite heavy rain eighteen hours or so before, there were no billabongs or creeks from which he could quench his thirst. Evaporation had left furrows of mud but no drinkable water. That would change, the further west he headed.

Mindful of becoming dehydrated, he reflected on the bush survival skills he was taught by his childhood friend, Mokiny. Brother of Yabini, the young woman he had murdered. He brushed that thought aside. Dismissed it; of little consequence, he decided. What was of consequence was his survival, so that he could mete out his own form of vengeance on her cousin.

In the next couple of hours, he would likely encounter the first of the small lakes that drained into Kooyarup. When he reached the waterway, he would start to look for a secluded location to make camp. Closer to the southern part of Lake Kooyarup would be best, as he had learnt this area usually had deeper fresh water. Hundreds and even thousands of years before, this area would have supported a significant number of First Nation tribes.

Boodjark again thought of Mokiny. He didn't know why these flashes of his childhood friend had suddenly passed across his mind. *Mokiny would believe the spirits of the Indigenous people would still be here, I'm sure. Bullshit, of course*, he thought. *Piss off, Mokiny. Leave me alone.*

Over the years, various surveys by archeologists had found a significant number of heritage sites in the region of Lake Kooyarup. For thousands of years, there had been an obvious connection to water for the

First Nation peoples. Rivers, creeks, lakes and swamps hold importance for food gathering and ceremonial purposes. Wetlands and several sources of moving water in abundance were attractive for hunting *yongkas*, *yerderap* (ducks), *djildjit* (fish), *kooyar* (frog), and *koonak* (marron or freshwater crayfish).

The country surrounding Lake Kooyarup and the catchment area for the many feeding creeks is rich with edible plants and animals. Boodjark learnt this from his visit to the lake with a group of prisoners assigned responsibility for maintenance of public facilities, including a bird hutch, a lake observatory and boardwalk, tree-planting and noxious weed control. He had also used the library's Internet search engines for research about soil types in the vicinity of the prison farm, purportedly for better contributing to the farming activities.

What he didn't know, but should have from the teachings of Mokiny's father, Uncle Mokiny Snr, was that the southwest region was rich in a cultural and spiritual connection to the Noongar people. The rivers and lakes were created by *Walgu*, he had been told. The bearded serpent still inhabits the rivers and rests in their deepest parts near Cottam Mills. *Walgu's* life exists and can be sensed in the creeks, the springs, and the shallow lakes of the river catchment area. People of the Dreamtime and Noongar people receptive to their culture can almost touch its life force.

Walgu has produced and maintained the sacred rivers and wetlands to nourish edible plants and animals and ultimately, to provide life to the people. That was just as true for the Indigenous people now as it was for their ancestors.

It's hot. I'm thirsty. No obvious sources of water. What to do?

It was early afternoon. Hardly a cloud blemished the pale blue sky. The sun had passed its highest point, its hottest point, but the hot air lingered. Boodjark rested in the shade of a tree for a short time. As he sat and glanced back between thick river sheoak trees, he thought he noticed a movement. His eyes narrowed, attempting to focus. Nothing.

He gathered himself and stood. Time to move on. Thirty minutes later, he meandered between sedge grasses and noticed the taller eucalyptus trees were less abundant. Ahead, there was a line of distinctive trees he had recalled from his childhood experience around Cottam Mills. He knew the melaleuca preissiana, more commonly known as the paperbark tree, was found almost exclusively on watercourses.

Those trees follow creek beds, he thought. Must be water nearby. Mokiny taught me to eat animal flesh for fluid if there's no water available. Hopefully I won't have to, although I will have to eat.

Within a short time, Boodjark walked adjacent to the tree line, ensuring he didn't step onto loose sand and leave footprints. He was following a creek line that drained into one of the smaller lakes of the Kooyarup complex of waterways. Ahead, as the creek turned in a northerly direction, he could see small pools of water. He would quench his thirst.

As he approached the first of the puddles, treading carefully onto clumps of reed and grass to avoid leaving any human trace, he suddenly stopped. There, right in front of him, was a set of fresh, animal footprints. He expected to see animal prints near the watercourse but not this animal. It was a dog.

Boodjark placed the first-aid kit on a fallen paperbark tree and edged towards the water, eyes darting in all directions. He knelt on a dense tussock and reached towards the water. That's when he heard it. The sound of water lapping nearby. About fifteen metres further along the creek stood what appeared to Boodjark to be the same dog he saw, earlier in the day, at Blissful Mountain Winery. It was lapping at water from the same pool.

Closer now and in the light of day, Boodjark thought the dog looked a little like a dingo. He had only seen photographs of dingos, but he thought this dog resembled what he had seen.

Hastily, Boodjark cupped his hands and with one eye on the dog, he scooped water, firstly onto his face and then into his dry, parched mouth. The dog stopped drinking and watched. Mouth open, tongue dripping water, he panted and watched.

Where in the hell did he come from? Was he following me?

Chapter 33

In Cottam Mills, Bessie's gardening provided calorie-burning moments. With spade in hand, she worked vigorously to prepare the ground. The multi-pronged rake scraped and smoothed the surface. Calories were not slowly burnt. They were utterly torched. Cast away like smoke to the sky, just as her perspiration plummeted to the ground.

On the same day as Boodjark's escape from prison, the day after the storm, Bessie worked in the garden. She knelt beside Mardoo. For the last forty-five minutes, they had prepared the ground and together planted zinnias on the path leading to the front porch of her house. Buster sat on the porch and watched the activity.

"The ground is still heavy from last night's storm," Bessie opined.

"The storm was horrendous, wasn't it?" Mardoo commented rhetorically. "It came from nowhere and caused some damage at our *karla*. But nothing that couldn't easily be repaired at daylight. Everyone in the community digs in to get the jobs done."

The pair worked quickly and as she planted the last punnet of zinnias, Bessie noticed Mardoo fidgeting. He appeared unusually nervous.

"Is something bothering you, Mardoo?"

Mardoo stood, deciding it was time to confront an issue that had bothered him for a very long time. Perhaps it was the attitude of his father, Mokiny Jnr, that morning or perhaps it was his *koondarm* the previous night, but something prompted him to seek answers from Bessie. Mardoo was anxious to know more about his family. His lost family.

"I need to know about Uncle Jimmy. I need you to tell me about my grandfather, too. My Pa doesn't talk. I ask him about family but he won't talk. I know there is something bugging him."

Bessie gazed into Mardoo's unwavering eyes and knew what she had to do. *I know your father cannot tell you but you should know. It's time to tell you the truth.* "Let's go to the river," she said solemnly, after a few moments of reflection. "I need to tell you about the sorry time."

"Tell me here."

"No. The river. You'll soon understand why. Wait by the car. I'll get my keys. C'mon, Buster," she said, patting her hip. "You can wait inside and we'll go for a walk later."

Ten minutes later Bessie reappeared, having quickly changed from her gardening clothes. She wore jeans, a black blouse and her long, dark hair that had been tightly tied into a bun was now loose, shining and flowing over her shoulders. She now wore modest jewellery. Imitation-pearl earrings given to her by her late husband on their wedding day.

The Cottam River flows peacefully through the middle of the town but the most attractive section of the river frequented by the local community was about three kilometres south of the town. Only a seven-minute drive from Banksia Street to the riverbank. There, Bessie parked her late model, two-door Ford Escort sedan. As she stepped out of the car, she had a sudden realisation and, as if seeing Mardoo for the first time, she looked deeper into his eyes.

Yabini's eyes. Dark, but sparkling and asking questions, just like his Aunt Yabini.

The pair walked slowly down the gradual embankment onto the beach, where Bessie bent and in her right hand gathered a handful of yellow sand. She led Mardoo along the embankment to a special part of the river. In the traditional time-honoured way of the Wilman Beelagu people, she sat on a large granite rock near the water's edge. She gestured to Mardoo to sit next to her. He skidded sideways onto the granite rock; a tiny boy who looked even smaller sitting atop a large and magnificent creation of nature.

They sat in silence for a few minutes before Mardoo quietly whispered, "You carry too much sadness, Aunt Bessie. I can see it in the lines at the side of your eyes. I can see it in your face but mostly your eyes."

This boy expresses wisdom years beyond his age. He's so perceptive.

Bessie looked to the distance. Down the river, past the bend to the left and the dogleg to the right. A kilometre look. Mardoo glanced at her from the corner of his eye but did not disturb her thoughts.

Without a word, she wiped the handful of sand under her armpits and then threw it into the river. To announce their arrival. So the spirits could smell her presence. She took a deep breath, filled her *walyan* and sucked in the cool afternoon air that drifted silently across the water. A gift of comfort from the spirit of *Walgu* and the Wilman Beelagu ancestors. She loved the river, especially this sacred spot where *Ngarngungudditj Walgu* rests. The Beelagu people regularly visit here for the tranquillity. For many, it's their church.

Bessie knew the law. The law that said she must show respect and throw sand into the river before talking to the spirits of the dead. An important custom passed down over the generations. A law that cannot be ignored.

Having respectfully waited a reasonable time after throwing the sand, Bessie began to quietly sing. She sang in the language of her mob, the Wilman First Nations people. A song calling to the spirit of her long-gone ancestors and her recently deceased family members. A song asking *Ngarngungudditj Walgu* to accept their spirit and, when the time comes, to welcome her spirit to the river. A song of respect. A song that announced their presence, that stated who she was and the purpose of their visit.

Abruptly, Bessie stopped singing and turned to little Mardoo. "Water has always been so important to our people. The waterways, wherever they are on Noongar *boodja*, have a practical – and more importantly – a spiritual significance. *Ngarngungudditj Walgu* created all the creeks, the rivers, and lakes for our people. *Walgu* created our laws and customs. We must never forget that, Mardoo."

Mardoo nodded and added, "I understand, Aunt Bessie. I understand it is important for us Wilman Beelagu people to respect and protect our environment."

"Yes, it is but it's much more than that, Mardoo. This special place is where the spirit of our Dreaming, the spirit of *Ngarngungudditj Walgu* rests. *Walgu* still rests here, Mardoo – do you understand?"

Again he nodded, but more slowly and wearing an impatient look. His much-older cousin, whom he respectfully called 'Aunty', knew Mardoo was eager to know more about family.

Bessie proceeded to tell Mardoo about his grandfather, her Uncle Mokiny Snr. "He was a very charismatic and wise man. He was *djenakabi* and *kabap*. His passing to the Dreaming was unexpected, sad, and too early. I'm sure it's one of the many things that haunted your father." Bessie paused and pointed to the river, "His spirit is here now, right here with *Walgu* and resting with our ancestors."

For several minutes Bessie described how her mother-in-law had been taken from her family as a small child and how that caused intergenerational suffering. How *wadjala* Government policies caused emotional and mental damage, and long-term scarring, as family connections were stolen. She forced herself to tell the story of her late husband Jimmy.

"Mardoo, Uncle Jimmy carried a pain too great for him to bear in the end. Your Pa carries another burden. You need to understand and be patient with him."

Bessie took a deep breath whilst contemplating how much to tell this young boy, then continued. "Before you were born, there was an unthinkable tragedy in Cottam Mills. A tragedy that had a profound impact on our family. It is why your Pa is sometimes difficult to talk to. I want you to understand why he is often so very sad. Moody. Your papa may not show his emotions. Like so many Noongars of his generation, especially men, he conceals them. He loves you more than you'll ever know Mardoo. He has high hopes for you. Says you can be whatever you want to be.

"I'm sorry, I digress. But I wanted to assure you of your papa's good intentions. Despite that, he cannot bring himself to tell you the sorry story but you should know."

For the next fifteen minutes, Bessie told Mardoo about the sorry time. She told him about his beautiful Aunty Yabini. That she was a ray of sunshine in the Wilman community. She told him that beautiful, sunny, bright Yabini had been murdered near the *djooroot* to his *karla*. The rape and murder of Yabini had emotionally scarred those who were close to her. Especially Yabini's brother. Mardoo's father.

There was a splash in the water a few metres from where they sat. They turned and watched a *djildjit* (fish) in the shallow water. In the clear water they could see stripes and as the fish turned, a distinctive red ventral fin. It was a redfin perch opportunistically hunting for yabbies, scrubworms or minnows at the edge of the reeds. Another splash and a ripple of water as the hunter swam away, having sated its hunger.

Bessie smiled at the good fortune the Cottam River and all waterways on *boodja* brought to the food chain and the Noongar people.

"The night Yabini was murdered, I was nearby. It was dark for most of the night but as if arranged by the spirits, there was a break in the clouds." Bessie told of a bright star, the brightest star she had ever seen. She told of a flash of *kilang* that reached to the sky. Not projecting down as expected but rising from the ground. She told of an extraordinary sensation she believed was a soul passing. A soul travelling to the Dreaming.

"That night I experienced a profound display of Noongar spirituality. I felt a soul passing. I saw the star that shouldn't have been there. Stargazers had another name for that star – Sirius, I think they called it, but Sirius doesn't appear in the sky until after midnight. Something extraordinary happened that night. I saw it. I felt it."

Bessie paused, allowing Mardoo time to absorb the significance of what she had just told him. Then, in a firm but quieter voice, as if to reinforce the intensity of her intuitiveness, she added, "On the night she was born, Uncle Mokiny and Aunty saw a very bright star in the sky. They named their baby girl Yabini." She paused again. 'Yabini' means 'star'."

For a short time they sat in silence until the slight movement of air across the water seemed to gain momentum. Mardoo had been gazing into the blue depths of the Cottam River but as quickly as the breeze lifted, he raised his eyes to Bessie and asked, "Did you hear that song just then, Aunty? Must be someone playing music further down the river."

Bessie smiled but didn't answer, instead telling her young cousin, "It was exactly sixteen years ago that Yabini was taken from us. A night just like last night, the only difference being sixteen years ago I saw the star. Sixteen years ago, I came here with family to ask *Walgu* to accept Yabini's spirit. To ask that her spirit be allowed to rest here in the Dreaming. She is here now, Mardoo, and that music was Yabini's song."

For a moment Mardoo pondered what he had been told. Then, in a serious tone, he said, "I understand why our mob gathers here, Aunt Bessie. I can feel it, too. Our river, created by *Ngarngungudditj Walgu*, is where the spirits of our ancestors rest."

Chapter 34

Eventually, Boodjark gathered the first-aid kit and carefully watching the dog, he set a course to be well clear of it. He manoeuvred past some reeds and sedge grass, past a stand of melaleuca trees and circled around the animal. He initially didn't look back but when about fifty metres from where he stopped to take his fill of water, he turned. The dog was nowhere to be seen.

He swapped the first-aid kit and joggers to his other arm and winced. The scratch was now inflamed and more swollen. *Change the dressing. I'll have to change it when I make camp.*

As he continued the trek, Boodjark occasionally stopped to strip bark from the largest paperbark trees. Without acknowledging the source of his information – he chose to forget any connection he previously had with Mokiny – he decided the long, wider strips of bark would be useful to provide shelter from the weather, ground cover for sleeping upon, and possibly useful to construct a fish trap in the lake or the river ahead. He would need food. Fresh raw fish would best meet his needs.

He walked on but after a short time again needed to rest. He left the edge of the creek to sit on a fallen, dead melaleuca tree that had been scorched by fire. It was wedged in the lower branches of a much larger melaleuca, which cast its shadow over the area. He stripped a layer of blackened bark from the log, placed his first aid kit and spare shoes on a tuft of grass at his feet, and sat on the clean timber of the melaleuca near the tree's base.

In the shade. Elbows on his knees, fingers steepled, hands touching long, unkempt auburn hair and resting on the crown of his head, he gazed at the grey sand, framed by the gap between his arms and legs. He felt unusually tired. Perhaps it was the release of adrenalin after his escape. Perhaps it was the unusually late night. Or perhaps it was something else… He felt a twinge of pain in his right arm. He closed his eyes.

With a shake of his head, Boodjark sat upright and forced himself to alertness. He knew he was on the verge of falling asleep. *Perhaps I did, momentarily*, his immediate thought.

Then he saw the dog standing nearby, with eyes fixed on him. *I didn't hear the dog. Stealthily appeared. Like a dingo.*

Boodjark stood and vigorously and aggressively waved at the dog, attempting to scare it away without making any noise. The dog didn't move but Boodjark felt a wave of nausea and vertigo. He steadied himself against the log before slowly moving away, continuing in a westerly direction. He peered over his shoulder. Silently, the dog ambled away in the opposite direction. The direction from which they both had come. Boodjark was satisfied the dog had either lost interest or he had scared it away.

Soon after, he came across an expanse of water. He knew it wasn't large enough to be the lightly saline Lake Kooyarup. He tasted the water. Fresh. It had to be Twisted Lagoon (coordinates approximately 34.5000° S, 116.7333° E), which was close to the larger lake situated amongst a string of smaller lagoons in the complex of waterways. He walked past the southern end of the lagoon and into a thick grove of trees. This is where he would build a camp, using branches from the abundance of *Kitja Boorn* (spearwood) trees surrounding the area.

The afternoon sun was still warm, even though several hours before it had commenced a slow trajectory towards the western horizon. No time to waste. Boodjark broke branches from the *Kitja Boorn* trees, saving the straightest for the purpose used by the First Nations people. The branches had traditionally been used to make spears for hunting purposes. Mainly for hunting smaller animals near waterways. The majority of twisted but surprisingly strong branches would be used to construct a shelter and, although he didn't think it necessary being hidden in the grove of trees, to provide a suitable camouflage.

Wearily, and now having developed inexplicable tremors, Boodjark sat on some of the paperbark he had collected, to steady himself. He raised his eyes to the tree canopy above and absorbed the unique character of the native Australian trees that surrounded him. He reflected briefly on the cluster of trees that fringed the small artificial lake at the school he had attended in Ditchingham. They were deciduous and would now be shooting new leaves.

These trees are different. They're real. Native Australian trees. More authentic than those grown at that private school. Why am I even thinking about that school?

He shrugged his shoulders as a gesture of bewilderment. Why would he contemplate such matters? Boodjark didn't normally care about the natural environment. He didn't have a connection to the *boodja*, or any connection to the beauty of his surroundings. Or even any spiritual discernment that might be capable of opening his eyes to what may be possible. Something was weird about this place. Something made irregular ideas enter his head, he decided. Silly thoughts festering.

Festering. That was it. It had started as a scratch but, after hiding in the sedge grass and reeds, it had become infected. It didn't take long. He slowly removed the plaster from his arm. The skin around the wound had become inflamed. A yellow streak marked the length of the scratch. His arm had started to ache and a red line crept along his arm towards his armpit. Poison.

Suddenly, he sensed he was being watched. His gaze was averted towards the base of a nearby tree, no more than five metres from where he sat. He hadn't heard it; hadn't any idea when it had arrived. But there it was, standing next to a tree that it could only get to by passing Boodjark. It stared, mouth open and panting quietly as if it had just sprinted a 1500-metre time trial. It was now evident to Boodjark that the dog, which he believed could be a dingo, had no intention of leaving him.

Again he felt nauseous and a feeling of light-headedness engulfed him. It was the poison. He had a childhood recollection of his father telling him if a dog licked a wound it would clean out the infection and heal. Lifting his gaze from the wound, he noticed the animal shaking its head, as if reading his thoughts.

Suddenly the dog panted more heavily. A strange pant. Irregular breathing. Simultaneously an image of Uncle Mokiny Snr – his childhood friend's father – appeared. Boodjark closed his eyes but the image remained as if glued to the back of his eyelids.

His new companion spoke. Boodjark opened his eyes and stared hard at the dog. He had to be hallucinating. The dog nodded. The voice of old man, Uncle Mokiny Snr, said, "Heal yourself. I will help you."

"How? How will you help me? The blackfellas in Palmyra told me you died."

"My body has gone but my spirit remains. Lives in the waters created by *Walgu*."

Boodjark looked at the dog in disbelief. The dog nodded again. Its panting became stronger.

I'm hallucinating. The poison. I'm goin' mad ... or ... I'm gonna die.

"No, you're not."

The voice came from the direction of the dog. It had changed its appearance and now definitely resembled a dingo. Boodjark recalled the meaning of 'mokiny'. In the Noongar Wilman language, 'mokiny' meant 'dingo'. Another flash from his childhood as if suddenly planted in his cerebrum by a transcendental being.

Uncle Mokiny Snr was not of mixed blood. He had the telltale signs of his initiation to manhood. The missing front tooth and scars on his chest. The animal had a front tooth missing.

As if it had been running, the dingo's breathing became harder, more irregular, before it again spoke. "I am *moorook* (magic man), *kabap* (healer). Place your *djaa* over the *bookarl*," the deep and comforting voice of Mokiny Snr said. "Place your mouth over the sore and suck the poison. When I tell you, spit it out."

Boodjark did as the voice instructed.

When he woke from a deep slumber, Boodjark sat upright on his paperbark bed and examined the wound. The redness and swelling had gone. The yellow streak of pus had disappeared. The light-headed feeling was no longer evident.

He rose and stepped outside his shelter. Semi-darkness greeted him. Glimpses of the sun rising in the east appeared between the trees. He had slept fourteen hours. It was bright enough for Boodjark to see he was alone. The dingo had gone without a trace.

Some of the First Nations people in the region of Lake Kooyarup believed that after a soul travels to the Dreaming, it can re-emerge at will, even in another body. Change its shape. Change its identity, its being.

It was possible for an Indigenous person's soul to morph into any bird or animal it chooses. Commonly, it morphed into an eagle and soared above the mountains inland from the coast, near the lake country. Surveilling the area for unwanted intruders. binocular vision made them powerful predators. One of the most sacred protectors of *boodja*.

Wedge-tailed eagles were less common on the coastal areas. To the First Nations people, their presence meant a spiritual renewal.

But there were choices. A soul might morph into a *ngoorlak*. A black cockatoo that announces the imminent arrival of bad weather, providing a warning to prepare for a storm. Or morph into a bronze-winged pigeon that could escape from danger with unbelievable speed. Most importantly, and most commonly, a soul might morph into a wild dog. A dingo.

In the dim light of dawn, Boodjark first peered to the sky and blinked to adjust his vision to the light. He then cast his eyes at ground level, between the trees and shrubs. But the dingo was gone. Carefully, he searched the ground around his shelter. There were no paw markings.

It was as if it had never happened but the presence of Uncle Mokiny Snr was as real to Boodjark as the *djidi-djidi* (willy wag tail) that sat on the spearwood branch nearby. The branch that poked from under the paperbark at the entrance to his shelter. The *djidi-djidi* stood unusually still. Like a sentinel.

The Wilman people believe the *djidi-djidi* is a portent to darkness. Its stubborn and unearthly presence would be accompanied by death.

Chapter 35

The six p.m. news bulletin conveyed the story. It wasn't the first news item. Obviously the media thought a story about an Australian Rules footballer being injured at training was more important.

In a solemn tone, the news anchor reported that a prisoner who had been incarcerated for the rape and murder of an Indigenous girl had walked out of a minimum-security prison. Bruce Prentice, originally from Cottam Mills, had served time in Palmyra but was in the Kolbang Prison Farm when he escaped.

"What was a man convicted of murder doing in a minimum-security prison?" the anchor asked, as if the murder and his conviction had only recently occurred. Not surprising for the media, the newsreader was conveying an opinion by her question, not merely reporting news.

"The justice system needs to take a good, hard look at its processes when a dangerous criminal can simply walk out of a low-security prison." A second comment seemingly intended to arouse concern in the community.

The scene changed from the newsreader in the studio to an aerial shot of Kolbang Prison Farm. The entrance to the Prison Farm was next, presumably to show the inadequate level of security for inmates who had committed the worst type of crimes. Then, to the front of the Abannerup Regional Police Station where a group of journalists surrounded a local senior detective.

"Prentice has a history of violence and should not be approached if sighted," Detective Inspector Wallace spoke directly to the camera. A photograph of Boodjark dressed in prison greens was displayed. The scar was clearly visible. "We have reason to believe he is heading to the goldfields. If seen, under no circumstances should he be approached," Wallace repeated. "Call Crimestoppers." The Crimestoppers telephone number scrolled across the bottom of the screen.

When did that happen? Bessie thought as she watched the evening news, a frown deepening across her normally smooth forehead. She sat comfortably in her living room following her cup of tea with Buster on the rear veranda. *Why the goldfields?* She gazed at Buster who looked alert with ears raised.

"As long as he keeps heading east, away from here," she told her pet.

Buster sensed the concern of his cynophilist Mum, rose from his mat and trotted to stand by her side.

"Its okay, Buster," she reassured the border collie, bending forward to pat his head. "The police will catch him before long." Bessie was attempting to reassure herself, not only her pet. Unsuccessfully.

In the days that followed the public announcement, the police were becoming frustrated at numerous reported 'sightings' of Boodjark. He was allegedly sighted in Silkspear, Barragup, Mooro, Mardella, Kurl-Kurti, Jimberlana and even in the State's northern Murujuga area, all within two days. Police resources were stretched thin.

The Trunning family shack had an old but reliable Panasonic television set sitting atop an older sideboard in the dining room. Mardoo thought the national news was usually too depressing to watch. He wasn't interested, and waited for the sports report. His parents habitually had the television switched to one of two commercial channels whilst dinner was being enjoyed. The evening news was background to the joyful sounds of deliciously cooked food being consumed.

Suddenly, the perturbed voice of the newsreader was heard to mention Cottam Mills. All eyes and ears turned to the television. Even Mardoo sat upright and was attentive when the newsreader reported the prison escape. Initially, it seemed the newsreader only wanted a sound bite to cause fear. *Fear must be good television*, thought Mardoo before the photograph of Boodjark appeared on the screen.

Mardoo didn't wait for the sports report. He excused himself from the table. It was six thirty p.m. and the sun had just slipped below the horizon. Enough light lingered to outline the *djooroot*. Mardoo darted away from the *karla*.

"Did you see the news, Aunty?" Mardoo breathlessly rushed the words when Bessie answered the front door.

"Yes, my dear. What bothers you?"

"The prison escapee, Aunty. Was that him? They said he had murdered an Indigenous girl. Was that the man that killed my Pa's sister, my Aunt Yabini?" Mardoo gasped for air.

"You mustn't be anxious, Mardoo. Yeah, that was 'im but the policeman said he was heading in the direction of Silkspear. We needn't be concerned. The police will catch 'im."

"Remember I told you about my *koondarm*? Why don't you and Buster come and stay with us in the *karla* until he is caught."

Bessie smiled appreciatively at her youngest cousin before again attempting to reassure him, "Thank you, Mardoo, but you needn't worry. I don't want you to make your father unnecessarily anxious. Besides, I have a guard dog."

They both looked at Buster, who vigorously wagged his tail in excitement at the attention he was receiving.

"You should go home before it gets too dark. If it makes you feel better, I will take Buster's mattress and blanket into my bedroom until that evil man is captured."

Not entirely convinced by his aunt's reassurance, Mardoo stepped from the front veranda, walked along the path past the recently planted zinnias, crossed Banksia Street, turned, waved and threw a kiss to Bessie. As if he was aware of his new responsibilities, Buster nudged up against Bessie's leg and licked her hand as she lowered it to pat him.

Chapter 36

To Boodjark, the two days and three nights he camped at Twisted Lagoon felt like a holiday. His first holiday for sixteen years. He was almost relaxed. Almost free. When the object of his escape had been achieved, he told himself, he would be free. Free from mental torment.

For now he had to take his time in gathering food for the long trek ahead. By day he would draw upon the bush tucker knowledge taught to him by Mokiny, when he was a boy. He scowled at the thought of an Indigenous boy giving him lessons.

That black kid taught me nuthin'. My dad was the best teacher.

Thoughts of his childhood, albeit a twist on the reality of it, were in part correct. His drunken, racist father taught him the worst of human values. But Boodjark couldn't see that. It was subliminal. He had rejected the opportunity to maintain positive and sound values directed his way by the Wilman Elders, especially Mokiny Snr, to devour an immoral, thuggish, blood-thirsty gangster lifestyle. A life of evil.

Even though his inner hatred, his warped and malevolent mind couldn't wrestle with a positive admission of the truth, as it had occurred in his youth, some lessons taught by Mokiny had been unwittingly absorbed and retained. But he would never acknowledge the source of his knowledge.

Strips of paperbark would be used to create a small dam and enclosure to trap freshwater fish. He knew how to create a trap but wasn't sure if the wetlands in this area hosted edible fish. If he were lucky with the waterways, the species would likely be the same as those he had caught in the Cottam River.

He was indeed lucky with the time of the year. In late spring, freshwater cobbler breed. During the breeding season, they migrate in abundance to protected areas of lakes and rivers, where they can readily find gilgies and western minnows to feast upon.

Boodjark had been taught how to trap black bream, redfin perch and cobbler in the Cottam River. The bream and perch could be conveniently captured in the early morning daylight, but their taste and texture was less to Mokiny's liking than the cobbler. They were, therefore, usually not hunted with enthusiasm, if at all.

Mokiny's favourite was usually caught at night, which pleased Boodjark. It was a regular practice to trap at night, when he was a very small boy. He was careful with the venomous fins but the delicate flavour of the soft white flesh, even eaten raw, made it worthwhile to pursue them.

A *djidi-djidi* sat nearby on the branch of a melaleuca, watching.

More hoping for good fortune than belief in his skills, Boodjark used the first morning of his 'holiday' to build a paperbark trap along the edge of Lake Kooyarup, where a creek entered. Tussocks of sedge grass cascaded over the edge of the lake's bank and into the water and their root mounds also created ideal fish and gilgie breeding habitats.

With a sharpened tip, the spear he had made from a spearwood branch made the ideal weapon with which to gather the fish. He had made several spears from the *Kitja Boorn* trees near his camp. He carried only two on this fishing trip: one to use for the kill and one as a spare and to carry the fish back to camp.

The moonlight was just sufficient for Boodjark to see the shadow of several large fish emerge from their shelter, cavities created by male cobbler. With poor eyesight, their feelers would hit the paperbark and then follow the edge of the wall held in place by spearwood branches.

Watched in silence by a *djidi-djidi,* on his first night he was able to spear three large fish that would provide several meals over the next few days. Using paper-bark strips shaped as a bowl, he also managed to scoop two of the nightfish species that would also make a tasty morsel. He used the screwdriver to kill the fish in the traditional Japanese, *ike jime* manner.

There was an abundance of bulrushes growing at the margins of Lake Kooyarup, Twisted Lagoon and the creeks feeding those water masses. The roots of bulrushes, known to the Indigenous peoples as *yanjet*, were a staple diet for them. In the dry country, it was most commonly harvested in autumn and early winter, when the sugar levels were highest. In the Lake Kooyarup region, it was also harvested in summer when the rhizomes contained sufficient sugar and starch to satisfy the needs of the *Minang* Noongar people.

Usually the labour-intensive *berniny* (digging) was the responsibility of the women. They would pierce the ground with a *warna* (women's digging stick), loosen the ground around the plants and dig the dirt away with the *moora* (blunt, flat end of the stick).

Boodjark was familiar with the *yanjet*. He knew it to be a nutritious and tasty food with a high content of mucilage, a solution with considerable health benefits. Fortunately, recent rain had softened the ground and made it easy for him to dig, using a *Kitja Boorn* spear. No need to craft a *warna*.

Traditionally, the *yanjet* would be mashed into a pancake and roasted on hot coals. Similarly, many animals would be covered with hot coals and roasted. The brush possum would be skinned and the fur stuffed into the animal for absorbing the juices from the meat whilst being cooked. This delicacy would be shared, mainly amongst the men who had hunted for the creatures.

As a boy, Boodjark had learned that a careful inspection of the bark at the base of a tree would likely reveal the presence of a possum. He could tell if the animal had descended and not returned. Using one of his shorter spears, he was able to extract an animal from its shelter in the hollow of a tree.

Although it was preferable to cook both the *yanjet* and the brush possum, Boodjart erred on the side of caution. Any sign of smoke would attract attention and the Bush Fire Brigade would surely arrive in number. Eating raw product wasn't an issue for him. He suspected there was possibly even greater nutritional value in the raw material. Additionally, the meat would provide enough liquid to prevent dehydration.

At Kolbang Prison Farm, offenders were permitted some limited computer time in the library. Boodjark had taken the opportunity to access the Internet and had studied the southwest countryside. He knew where the creeks, rivers and lakes were roughly situated in the direction of Cottam Mills.

He was comfortable in the knowledge there would be no shortage of food or water. He knew where the best source of bush tucker would likely be, as he made his way to where he believed he would become free.

In the early morning of the third day, he commenced the long walk from Lake Kooyarup.

Yanjet roots were plentiful. The creeks held enough gilgies to feed an army. He had even managed to scare a *yerderap* (duck) from its nest and steal the eggs. It was also the right time of the year for harvesting *kwonding* (quandong). Using a concave-shaped river rock to hold the seed and another rounded rock, Boodjark was able to crack open the seeds, revealing a delightfully edible and healthy white flesh.

The trek would take about a week. It wasn't a challenge. Boodjark had planned well and the many hours spent in the bush on a daily basis as a boy had educated him more than sufficiently. "The university of bush living,' he had been told by the black kid, Mokiny Jnr. He shook his head vigorously in an endeavour to free his mind of that thought.

Towns were to be avoided, however tempting it might be to break into a food store at night. Several farms en route were skirted. There would be no trace of human activity anywhere to be found.

On the fifth day, as he walked, he surprisingly thought of the life that might have been. What if he hadn't joined a gang as a teenager? What if he had finished his apprenticeship? What if he'd been honest with his mother? His mother. Well, she's dead now, so forget that.

He again shook his head vigorously, as if to dispel the thoughts and permanently erase them. Prevent them from ever existing. He decided the questions didn't bear thinking about.

He couldn't turn back the clock. The 'what ifs' would be too numerous to think about. Confusing. He had enjoyed a good life with the gang of white boys. He was well liked by his buddies back then and they shared exciting times. A satisfying life in many ways. He had a sense of purpose back in the day.

There was only one 'what if' to think about now. *What if I don't succeed in this mission?* The one thing that made his raison d'etre worthwhile. He would succeed. He had to. His life would be meaningless if he didn't make well on his promise to himself years ago, as the bitch left the courthouse.

She was the reason my freedom and exciting lifestyle came to an end. I will end her happy existence like she ended mine.

Don't get mad. Get even he had said. He said it again now as he walked. Boodjark never took responsibility for the murder.

Yeah, me and me mates had raped that girl but she had invited it. The way she dressed, the way she looked at people. Her demeanour. All of the white boys in town had wanted a piece of her. I was the lucky one.

But he was unlucky to be caught. And she was unlucky to have a soft skull. He didn't mean to kill her, just silence her. *Too bad*, he thought. *Just rotten bad luck.*

Chapter 37

The state-wide search, which had focused on the goldfields region, entered its tenth day. The police had stopped traffic on the main route to Silkspear. They had interviewed each of the offenders at Kolbang Prison Farm, some on several occasions. Nothing. No leads. No luck. The search continued but it was now mainly in response to public 'sightings'.

It was Yabini's thirty-first birthday on the day the fugitive arrived at the outskirts of Cottam Mills. He would find the woman, serve up his version of justice and retreat through the bush to find concealment somewhere in the valley. He'd never be found. Free of his demons, at last.

It was after midnight. Bessie hadn't slept. Tossed and turned. Her overhead fan wasn't operating. Another of the regular brownouts cut power to large sections of Cottam Mills. Street lights were out. Banksia and surrounding streets were in complete darkness.

Buster growled. He had heard something foreign. Something unusual for this hour of the night in quiet Banksia Street. Bessie heard it, too. It sounded like metal scraping against metal. Possibly the movement of tight, rusty hinges.

Silence, followed by the sound of footsteps on the stairs at the rear of Bessie's house. A new sound. The stairs groaned. Mardoo hadn't nailed down the boards. Buster growled again. The sound stopped. Bessie listened intently.

There it is again. Buster is tense. Ears pulled back hard.

The movement was slower now. Hesitating. More boards groaned.

Bessie cautiously moved to the bedroom window that opened onto the rear veranda. The window was covered with vertical blinds with blockout fabric. She slowly pulled one of the slats towards her to open a five-centimetre gap, sufficient to see the rear staircase and part of the veranda. Someone was standing about three-quarters of the way up the stairs. In the dim moonlight she could just make out a tall, thin figure. He didn't move. The light wasn't sufficiently bright for Bessie to identify the intruder.

Where the stairs abutted a beam at the side of the staircase, there was more support and boards not firmly fastened were less likely to move and make a sound. Boodjark moved his left foot sideways to the edge of the second-last stair to avoid any more noise.

Bessie watched, unsure what to do. With the power out, the lights wouldn't work. Should she scream in the hope she might arouse the neighbours? What if it was a relative in need of assistance? She'd look foolish. But the shape of the shadow didn't look like anyone she knew. No phone. *What to do?*

As Bessie was considering her options, a very bright star suddenly appeared in a break between the clouds. It cast sufficient light on the rear of her house for Bessie to catch a glimpse of the stranger's face. It wasn't a face she recognised. A dark, rugged face, deep-set eyes, and an aquiline nose. A red beard and stringy unkempt hair swept forward and concealed the man's most distinctive feature, a scar the length of his cheek.

Buster couldn't see the intruder but he sensed Bessie's anxiety and unleashed a ferocious bark. A bark loud enough to wake the now-extinct wolf from which domesticated dogs have descended. For a small dog, he made a surprisingly loud and vicious sound. He would protect his cynophilist no matter what.

He rushed from the bedroom, along the passageway and skidded on the linoleum into the kitchen-dining room. Still barking, Buster ran hard and launched himself at the kitchen door that exited onto the veranda. Light in weight, he made no impact. He crossed to the opposite side of the kitchen and stood near the entrance to the passageway. The hair on his back bristled. Hackles stood erect.

Bessie entered the kitchen, patted Buster and retrieved a carving knife from the drawer of the kitchenette that stood against the wall near the passage door. The only weapon available to her, should she need one.

Buster had a different idea. He again charged at the kitchen door and jumped to rattle it on its hinges, barking as he did so.

There was no attempt to conceal the sound of his footsteps on the groaning floorboards and stairs as the intruder retreated. Boodjark was concerned the commotion might arouse a reaction from the neighbours. He would return.

Bruce Prentice had been befriended by Mokiny Jnr and taught bush survival skills. Mokiny Snr had taught him positive human values. His own father had taught him conflicting values and the worst, most despicable attitudes. Attitudes that had been reinforced by his peers at school.

Peer pressure combined with his own sense of worth produced a teenager who believed he could be accepted as an equal only if he stood out by doing something he thought was brave. But it wasn't brave. It was cowardly, and for that he was incarcerated in a prison system that served only to reinforce his learned behaviour.

Imprisonment at Palmyra top-security prison reinforced the worst skills and attitudes that he had acquired as a teenager. Fellow offenders gave him lessons in new techniques to commit the crimes for which he had served time as a juvenile.

Above all, he was encouraged to never accept responsibility. Never accept that the police and the Courts would deliver proper justice and peace of mind. Never admit defeat.

Boodjark returned to 31 Banksia Street an hour later.

Chapter 38

Someone must have borrowed Bessie's car. She's always home on rent collection day. Rent Man thought it unusual that Bessie would let someone else drive her car. Must be someone special.

He knocked on the front door but there was no response. *Must be out the back.*

Rent Man walked along the side of Bessie's house. The side gate made a screeching noise as he opened it. *Hinges badly need oiling.* He adjusted the leather bag slung over his left shoulder, walked extravagantly to the stairs, and ascended them two at a time. He walked many kilometres each day and was a fit man.

Near the top of the stairs, he stooped and cast his eyes around the rear yard for the first time. He noticed a well-kept vegetable garden but Bessie wasn't in sight. At the top of the stairs, Rent Man saw the kitchen door hanging loosely. It appeared to have been smashed open.

"Bessie, are you there?" Rent Man yelled.

No response. He pushed on the door and the shock of what he saw hit him hard. It looked as if someone had thrown red paint around the room. Then he saw Buster on his side against the kitchenette. It wasn't red paint. He looked past the lifeless dog and saw Bessie lying horizontally on her back, eyes wide open, torn clothes where blood had gushed from numerous wounds.

Rent Man retreated to the veranda edge and vomited over the balustrade.

Chapter 39

Now that Boodjark had achieved his objective, something he had planned for about fifteen years, he had an empty feeling. It wasn't as liberating as he thought it would be.

In the early hours of the morning, he used Bessie's car to drive south of the town. He went to the river to wash blood from his hands and arms and thoroughly scrubbed the knife with wet sand.

Beyond revenge, he had no plan. His mind had been set on the initial escape and was blinded by his desire for revenge. Long-term freedom was not considered. He had a rough idea of the area he might retreat to. Thick bush in which he could hide. But where to go next?

They won't get me. Too clever for the cops.

Boodjark recalled exploring remnant mine sites and derelict buildings in his youth. He couldn't remember the name of the mine he would choose but decided it was the most isolated and difficult to access of all the abandoned mines in the area. Hunkering down there would give him time. Time to plan something more permanent.

Time for the coppers to lose interest. I could live there until they give up.

Mentally, he reassured himself. There was no reason for the police to link the murder of an Indigenous woman in Cottam Mills with him. It was just one of those things that happened. A burglary gone wrong. A break-and-enter interrupted by the victim.

The cops wouldn't spend much time on it. Probably a fight with another black fella. Such was his thinking. He was confident the authorities would still be stopping vehicles in the goldfields area.

He wore gloves to ensure he didn't leave fingerprints. Drove Bessie's car to the river. To the place she believed was *Walgu's* resting place. He didn't respect that spiritual belief. He recalled that it wasn't unusual to see her car parked there. To Boodjark, her regular visit to this water was inexplicable.

Kinda freaky, he thought. *Why the obsession with the river? Who cares.*

From the wide expanse of Cottam River where *Ngarngungudditj Walgu* rested to Boodjark's destination was about ten kilometres. He would walk double that distance through the bush, avoiding sand. His footprints would be too easily spotted in the grey sand of the forestry tracks. In the undergrowth, he could cover his tracks more effectively.

Just over six hours after dumping the car, Boodjark emerged from the thick bush into a clearing near a three-metre, chicken-wire fence. It had several strands of barbed wire on top. Several signs spaced at about five-metre intervals warned of danger beyond the fence line. Nearby, there was a large gate bearing a more serious warning. A sign with a picture of a black stick figure surrounded by a red circle. A red line crossed the circle. Beneath, there was a bold capitalised warning, "NO ENTRY" and below that, "Authorized persons only."

Childhood memories flooded back. *Been here. Years gone by. Sometimes on my own and sometimes with that black kid. Nobody else would come here. A long-forgotten mining operation. The best place to hide and rest. Plenty of bush tucker around here, too, if I remember correctly.*

Boodjark circled the area, walking cautiously near the fence and stepping on hard surfaces to avoid leaving footprints. He remembered a gap in the fence that he had created many years before but was unsure precisely where. Eventually he found it. Nearby, perched above the gaping hole in the wire, sat a djidi djidi. It chirped and wagged its tail as if welcoming him to the compound. Perhaps it was.

As he carefully manoeuvred his body between the intertwined strands of wire, the djidi djidi defecated. It just missed Boodjark. He noticed the projectile pass within centimetres of his outstretched arm that held the wire apart. "Little shit!" He mouthed the words.

While Mokiny, his family and friends grieved, Mardoo had a strong calling to assist the police, just like his Aunt Bessie had sixteen years before.

A blue and white band of tape secured 31 Banksia Street from the public. Several police officers carefully combed the yard at the front of the house, looking for evidence.

Mardoo believed, together with his friends Ozzy and Ace, they might be able to assist the police. They certainly didn't have a shortage of confidence. The boys approached a group of people lingering across the street from the crime scene and stood within close proximity. Not too obvious, just within earshot.

"It happened last night," one man said with a forlorn look. "About ten o'clock. I heard a scream from my house just over there" – he pointed to his house diagonally across the road. "I called the police."

A second man said police officers had been there since before sunrise. "I walked my dog this morning and the police were here in number then. More coppers than we have in town. My guess is they've brought some from Ditchingham."

The first man's neighbour, a woman with greying hair and freckles spread unevenly across her face, added, "I tried to call the police, too. The call was diverted to Ditchingham and the operator asked if my call was about the 'incident' in Banksia Street." The woman waved imaginary air inverted commas as she spoke. "She said it had already been reported and the police were on their way. She didn't even take my details, although I suppose these days they have technology that could trace me."

The conversation was muted for a few minutes before the first man broke the silence. "A terrible thing to happen in our town, eh? That black woman who lived there seemed pleasant enough. Never spoke to her, mind you. The quiet type. Didn't cause no trouble but ya never know what goes on behind closed doors."

'Pleasant enough.' That's my Aunt Bessie you're talking about. Mardoo's grief was silent but he couldn't hold back the tears.

First man seemed more knowledgeable about the events. Ozzy edged closer to hear what he had to say.

"The senior sergeant in charge told me he would need a statement from all of us near neighbours. I s'pose we'd best hang around. I haven't got much to say, though. I just heard the scream. I looked outside but didn't see anyone."

The second man also seemed knowledgeable. Ozzy edged closer still. "There have been detectives inside the house for some time now. One came out a short time ago and walked to the garden, where he had a technicolour yawn."

The first glanced sideways at Mardoo and translated, "A chunder. He vomited."

"I know what a technicolour yawn is," Mardoo growled, still smarting from the stranger's earlier comment.

The second man continued, "Apparently it was a pretty horrific scene inside. Blood everywhere. Some bloke lost the plot, I reckon. Insane. Although the cops think it might be a burglary gone wrong."

A man strangely dressed in jeans, a polo shirt, a waistcoat and joggers walked next to the side of the house. He backtracked and moved to the front, never lifting his head or taking his eyes from the ground.

"I heard someone say that man is a blacktracker," Ozzy shared his intelligence with Ace in a whisper. "He has been covering the ground around the house, looking at the ground and then backtracks. Must be looking for ground marks, footprints or something."

Mardoo shook his head. "But the problem is this bloke is not from *boodja*. He's from another mob in the north. He doesn't know this ground. No good. Let's go," Mardoo urged. "I reckon we know the bush better than anyone around here. He'll be hiding in the bush somewhere. I have a feeling I know where we can find him."

Ozzy's voice carried more than a hint of incredulity. "And then what, Mardoo? Do three boys make a citizen's arrest? Do we ask a madman carrying a knife if he wouldn't mind, please, coming with us to the police station?"

"Let's see if we can find where he is hiding and tell the police," Ace suggested. "Mardoo, you are the best at detecting animal footprints in the bush. A man's footprint would be easy for you. You're the best."

Mardoo stood still, seemingly gazing into space through the blur of moist eyes. Suddenly he was back and ready to share his thoughts. "The murderer has headed south. As you know, the bush is closer and thicker south of the town. And there are the old coalmines, too. If he is a local or has lived here in the past, he would at least know where the heaviest bush is. He would be hard to find there. I'm certain he knows the bush."

"Struth, we've even been lost in that country," Ozzy interrupted. "Some of that bush is even too difficult for a horse if the police bring in the Mounted Division, but I reckon a bloke on foot could do it."

"Let's go to the river and work our way south from there."

The boys worked their way along the bank of the Cottam River, but other than an occasional *yongka* there was no activity to be seen. Mardoo was unable to identify the murderer's footprints. The fact he couldn't get inside the area that was cordoned off made it difficult to know what to look for.

Chapter 40

Over the next twenty-four hours, police knocked on doors in the neighbourhood, seeking information. Any information. They needed to determine a motive.

Unfortunately, in a small community, rumours often abound. The first rumour started mid-morning, soon after the police commenced their search. Someone had helped him escape, it was suggested. Perhaps an unsuspecting traveller had picked up a hitchhiker leaving town. Perhaps he hitched a ride on one of the coal trains bound for the coast.

Mardoo intuitively knew none of the rumours to be close to the truth. He returned to the crime scene at night on the second day of the search. He had begged his parents to allow him a very short time out of their *karla*. "Thirty minutes. I can't get into any trouble in thirty minutes. I promise to be home by ten o'clock."

Mardoo stood across the road in the darkness and gazed at 31 Banksia Street. It was still cordoned off by crime-scene tape. Deep in thought, he considered all the processes he believed the police would have gone through to locate the murderer.

Exhausted all options. They shouldn't have used a tracker from the north. Police have searched the bush. They've knocked on doors nearby. Searched the riverbanks, the swamps, and unoccupied houses. Established a dedicated, focused team. Mardoo ticked them off in his mind.

Nothing has been successful. Forty-eight hours and no sign of him.

Returning to his *karla*, Mardoo found his father sitting by the camp fire, head bowed. His grief was overwhelming. Mardoo wanted to talk to him, to implore his father to accompany him to the police control centre so he could convince them of his belief. Mokiny waved him away. "Go to bed," he insisted.

"It's important," Mardoo urged. "I know who the murderer is. I can find him."

Mokiny didn't want to talk about the murder. The loss of his sister and now his cousin was too much. "I said go to bed. If the cops can't find him, how in the hell can you?"

Without completely understanding how he arrived at such a conclusion, Mardoo's innermost feelings, the very fibre of his soul, told him the man who murdered his cousin was the same man he saw in a *koondarm*. A man with a scar the length of his face. He saw the photograph of that man on the television news.

Mardoo decided he needed the support of his friends. It had always been obvious to him that people of colour were treated differently. He would take Ozzy and Ace with him to the police station. Their presence might give him credibility.

A nervous voice uttered, "I know who committed the murder." Mardoo fought to hold back his emotions.

Senior Constable Fraser stood behind a bench and looked down deprecatingly at Mardoo but said nothing. Gradually, a smirk crept across his face.

"The same man who killed my Aunty Yabini. He has escaped from prison. I saw it on the news last week."

There was a lengthy silence as Fraser looked at each of the boys from head to toe. The boys were fixed to the spot in front of a long, timber bench with impact-resistant Perspex fixed thereto as a security screen.

None of the boys had previously been inside the police station. Ozzy and Ace cast their eyes around the reception area, attempting to absorb the sense of being an officer of the law. Mardoo stared at a board to which were pinned several photographs of 'Wanted' people. None were the man referred to as Bruce Prentice, on the nightly news.

After a time, in a firm and uncompromising tone, Fraser quietly said, "Go away, boys. I'm busy. We're understaffed and overworked. I don't have time for your nonsense." Pointing at the small, nervous boy, he added, "What would you know, a little black fella?" The derisive tone of dismissal.

"But sir, I do know, believe me."

"I said go away boy. Don't waste my time. Go away or I'll lock you up for obstructing the police."

"His name is Prentice. He lived here many years ago. He killed my aunty."

"What evidence do you have to support that supposition?" Senior Constable Fraser asked and raised his voice aggressively. "Don't waste my time, I said. Prentice was last seen near Silkspear yesterday. He couldn't be there and here at the same time. Don't be ridiculous."

"I know where he's hiding," Mardoo insisted, but he knew that if he told the policeman that he sensed where Prentice was, he would be laughed out of the police station.

Heads nodded. Both Ozzy and Ace acknowledged Mardoo's intuitive sense. Nothing more than subconscious reasoning. Their facial expressions were as convincing as possible but not convincing enough for Senior Constable Fraser.

The policeman thought the reaction to be humorous. He laughed. Then, returning to his more serious persona, "You've said nothing to convince me. Nothing. No evidence to support your ridiculous assertion, so piss off and leave us to do our job."

Another police officer sat at a nearby desk and appeared to be working at a computer, transferring or double-checking information, running the index finger of his left hand down a document and punching the keys with his right index finger. He stopped and raised his head in surprise at Fraser's insensitive reaction and emitted a quiet grunt of disapproval. Then he raised his eyes even further. To the ceiling. He looked as if he had just been told his holidays had been cancelled.

"We build too many walls and not enough bridges," the policeman said quietly, quoting Isaac Newton.

His colleague at the counter heard the comment. His face became tinged with a Topaque blemish but without its sweetness.

As an afterthought, Fraser surprisingly decided to give an explanation. "We have knocked on all of the doors in the neighbourhood. Combed the area for evidence. Spent some time respectfully questioning everyone in the Indigenous camp. We thought the incident might have been the result of a B and E but now we're not sure."

Head down and eyes still scanning the document on top of his desk, the other Police Officer muttered, "Break and enter."

Fraser continued, "We've been thorough. There's no apparent motive for the incident."

There's that word again, thought Mardoo. *Incident.*

"No motive," Fraser repeated, "leads us to think it might have been someone from your community."

Yeah, it had to be another black fella, didn't it? You've spent an inordinate amount of time talking to people at my karla.

Chapter 41

The police were thorough. Several days were spent dusting for fingerprints inside Bessie's house, as well as externally on windowsills, doorknobs, and the balustrade. Only Bessie's and Mardoo's fingerprints were found. They were sent to the National Fingerprint Database to check for matches. Negative.

Police turned the yard upside-down and the house inside-out. All residents in Banksia Street and the surrounding streets were questioned. The Indigenous people at the local camp were questioned on numerous occasions. The questions were the same and the responses didn't change.

There were no leads. There wasn't a trace of evidence to be found. No motive to provide an explanation and a potential direction for the investigation.

Neighbours had variously reported to the police that Bessie was "pleasant enough". "Never any noise from that house". "Kept to herself, except for a young boy that visited and helped with her gardening". "A quiet type". "She seemed shy". "Just said 'hello' if she was passed in the street. Nothing else".

"Perhaps a little eccentric," her immediate neighbour at number 33 had said. "She would often sit on her rear verandah in the early evening and you could hear her talking to someone. But she was always alone. There was nobody there. Yeah, a little eccentric."

Without an obvious motive, without a suspect and without the slightest piece of evidence, the police continued with more intense questioning of the Indigenous community.

For a short time, they suspected Mokiny might be implicated in the crime. His reluctance to talk to the police raised suspicion. When he ventured out of his shack to the community meeting area and saw detectives or uniformed police in the *karla*, he walked sullenly away.

Most of the time, Mokiny remained in the family shack at the *karla*. The loss of another family member was almost unbearable. He ignored police questions and even when they told him Bessie's car had been found, parked by the Cottam River with the keys still in the ignition, he didn't respond. Nothing made sense to him. Time to grieve. Time to be left alone. Time to think.

Mardoo overheard a police officer tell his father about the car. "How do you explain that, Trunning? The car was found four kilometres from her home. Where the body was found. Did you leave it there? The car, I mean."

"Why are you asking these questions? You don't understand do you?" Mardoo challenged. "Do your job. Leave our family alone!"

For the first time during the police grilling, Mokiny raised his head and peered through narrow eyes at his son. He merely gave an almost imperceptible shake of his head. A signal for Mardoo not to goad the officer.

Eventually, the police Aboriginal Liaison Officer intervened. "I need to talk to you privately," he said. It was necessary for him to explain to his colleague the need for respect and for him to understand culture and grieving.

"Mr Trunning cannot possibly be considered a suspect," he offered politely. "You have misunderstood his reluctance to talk. You must understand: the Trunning family are grieving deeply. I can see that. You need to back off."

Mardoo knew why the car was at the river. He had told the police but they wouldn't listen. A *wadjala* is killing his family. His aunty was first. Now his cousin. Who's next? He had seen the killer in his *koondarm*. He couldn't explain that to the police and maintain a semblance of credibility.

They talk about motive. What's the motive? Is it based on race? Is it something else?

He remembered his Aunt Bessie's truth-telling by the river. She had told him of her vision, just like his *koondarm*. She had been the soul prosecution witness to the murder of his Aunt Yabini. He knew the two tragedies were connected.

Aunty would have been thirty-one years of age now. First Nations people attend way too many funerals. My Pa has grieved for sixteen years. He will never recover from this.

Chapter 42

"I've got to make this right," Mardoo told his friends. "The police won't listen to me. I get that. A little black kid. So I'm gonna deliver him to the cops."

With Ace nodding in vigorous agreement, Ozzy told Mardoo he wouldn't be alone. "We're coming with you," he insisted. "Strength in numbers and strength in this, too." He extracted a semi-automatic Colt 1911 pistol from a small leather bag tucked into the small of his back and waved it in the air. "I borrowed it from my grand-dad's gun shop. It's old but it'll do the job."

"Yeah, threatening," said Ace, "if you need it." Ace remained skeptical that Mardoo would be able to find the killer and even more skeptical that he would deliver him to the police. *I know he is an intelligent and skillful lad but he might be dreaming this time.*

Mardoo found the path Prentice had walked. It was barely visible to the uninitiated but Mardoo saw a broken twig pushed slightly into the earth where a heavy foot had stepped since the last rains. Ten metres on, a leaf was overturned. Wet from night dew, the leaf had stuck to the sole of a shoe and then found separation on a patch of dry ground. The direction Prentice was heading was confirmed by a slight heel and toe indentation.

A male foot. Size eleven, he thought.

They walked in silence, Ace still doubtful that the markings Mardoo had identified as Prentice's were truly his. Ozzy was never in doubt. He knew Mardoo had an uncanny ability to see things the normal eye could not. Certainly *wadjala* could not.

As they approached the fence surrounding the abandoned Kitty Valley Mine, a djidi djidi suddenly appeared. Beyond the fence line. It skimmed close to the surface of the rocky ground in front of the boys, stopped, and silently flicked its tail from side to side. It then reversed and skittered back in the direction from which it had come, dropped to the ground about ten feet away from the gaping hole in the fence and watched the boys.

Before entering the compound, Mardoo stopped and stared at the small bird. Right there was confirmation of his innermost belief. *Djidi djidi. Death.*

Everything was still. No wind. No rustle of leaves in the trees. Unusually, no sound from the djidi djidi. An eerie silence.

It was late afternoon. Long shadows were cast from a gantry to the left of a cluster of old buildings. Buildings long abandoned. Crumbled bricks lay at their base. Rusted corrugated iron was scattered nearby. Weathered timber window frames split and sagged. The glass the frame had once held in place was scattered amongst the bricks and mortar.

The boys silently squeezed through the gap in the wire-meshed fence. Mardoo gazed at the ground as he did so and detected small indents in the ground where pebbles had been disturbed.

Inside the compound, the boys stopped and surveyed their surroundings. Memories of their last visit to Kitty Valley returned. Ozzy and Ace visibly shuddered. Mardoo felt his skin crawl and sensed goose bumps on his arms. Without explanation, he was suddenly engulfed by a strange sensation. As if his heart was placed on pause. Unexpected, unearthly.

The ruined buildings and the towering gantry inspired an uncomfortable eeriness.

"You two wait by the gantry," Mardoo instructed.

"No. We're not leaving you alone," Ozzy whispered.

"You must. I have to deal with this."

Ozzy was anxious for his friend. "Please, Mardoo," he urged and pointed towards the adit. "If he is in there, I fear for you. He is evil personified."

"It's important to me," Mardoo pleaded earnestly in a low, husky voice. "Important for my family."

Ozzy reached behind his back and retrieved the Colt 1911. "Take this."

Mardoo hesitated and Ozzy thrust it forward. He gripped his friend's right hand and pushed the weapon into his palm. "If you need to use it, give the trigger a firm squeeze. This one doesn't have a fine trigger. Be careful."

Mardoo turned and walked slowly to the decline that had been their exit point the last time they were at the mine. He stopped about three metres in front of the entrance and took a deep breath. He was resolute in his decision but was nervous, nevertheless.

As Mardoo entered the darkness of the decline, the djidi djidi briefly hovered above him and then flew away and perched on the pile of bricks. Was death mysteriously hanging over Mardoo?

Boodjark had chosen an adit off the major decline to establish his camp. The adit was situated near the bottom of the same shaft the boys had fallen down when last they visited the mine. It would be the perfect refuge. A sanctuary that would be his alone for as long as required.

From there, Boodjark could exit the mine at will in the dark of night and replenish his food cache from a nearby farm or from nature's garden. A safer place could not be found. This was perfect. Eventually the police would end their search.

Still fully above the horizon, a glow of orange light came from the setting sun west of Kitty Valley, but it softened and flickered like a candle as it passed through the trees. It softened even more as a full moon crept in front of the sun as it descended. A full solar eclipse. Sharp light would soon surround the moon but the earth would temporarily be bathed in darkness, earlier than expected.

Boodjark thought he heard a noise. *Footsteps? Or just coal cracking.* He held his breath and listened intently. *There it is again. Footsteps.*

He rose to his feet and felt his trouser pocket for the knife. He pushed his back against the coalface. The steps were slow but coming closer. He looked up the shaft but it was now completely dark outside.

Small, light steps. Perhaps a wallaby.

Mardoo thought he could hear breathing. He stopped. Another piece of coal fell further along the adit. It was utterly black. Mardoo's hand slid along the side of the tunnel and he took another step. Pistol firmly gripped. Nozzle pointed ahead.

Suddenly, an exceptionally bright light beamed down the shaft into the open area at its base. Simultaneously, Boodjark and Mardoo looked up and could see strong rays of light from a star.

Boodjark dropped his eyes and could see the intense and determined look of a small Indigenous boy pointing a firearm at him. He smiled contemptuously. He wouldn't be intimidated by a mere wisp of a boy. He took a step towards Mardoo and barked, "Give me the gun."

"Get back."

The weapon was shaking in Mardoo's hand.

Boodjark took another step forward. And another step. The knife flashed at waist level.

Mardoo eased backwards, unsure if he could shoot this man. Any man. He had killed animals and tried to visualise the man slowly approaching him as a wild pig. That would make it possible to shoot him. The face changed with boar teeth protruding from a mocking, distorted mouth. But then it changed back to a scarred, rugged vulpine face that held no semblance of care. The features of a dying man.

Pull the trigger, Mardoo, he told himself. *I can't. Am I to die instead?*

The light was still bright. Bright enough for Boodjark to see an Indigenous warrior emerge from the shadow behind the boy. He had ochre warpaint striped across his broad chest and across his forehead. His hair was held back by sinewed tendons from a kangaroo leg. The same tendon strips that held a spearhead tightly in place on the end of the spear he held at head height.

Boodjark was frozen. His eyes bulged in disbelief. Mesmerised.

The spear hit him at the top of his chest, deflected off the clavicle bone and lodged in his throat. He fell backwards, gasping for air. The light shone directly down the shaft onto him.

Boodjark opened his mouth and uttered his last word. "Mokiny!"

More coal cracked along the adit, followed by a rumble as material started to fall more seriously.

"Lets get out of here!" Mokiny yelled to his son. They turned and ran along the tunnel and up the incline.

Judgments had been given. Judgments for which Boodjark had been imprisoned. Crimes had met with punishment. There were crimes for which he never faced judgment. Crimes escaped. The earthquake delivered the final judgment he would ever face.

It was reported to have measured 6.2 on the Richter scale and was centred thirty-one kilometres directly underground of the Kitty Valley mine. The mine would be closed forever after the massive cave-in.

Mokiny and the boys sat on a log about a hundred metres away from the collapsed gantry.

The moon had passed across the sun and the fading glow of the red ball revealed a plume of black dust that hung in the air. Complete darkness was almost upon Kitty Valley again but there wasn't a star to be seen.

Mardoo was first to speak. "How did you find me? That was incredibly brave, Pa."

Mokiny didn't immediately answer but smiled warmly at his son.

"Pa?"

"It's in the genes, Mardoo. It's in the genes. I think you know what I mean."

Mokiny looked fixedly at where the mine's main tunnel had been. Swirling black coal dust prevented its visibility. Pearl white teeth were highlighted in the near darkness. He was still smiling when he said, "That fella now has black skin, too. If an archaeologist digs him up in five hundred years, he will find bones the same colour as my bones if they were to be dug up."

Mardoo's gaze was fixed on his father. *Profound, Pa*, he thought.

Mokiny continued. "A brown egg and a white egg. Break them open and what's inside? They both have a yellow yolk and they both have translucent albumen. Humans are the same. It's just that some of their insides become twisted in life."

He then stood, stepped away from the log, and turned his back to the mine site. He raised his arms, inviting the three boys towards him. For a long moment, they embraced.

"Let's go home now, boys. Tomorrow we'll go to the river and ask *Ngarngungudditj Walgu* to allow cousin Bessie to rest there with the spirits of our ancestors. To set her spirit free. To join Yabini. To join Jimmy. In peace."

Noongar words used in Star of the South

balak [xanthorrhoea plants]
barding-iny [hop]
the Beelagu [River People]
berniny [digging]
birok moordang worl [early summer night sky]
boodja [country]
boodjark [maggot]
bookarl [sore]
boonda [true]
boongari [south]
danjoo koorliny [walking together]
dileri [bluetongue lizard]
dirdong [spring]
djaa [mouth]
djenakabi [lawman]
djidi-djidi [willy wag tail]
djildjit [fish]
djinack [evil spirit]
djindang [the stars]
djoodiny [joey kangaroos]
djooditj [wild cat]
djooroot [track]
dombart yabera [lonely walk]
doordok [pigs]
kaa-kaa [kookaburra]
kaanya [a soul]
kaat wara [sick in the head]
kabap [witch doctor, healer]
Kambarang [spring]

ka-rda [racehorse goanna]
karla [camp]
Karla koorliny [coming home]
karla djooroot [track]
kedaluk [night-time]
kep [water]
kep boolarang [much rain]
ket-ket [in a hurry]
kilang [lightning]
Kitja Boorn [spearwood trees]
kolbang [go forward]
kongal [south]
koolbardi [magpie]
koonak [marron]
koondarm [dream]
koorlamidi wadjala [young white men]
koorni [frog]
kwernt [bandicoot]
kwobali kaanya [a very good soul]
kwoka [wallaby]
kwonding [quandong]
maam yok [aunty: father's sister]
mar [the wind]
maar wirnkoorl [the westerly wind]
malkar [thunder]
maran [freshwater crayfish, marron]
marany [non-meat food]
mardoo [mouse]
mayat [red gum sap]
Minang [the southern-most Noongar language group]
mokiny [dingo]
moora [blunt, flat end of the stick]
moorook [magic man]
moort [family]
ngadi ngadi mar [wind is picking up]
ngany moort [cousin]

ngoony [brother]
ngoorlak [black cockatoos]
ngwir [possum]
nyidiyang [ancestors]
nyorn [sorry]
wadjala [white men]
waitj [emu]
walyan [lungs]
wara [bad]
wara-wara maaman [wicked, ugly man]
warna [women's digging stick]
warra wirrin [bad spirit]
wern [spirit of the dead]
Wilman [Noongar language group]
yabini [star]
yakkan [freshwater turtles]
yanjet [bulrush]
yerderap [ducks]
yongka [kangaroo]
yoolart [skink]
yoorn [bobtail goanna]